GRAVE
INTENT

ALSO BY ALEXANDER HARTUNG

Until the Debt Is Paid (A Jan Tommen Investigation)

ALEXANDER HARTUNG

TRANSLATED BY
STEVE ANDERSON

amazoncrossing

Previously published as *Vor deinem Grab (Ein Jan-Tommen-Thriller 2)* by Amazon Publishing in 2014 in Germany. Translated from German by Steve Anderson. First published in English by AmazonCrossing in 2016.

Published by AmazonCrossing, Seattle

www.apub.com

Amazon, the Amazon logo, and AmazonCrossing are trademarks of Amazon.com, Inc., or its affiliates.

ISBN-13: 9781503950658
ISBN-10: 1503950654

Cover design by Marc Cohen

Printed in the United States of America

Prologue

Police Emergency Call—7:47 p.m., June 22, 2013

"I'm standing at my own grave." The voice was shaky and hard to understand over the phone.

"What was that?" Emilia asked.

"There's a grave here. With my name on it."

Emilia hated the late shift on Saturday. The drunks were always having their little fun, calling the police and trying to pull her leg.

"Is this some kind of joke?"

"No, no," the man said, sounding confused.

Emilia took a deep breath. She couldn't let herself get worked up—these calls were recorded, after all.

"Can you tell me your name?"

"Bernhard Valburg."

"Thanks, Herr Valburg. Where are you?"

"At the cemetery."

"Which cemetery?"

"Dorotheenstadt Cemetery," the man said, though he didn't sound certain about it.

"Good, Herr Valburg. And you're standing at your grave right now?" Emilia asked. Maybe the caller was some junkie tripping out.

"I went to the cemetery this evening. It's my departed wife's birthday tomorrow. I always gave her roses when she was alive. Peace roses. She loved those, the yellow ones tinted with pink at the edges . . ."

Emilia heard Bernhard Valburg swallow hard.

"I didn't notice anything at first, but then, when I went to get water for the watering can, I saw a newly dug grave. About a foot and a half deep—not near deep enough for a coffin. With a wooden cross, and a name painted on it."

"Your name?"

"'Here lies Bernhard Valburg,'" he read out loud. "'Born December third, 1959. Died June twenty-third, 2013.'"

"So the date of death is tomorrow?"

Instead of a reply, only a sob came over the line. She wasn't dealing with some crazy guy. This man feared for his life.

"Herr Valburg?"

No answer. Emilia nervously bit her lower lip. "Can you hear me?"

"Yes." His voice was just a whisper now.

"Is someone else there?"

"I'm all alone. I always go to the cemetery this late. Because it's peaceful."

She had to help him, but all the available units were out on calls just then. And since there didn't seem to be any immediate danger, it could be up to a full hour before officers got to him. Far too long. She had to get this Bernhard Valburg out of the cemetery. Otherwise the guy was going to lose it.

"I suggest you use your phone to take a picture of the grave and the cross with your name on it. Then come on down to the station and report the incident to an officer here. They'll look into it, get in touch with cemetery management. Maybe one of the staff saw something."

Silence.

"Herr Valburg?"

It took a moment for him to answer. "Yes."

"Are you following me?"

"Sorry, yes," he stammered. "Give me a moment. I'll take a picture and come down there."

"Great," Emilia said, relieved. The man's voice sounded stronger now, not as shaky. He seemed to be pulling himself together.

"Is there anything else I can do for you right now?"

"No. Thank you."

He hung up.

The call from the cemetery was the last one Emilia got that night. Her shift ended shortly afterward; she left for home as soon as a colleague arrived to replace her.

But she would never forget Bernhard Valburg's frightened voice. The man never reached the police station.

Chapter One

A person's house says a lot about him, Jan thought as he looked out a full-length living-room window onto a Japanese garden. A flagstone path led around a little pond. The placement of the slabs was so precise that it looked like they had been set with a laser. Beyond the pond were a small lawn and bushes in various shades of red, all aligned symmetrically. It would have been the ideal yard if only someone had been caring for it. But weeds grew between the stone slabs, a green film of algae stretched across the pond, and the overgrown bushes crowded the unmown grass.

The living room told a similar story. The walls were coated with a silvery plaster that blended in with the marble flooring. A crystal chandelier hung above a polished cherrywood table, its glass clinking softly from the breeze coming in through an open window. Picture frames, still wrapped in brown paper, leaned against the wall, as if the owner of the house had no time to hang them. Near the table stood a rickety folding chair that looked more like it belonged in an IKEA showroom than on a lavish marble floor. The flat-screen TV was set on a cardboard box, its stand secured with duct tape. Cords ran through the room and into a socket in the open kitchen, as though the electrician had run out of outlets right in the middle of the job.

A young female police officer was shining her flashlight along the window frames, searching for signs of breaking and entering. Her dark hair was neatly braided in a single plait, and she wore only a little makeup, no perfume. Although nothing about her looked suggestive, her dark complexion and elegant features gave her the aura of a mystical beauty more suited to ancient Egypt than to the Berlin police.

Jan reached in his pocket, took out a stick of chewing gum, and stuck it in his mouth. Given that he'd been awakened shortly before five this morning, he hadn't had a chance to see to his personal hygiene. At that hour he'd just been glad to get out of the house with matching shoes. But bad breath could wreck their first encounter.

He straightened his hair and went over to the officer.

"Detective Jan Tommen," he said to her, holding out his hand. "I'm running the investigation for this case."

"Marie," the woman replied, shaking his hand. She didn't look impressed.

Jan cleared his throat. "Did you know the victim, officer?"

"No. I've been on night shift. They sent me over here after the body was found. The front door was open, so I went on in. When I saw the blood, I called for the crime-scene investigators."

"How long has the victim lived here?"

Marie set down the flashlight and pulled her cell phone from her pocket. She swiped at the display a couple of times before answering. "Sixteen months."

Jan was gazing at her phone in wonder.

"A new notes app." She showed him the screen. "I can enter notes and comments, pull in e-mails and briefs, then I copy it all onto the computer to create my preliminary report."

"Ahh," Jan said stupidly. He refrained from reaching into his pocket and pulling out his little notepad. He'd catch up on his notes when he wasn't being so closely observed.

Marie nodded at him, picked up her flashlight, and continued her search.

"So, over a year now," Jan added, amazed. The place looked like the victim had only just moved in. Which meant the owner was either lazy, really busy, or never home. Who buys high-end furniture and has a Japanese garden installed only to let it all go to waste sixteen months later?

Jan couldn't wait to see what his investigation would bring to light. The first order of business was to learn more about the crime scene. He went over to the big table and knelt down next to the folding chair. A crime-scene tech was there now, taking a sample from a large dark stain.

"Can you tell when the man was killed?"

The tech shrugged. "Not from the blood sample."

"When can you know if this was the actual crime scene?"

"Shouldn't be too hard. We'll compare this blood with that of the victim. If it matches, we can safely say this was the place. Zoe can help you with cause of death. She's with the body now."

"Thanks," Jan said, pulling out his flip phone. He made sure Marie wasn't looking in his direction, then punched in Zoe's number. He really needed to buy a new phone when he got the chance. His was four years old, an eternity these days.

Zoe picked up on the third ring. "What?" she barked into the receiver.

"And a good morning to you," Jan said, smiling. There were some things a person could count on. Zoe being in a foul mood at this hour was as sure as the proverbial *amen* in church.

"What's so good about it?" she snapped, annoyed. "It's six a.m. I haven't had coffee yet and didn't even have the chance to shower. The garbage truck broke down in front of my place, so it took a full forty minutes to get here. It's raining, and here I am at a cemetery that was built before electricity. We had to patch together four extension cables just to get power to a lamp, which held for five minutes before the old prewar fuse went and blew. I had to hold a flashlight between my teeth just so I could tell corpse from tree."

She let out a deep sigh.

"Plus, I'm standing practically up to my knees in mud, and it's ruining my shoes."

"Your shoes?"

"You know Christian Louboutin?"

Jan wasn't sure. "That the new guy in Forensics?"

She let out a crabby growl. "And just when I think it can't get any worse, the phone rings and a bonehead like you is on the line."

"Sorry to disturb. I just want to know if you have cause and time of death yet."

"Dead guy's noggin is half-buried in the ground, the rain has turned this place into a swamp, and my colleagues in Evidence won't let me turn over the body until each and every earthworm is catalogued."

Jan heard a lighter click.

"Zoe, I wouldn't be bugging you if I didn't know that you can tell more from one glance than your colleagues can with a three-hour autopsy."

Silence on the line. Jan hoped he'd taken the right tack with flattery.

Then she said, "I'm thinking his skull got bashed in yesterday evening."

"Thanks," Jan said. "I'll check in again later."

"If you must." Zoe hung up.

Jan went into the kitchen, turned away from the crime-scene investigators, and pulled out his notepad and pen.

Victim: Dr. Bernhard Valburg. Residing at Dorenstrasse 24a since January 2012.

> *Cause of death: Beating*
> *Date of death: June 23, 2013*
> *Likely scene of crime: Living room*
> *Where found: Dorotheenstadt Cemetery*
> *Perp: Unknown*

Jan shoved the notepad back into his jacket. Time to start investigating.

.   .   .

Zoe leaned back on the bench and blew cigarette smoke into the air. Her blonde hair ran down her shoulders in unkempt strands. Her black leather jacket shone from the damp, and her tight-fitting jeans were spattered with mud. Dark-brown pumps with red soles stood on the bench next to her. Her naked feet rested atop the silver case where she kept her most essential instruments. Thanks to an overhanging oak, this was the only spot in the cemetery that was more or less dry.

A few months ago, she'd been bored to death in Forensics. Day after day she performed autopsies in the same stark room with the same boring people. Working with Jan had finally given her the opportunity to be part of a proper investigations team. Still, she had imagined it was all going to be a lot cooler, somehow.

What she hadn't imagined was waking at five a.m., rushing to a cemetery in the rain, and standing with a flashlight in her mouth, eyeballing a corpse. And certainly not at the expense of her six-hundred-euro Louboutins.

At least it was summer. She closed her eyes and dreamt of a coffeehouse with espresso brewing, fresh croissants, cherry jam, and maybe a layer of salted butter . . .

"Dr. Diek?"

A voice pulled her back to the rain-soaked cemetery She opened her eyes, not bothering to conceal her irritation.

A young man stood before her. Judging by his smooth face, he was just barely eighteen. He wore white protective coveralls spattered with mud, leaving only his face exposed. If the overalls had been blue, he would have looked like a giant Smurf. The guy's name was Roger, Robin, something like that.

"What's up, Robin?"

"My name is Romir."

"Whatever."

"We've finished searching the crime scene. You can move the body now, if you like."

"That mean you guys are taking a break till I'm done?"

The young man nodded.

"Perfect." Zoe stood, pulled out a ten-euro bill, and pressed it into the young man's hand. "Go get coffee, then. Black, no sugar. And bring a couple of croissants."

The guy stared at the bill in his hand.

"I'm not going to start till the sun comes up, anyway. You've got enough time to grab me breakfast."

Zoe sat back down, set her feet on the case, and closed her eyes again.

"It won't be light for another half hour."

"Right, and that's how long I'll be sitting here."

"According to regulations, you're supposed to—"

"Don't care."

"But—"

"Roger, look. My blood-sugar level's about to bottom out. A condition that makes it extremely dangerous to be anywhere near me. For the morale of the unit and your general health, I need something to eat, and soon. Because inside this lovely case under my feet here? I have enough scalpels to create a dozen new crime scenes."

Zoe raised a merciful hand and waved the young man away. She heard him head off muttering, "My name is Romir."

Zoe descended back into her dozy half-coma. The sun still had not risen above the horizon. The rain had likely washed away all the good clues in this mudhole. But that bonehead Jan was right. She had an eye. She would find something.

Chapter Two

Chandu felt a bit hesitant entering the offices of Kripo—
Kriminalpolizei, the Berlin Detective Division. A bouncer and debt
collector, he never imagined he'd be coming here of his own free
will. He tried to act inconspicuous, which wasn't exactly easy, considering his size, his broad shoulders, and his imposing upper arms.

There was more action in the lobby than at a shopping mall on
a Saturday afternoon. No matter where Chandu stood, he was in
someone's way. A panting woman loaded down with files bustled
past him. He thought he heard a baby crying. Two uniformed officers escorted a drunk into the station; the man wasn't done with his
treatment and gave his aggravation free rein. Chandu was standing
at a bulletin board, trying to get his bearings in this chaos, when a
man approached him.

"You must be Herr Bitangaro," he said politely.

"I am, sir," Chandu replied, trying to hide his unease. The man
was wearing a dark suit with a red silk tie and a pocket square. He
looked like an old-fashioned dandy, his shiny hair slicked back with
pomade.

"My name is Patrick Stein." When he shook Chandu's hand cordially, Chandu could barely contain his surprise. Evidently Patrick Stein was overlooking the fact that the two of them had squared off in a parking garage eight weeks ago, when Chandu had almost blown a hole in the man's forehead. "I recognized you right away," he continued. "Not many people have such a . . . an imposing exterior."

"Uh, thanks. I'm working out . . ."

"If you don't mind me saying, Herr Bitangaro: you were a huge help to Jan in his last case. Your efforts really contributed to our solving the investigation."

"Don't mention it. But Jan, he—"

"Since you more or less belong to us now, I assume you're here about the new case."

"Well, to tell you the truth, I'm really not too sure why I'm here."

"We could use your talents."

"Uh . . . okay. I guess that's good. What are we—"

"A most unusual murder."

"So what do I . . . Who are we—"

"I'm almost envious of you getting it, but I have my own case to see to." Patrick glanced at his watch and sighed. "Time flies. Nice talking with you, Herr Bitangaro." He shook Chandu's hand again. "If you ever have questions, you can always come to me." He added a nod and headed off down one of the many corridors.

"Telling me how to find Jan would have been nice," the big man muttered.

Once Patrick was gone, Chandu pivoted in place, hoping to see Jan or some other familiar face. He again had the sense of being in a crowded shopping mall, only now he felt like a three-year-old who'd lost his mother. He balled his fists and cursed at length—in his native Kinyarwandan, for safety's sake. He was among cops, after all.

He made his way back to the lobby and was scanning a directory sign when a young woman came up next to him. She was three heads shorter and wore a tight green T-shirt that accentuated her athletic body. But her serious expression and her dark hair pulled back in a neat ponytail made her seem forbidding and severe. Of course, the pistol and pepper spray only added to his impression. Women with weapons spooked him.

"You look a little lost," she said in a kind voice. "Are you new here?"

Chandu considered making a sarcastic remark but then realized how he must appear to this woman. He was wearing biker boots, torn jeans, and a dark leather jacket. Add the tribal tattoos on his forehead, and he must seem as foreign to this female cop as she was to him.

"I am." He smiled widely. "Thanks for asking. Could you tell me where Jan Tommen conducts his meetings?"

"Aha, you must be that Chandu fellow."

"Yep, I am that Chandu fellow." He wondered if there was a poster with his image and name on it somewhere in the station.

"I heard about you."

"You're not the only one." Chandu had no idea what Jan had been saying about him, but it didn't exactly help his line of work when every cop in Berlin knew who he was.

The woman was eyeing him up and down. "Hmm," she muttered. She seemed to like what she saw.

"The conference room?" Chandu said, unnerved by her thorough inspection of his body.

The woman flinched and went back to being all business. "Uh, go down that hallway all the way to the end. Take a right; second door on the left."

Chandu walked past the woman. He could feel her watching him until he was all the way around the corner.

Max was waiting for him in the meeting room. Seeing a trusted face put him immediately at ease. "Hey there, Max." He gave the young computer freak and sometime hacker a friendly pat on the shoulder.

Max's long hair stuck out in all directions. His pants were too short for his skinny legs, and those green sneakers he never took off were probably part of his feet by now. The only aspect of his appearance that had changed in the weeks since Chandu had last seen him was his T-shirt, which was bright red with the word *Bazinga* in large black letters.

Max looked up, grinned, and then turned back to his keyboard. "Be done in a sec. Just have to finish connecting to Forensics."

"Don't let me disturb you," Chandu said and went over to a bulletin board near the door. On one side hung photos of a large home. The stark rooms were shot from various perspectives. Next to them were images of a cemetery. The body of a man lay facedown in a rectangular open grave that looked freshly dug. Next to the grave stood a simple wooden cross on which was painted a name, date of birth, and date of death.

Jan had left comments on the photos with little Post-its. On the living room, one note read CRIME SCENE? Jan had noted MURDER WEAPON NOT DETERMINED on a grisly close-up of the back of a completely shattered head.

Chandu was looking over a map of the cemetery when Jan strode in.

"Good morning, old buddy!"

"Morning." Chandu gave Jan a big hug with his massive arms. Then he stepped back and took a good look at his friend. Jan had surely been up all night. His thatch of brown hair hadn't been combed, and his shirt was wrinkled, but that mischievous grin of his—like that of some teenager who'd pranked his schoolteacher—outshone his weariness.

Jan was an experienced investigator, but in his last case he'd come under suspicion of murder himself. He had gone into hiding at Chandu's place, and the whole episode had been incredibly rough on Jan. Chandu wasn't sure if he was ever going to be the same "good old Jan" again.

"How does it feel to be working for Homicide?" Jan asked.

"Don't go exaggerating, now," Chandu replied. "I'm just a freelance informant."

"Admit it. You're getting off on it."

"On what?"

"Being in Homicide."

"The last time I was here, I was questioned about the murder of a pimp. They suspected me of being a henchman for the Russian mob—not to mention what they said about me being a debt collector. So to answer your question: *no.*"

Jan changed the subject. "Are we all here?" he said.

"We are," Max answered, turning his laptop around. The screen showed Zoe over in Forensics, in the pathology lab. She had her long hair pinned up and wore a white lab coat. Her eyebrows were perfectly plucked on her flawless face, and her dark-brown eyes blazed with mystery even through her thick safety glasses. Chandu lamented that she swung the other way.

"Well, I see the Three Stooges are back together," she said.

"Glasses don't work on you," Chandu said, taking a chair across from the laptop.

"Shut it, Mr. T."

"Ah, my little honey. I've missed you."

"Well, the feeling is decidedly not mutual. And don't call me your little honey."

"I really hate to break up this heartwarming reunion," Jan said, "but it seems we've been assigned a murder case—and it's a pretty unusual one."

"That's what I hear," Chandu said.

"From who?"

"Your bosom buddy, Patrick Stein."

"Patrick?" Jan asked in confusion. "How did you . . . and he—"

"Long story," Chandu said. "I'll tell you later. So, why is this case so unusual?"

Jan pointed to a whiteboard propped on an easel. "Our victim is Dr. Bernhard Valburg. Fifty-three years old. A lung specialist with his own practice. Two days ago he's at the cemetery to tend to his wife's grave site. There he discovers an empty grave and a wood cross with his name on it."

"Whoa, that's macabre, man, real macabre," Max remarked.

"It gets better. The wood cross has the day he dies on it. That's too much for Bernhard Valburg, so he calls police emergency."

"And you guys didn't protect him?" the young hacker asked.

"Now we know better, but at the time it just looked like some kind of sick prank. The woman at the call desk suggested he come in to the station and talk to an officer about the incident. But he never showed."

"Why didn't you follow up?" Chandu asked.

"You have no idea how many prank calls and nut jobs call that number. Saturday nights, all hell breaks loose in Berlin. Patrols are on calls nonstop. Plus, you can't go putting every victim of a sick joke under police protection."

"But this joker was getting serious."

"No one could have known that."

Jan pointed to a photo of an elegant home with a landscaped garden, a spotless white garage, and a footpath laid with bright marble slabs.

"The crime scene, presumably his home on Dorenstrasse. We found his blood on the floor of his living room." He turned to Zoe. "How far along are you with the autopsy?"

"We're not quite finished, but I'm getting the gist of it." Zoe took off her safety glasses. "Bernhard Valburg was beaten to death. We're working on determining the murder weapon, but I'm betting it was a hammer. A blow smashed the top of his skull and penetrated deep into his brain. Blood at the crime scene included brain mass, which tells us the victim was murdered at home. He died immediately."

"There is one other small matter," Zoe continued. "The victim had his eyes gouged out."

"His eyes gouged out?" Jan asked. "Why in the hell would someone do that?"

"No idea. Why don't you swing by and ask the dead guy."

"Gouged out with what?" Chandu asked.

"When you're dealing with vitreous bodies, it's tough to say. I'm guessing a screwdriver or something similar."

"Anything else out of the ordinary?"

"Not externally. Still running tests for alcohol, drugs, poison—all that fun stuff."

"Now we know where and how he died, but how did the murderer get the body to the cemetery?" Chandu asked. "From the photos, I'm guessing this Bernhard Valburg was over two hundred pounds."

"Two hundred and twelve," Zoe confirmed. "No one just heaves weight like that over a shoulder real quick."

"It's a good first question," Jan said. "The more intriguing one is *why*. The murderer went to great risk digging out a grave like that. It wasn't enough just to simply murder his victim. He bashes in the man's skull at home, gouges out his eyes, and transports the body to the grave. Even in the middle of the night, tons of people could have observed him doing it. He even creates a gravestone to warn his victim that his death will occur on June twenty-third. Now, the victim, Bernhard Valburg, could have locked himself inside his home out of fear or hired a security firm or flown to Hawaii, even. Why didn't he?"

"You're saying the murderer knew his victim?"

"Bingo," Jan said.

"What?" Zoe's voice blared from the laptop speaker.

"This murder's got a lot of personal aspects," Chandu told her. "First, the killer had to know where Valburg's wife is buried. Then, he knew the guy's birthday and where he lived."

"Another good indicator of a personal murder is all the extra effort made," Jan continued. "Digging a grave a foot and a half deep takes time, especially when you don't want to be seen doing it. Then there's the cross, carrying in the body. This was long in planning."

"Did your guys question the cemetery staff?" Chandu asked.

"Yes. No one saw a thing. The last one there called it a day at six in the evening. The cemetery is far too large for personnel to check all the graves every day."

"Surveillance cameras?"

"They don't even have power," Zoe cut in. "Our spotlights fried the fuses. I had to wait till the crack of dawn before I could see anything."

"What about the cross?" Chandu asked. "Fingerprints on it?"

"None," Zoe replied. "We didn't find DNA either. The murderer left no clues behind. My colleagues are testing a few other samples, but I'm not optimistic we'll find anything. The rain didn't make it any easier."

"Who did the grave site belong to?" Max asked. "Did the murderer dig out one that was already there?"

"Bernhard Valburg had reserved that grave site for himself," Jan replied. "He wanted to be buried next to his wife."

"So we got nothing," Max said.

"Apart from a mad killer who's still on the loose," Zoe added.

"Where do we start?" Max asked.

"I'll head over to Bernhard Valburg's office," Jan said. "Maybe his staff can tell me something. I'll get a list of patients too."

"I'll hit the underworld," Chandu said. "Valburg wouldn't be the first doctor to deal prescription meds, take drugs, or get addicted to gambling."

"They're looking at the computer from his house," Max said, "but I'll take a look. Before that, I'll root around the police database to see if the doctor drove too fast or got in some other trouble."

"I'll have a smoke first," Zoe said. "Then order a pizza and hit the sack."

"Great," Jan said. "So we all have important things to do. Let's meet tomorrow afternoon again, right here?"

"No can do," Chandu protested. "Police stations creep me out. Besides, I have my reputation to keep up. Let's do six p.m. at my place. I'll cook us up something tasty."

"Nothing with insects, though," Zoe said.

"For you, sweetheart, I have a roll of Smarties lying around somewhere."

Zoe narrowed her eyes and was about to comment, but thinking quickly, Max shut the laptop.

"Till tomorrow," Jan said.

Max raised one hand in salute as he yanked the cable from his laptop with the other.

"Happy hunting," Chandu said and left the room.

Back out in the hall, he looked around warily. The police-woman in the tight T-shirt was nowhere to be seen, so he hurried off, squeezed past a group of cops, then crossed through the lobby without drawing attention to his fast pace. He slipped out the front entrance and onto the street, breathing an audible sigh of relief. It was a weird feeling, working for the other side.

．　　．　　．

Bernhard Valburg's practice stood in a quiet suburb of Berlin. Single-family homes lined a street free of traffic, the sidewalk punctuated by narrow beech trees. Cherry laurel greened the entrance, where a sign was taped to the glass door: "Practice Closed Until Further Notice."

Still, Jan could see a light on inside, so he pressed the bell. A moment later, a woman in a white lab coat opened the door. Everything about her fit the mold of the long-serving doctor's assistant. She wore her hair pinned up and just enough makeup not to be intrusive. She smiled, but her tear-filled eyes told a different story.

"Yes?" she asked wearily.

"Detective Tommen." Jan showed his badge. "I'm from Berlin Police, and I'm working on Dr. Valburg's murder."

"Vanessa Ziegler," she told him, opening the door all the way. "I was Dr. Valburg's assistant for twenty-three years."

Jan stepped inside the office. A mountain of files was piled on the reception desk. Hastily scribbled notes lay next to the telephone. The aroma of fresh coffee mixed with the musty smell of file folders.

"I have to tell the doctor's patients about his death," Vanessa explained. "I'm trying to assign some to other pulmonologists in Berlin."

"How long have you known?"

"Since earlier today. Dr. Valburg had me listed as an emergency contact." Sighing, she pointed to the files. "And when I'm done with all that, I'll have to straighten up the offices for his successor, including getting all the personal items removed and shredding a lot of files."

"Do you know who his successor will be?"

She shook her head. "I don't have anything to do with that. The practice is in good shape, and Dr. Valburg had a spotless reputation. Whoever takes over is going to have it easy. There aren't many pulmonologists looking for a practice, so it could take a while."

"How was your relationship with Dr. Valburg?"

"He was a good boss. We bickered, sure, but I liked working here."

"What are you going to do now?"

"Hit the unemployment office. Hope there's a position available." She shrugged. "It's not easy when your life changes course overnight. I was hoping to stay here till I retired."

Vanessa was having trouble holding back the tears, and she turned her face away. Jan waited till she pulled herself together. She took a deep breath, then faced him again.

Her smile was back. "So how can I help you?"

"I need a list of Dr. Valburg's patients."

"Don't you need some kind of official warrant for that?"

"I actually do." Jan winced a little. He'd been hoping to leapfrog over that paperwork.

"Well, doesn't matter to me. If it helps find the murderer, then I'm happy to do it." Vanessa went into the neighboring room, started up the computer, and hit a few keys. "How do you want the list? Should I print it out or send it to your e-mail?"

Jan's cell phone rang before he could reply.

"Yeah."

"It's me, Max. I found something interesting."

"What've you got?"

"I entered Bernhard Valburg's name in the database and got a hit."

Jan pulled his notepad from his pocket and sat in a waiting-room chair. He wrote down every detail Max gave him. Two minutes later, he'd forgotten about the patient list and was hurriedly saying good-bye to Vanessa Ziegler.

"I'll be back," he said quickly, "that or call."

On the way to the car, he dialed Chandu's number. For the next round of questioning, he would need his friend's help.

·   ·   ·

Max strolled happily over to the candy machine and pressed the lever for a bag of gummy bears. He wouldn't have believed that doing an internship with the Berlin Police could be so much fun.

The guys in IT were *almost* as good as he was. His system access came with a tracker that showed them his every keystroke and mouse click. That way it would be impossible for him to pull some scam or use his access for something other than his official assignments.

It took him two days before he noticed it. But these cop geeks simply were not Maximum, the master hacker.

First thing he did was copy the top-level administrator's password. "NCC-1701" was easy enough to crack—as if he had never seen a single episode of *Star Trek*! That night he created a new user account, one that couldn't be traced, and then he quickly programmed in a back door to the system so he'd be able to get into the cop server when his internship ended.

He also tagged his file. Whenever someone pulled it up, he would receive a message with the name of the person opening it. That way he'd be warned in time if someone were investigating him.

Whistling the Imperial March, he went back to his desk. He was probably the only superhacker in the world with ongoing access to a cop server.

His phone was vibrating. Probably Jan with another question. He looked at the screen and froze. His sister had texted him.

In B this weekend. Coming Sat eve. xo Mira.

"Goddamn," Max cursed. His weekend was screwed.

. . .

Jan was waiting on the street corner as Chandu stepped out of the taxi.

"You're not driving?" Jan asked him.

"You sounded so worked up on the phone, I took off right away. Wasn't any time to get a . . . loaner. What kind of clue is so hot you pull me off my own investigation?"

"Over there is the office of a Dr. Aaron Ewers. A cosmetic surgeon."

Jan gestured at a garish building. Before it rose a little lane of blooming trees amid a lawn landscaped with a fountain and precisely trimmed shrubs. The rounded front entrance was all in glass.

Chandu nodded. "The Botox biz appears to pay off big-time. Why are we here?"

"The good doctor once threatened to kill our victim. Apparently Bernhard Valburg had set tax-fraud investigators on him. And they, annoyingly, caught some things that ended up reducing the clinic's profit."

"So why do you need me?"

"Max found not only Bernhard Valburg's claim of a death threat—he found others' claims too. This Dr. Ewers is bad-tempered and has little respect for authority. He faced five charges of insulting an official before a judge eventually slapped a suspended sentence on him. He may not respect me, as a police officer, but he might just be a little more intimidated by a six-foot-six tattooed black guy with giant arms."

24

"I feel like I'm being judged by my appearance," Chandu grumbled with a twinkle in his eye.

"It happens," Jan said, smiling.

"It's always a pleasure working with you."

"Don't be so sensitive. Got your fake badge on you?"

"Sure do," Chandu said. "It's scored me a few free drinks already."

Jan raised his eyebrows in disapproval. "We should have a talk about the exact meaning of the word *responsible use*."

"Those are two words."

"Fine." Jan waved away the thought. "Let's head on in. Try to act as threatening as possible. It's the only way to reach a person like this. Maybe he'll even cave."

"Sounds like fun."

. . .

The foyer fulfilled all expectations set by the building's exterior, from the shiny gray granite floor, to the soft piano music flowing from concealed speakers, to a faint aroma of artificial citrus. An attractive young woman sat behind the stark white reception desk, which was graced by two substantial floral arrangements and a bowl of expensive candies.

"Welcome to Ewers Clinic," the woman said through her immaculate teeth. "How can I help you?"

"Berlin Police, Detectives." Jan set his badge on the counter. "We have an appointment with Dr. Ewers."

The woman looked at a screen. "I don't have an appointment here. When did you—"

"Thanks. We'll find our own way." Chandu grabbed a handful of candies from the bowl and stuffed them in his jacket pocket.

"Dr. Ewers, room one zero four," Jan read off a wall directory.

"One moment. The doctor is in a consultation."

"Not anymore." Chandu popped a candy into his mouth and let the wrapper fall to the floor.

As they headed for the room, the woman hurried out from behind her desk and tottered after them in her too-high heels. She scolded Jan and Chandu, "This is outrageous! You can't just come barging in here."

"Sure we can," Jan told her. "This is a murder investigation. Whatever Dr. Ewers is doing can't be more important than that."

"There it is." Chandu pointed at a door, pulled down the handle, and went in with Jan.

· · ·

A man in a white doctor's coat sat on a pale leather sofa in the elegantly appointed room. He had short, thinning hair. The tawny color of his face seemed fake, almost like makeup.

A middle-aged lady sat across from him. Judging by the jewelry on her hands and neck, she was quite well-off.

The doctor balled one hand into a fist and pursed his narrow lips together. "How dare you!" he bristled. He threw the receptionist an accusing glance.

She began, "I couldn't stop them—"

"Leave my practice at once," the doctor told Jan and Chandu. "Or I'll call the police."

"They're already here," Jan said, showing his badge. "We have questions that can't wait."

"Well, I'm in a consult."

"Not anymore." Chandu approached the middle-aged lady. "Here, something for you to nosh on." He pressed a few candies into her hand. "Your boobs will have to wait."

Clearly not used to this sort of treatment, the lady emitted a startled gasp, rose from the sofa, and left the room.

The receptionist stammered an apology and meekly followed the lady out.

"This will cost you your job," the doctor snapped at her. His bronze face had turned red, the knuckles of his tight fist squeezing white. Jan could easily imagine how those threatening incidents had happened.

Jan turned to Chandu. "Did you hear that?"

"Hear what?"

"He just called me an asshole."

"Now that you mention it, I did notice."

"Stupid of him."

"Really stupid."

"Especially when he's on a suspended sentence for insulting officials."

"What's going on here?" the doctor broke in. "This is outrageous. I'm going to—"

"Take it easy!" Chandu roared at him. "Sit yourself down and answer our questions, or we'll run you down to the station. Our colleagues would be happy to see you again."

Chandu took a step forward and pointed silently at the sofa. The man sat, clearly intimidated, and Jan positioned himself in the seat across from him.

"Are you Dr. Aaron Ewers?" Jan began.

The man nodded.

"Do you know Dr. Bernhard Valburg?"

Another nod.

"Do you know what happened to him?"

Again a nod.

"We appreciate it when a man speaks to us," Chandu said.

"Yes," the doctor said softly.

"So tell us about the death threat to Dr. Valburg,"

"It wasn't me."

Jan took his notepad from a pocket. "But it is suspicious that you called Dr. Valburg a few weeks ago and left him a message where you threatened to bash in his skull."

"Stupid, more like," Chandu commented.

"And now guess how Dr. Valburg died."

"It was not me," the doctor repeated.

"You'll have to pardon me if I can't simply take your word for this, especially considering your little hobby of insulting officials."

"I get angry easily," the doctor offered. "Believe me, I'm aware of that. But I've never assaulted anyone."

"There's always a first time," Chandu said.

"I can understand your anger," Jan continued. "Bernhard Valburg was a colleague of yours, but *his* patients didn't come from Berlin high society. Instead of allowing you to bask in your success, he goes and fingers you. That can make a guy angry."

"Outrageous," the doctor said, fighting his fury.

"How did you know it was Bernhard Valburg? His tip-off was anonymous."

"It's a long story."

"We have time," Chandu said. He took a candy from his pocket, unwrapped it slowly, popped it in his mouth, and let the wrapper fall to the floor.

"Bernhard and I studied together at Berlin University. For him, becoming a doctor was a calling, a duty to alleviate suffering. For me, it was always just a job, an opportunity to earn money, have a nice life. We were at odds from that very first semester on. He couldn't understand why I'd want to be a cosmetic surgeon. Our studies were barely over before we starting seeing each other at medical conferences . . . and other events."

Dr. Ewers folded his hands together, staring at the floor. "The last time we ran into each other was at a reception. I'd bought a round; I was having my best year ever as a doctor and wanted to celebrate. Instead of leaving me to drink with my friends, Bernhard came over and started going on and on about a doctor's obligation to society. Talking about ethics and bitching about cosmetic surgeons. As drunk as I was, I just laughed at him, comparing my practice to his, making fun of national health-care patients."

"The classic competition—my dick's bigger than yours," Chandu remarked.

"Call it what you will, but this time it hit a nerve. Bernhard lunged at me, knocked the champagne glass out of my hand, and blatantly threatened that there would be consequences. A week later, the tax man was at my door."

"Which cost you some money?" Jan asked.

Dr. Ewers nodded.

"How much?"

"Too much."

"What's too much?"

"I had to sell one of my houses and give up my share in a private jet."

"Alas, cruel fate," Chandu said.

"Where were you last Sunday evening?"

"At one of those conferences. In a hotel downtown. My assistant can write down the address for you."

"On a Sunday?"

"National conventions are always on weekends."

"What was the focus?"

"It wouldn't interest you." Dr. Ewers waved away the thought. "Thoroughly boring stuff. But you have to be seen at these things, keep up appearances. I was actually preparing for another round with Bernhard; I was surprised he wasn't there."

"Did anyone see you at this conference?"

"I can give you a list of my colleagues who saw me. I spent the evening there, then an old friend from Brazil came to visit me. We drank until the hotel bar closed, around three a.m. I could barely stagger over to the taxi stand after that. Ask the concierge who was on duty then."

"Hm," Jan said. "That's it for now. We reserve the right to come back if we have further questions. It would be nice to be given a warmer reception next time."

Ewers glared at the two men but nodded obediently.

As Jan and Chandu turned to leave, the doctor called after them.

"You know something? Bernhard was a pain in the ass, but I'll miss him."

His words seemed genuine.

"Don't you worry," Jan replied. "We'll find the murderer. We're just getting warmed up."

They left the room.

"You don't think he was the murderer," Chandu said on their way back outside.

"What makes you say that?"

"You let him off the hook too quickly."

"I can't say exactly what it is," Jan began. "Guys like him, they think the world belongs to them. They love exercising their power over others, bullying everyone around them. Dr. Aaron Ewers is quick-tempered and touchy, probably beats up his wife and screams at his staff. But preparing a murder for days on end, digging out a grave, depositing the corpse, gouging the eyes out . . . None of that fits this asshole's style. I'd trust him to beat someone to death in a fit of rage, but anything beyond that is too calculating for him to manage."

"Maybe he's cleverer than we think."

"Possibly. I'll check his alibi, but to my mind, he's off the list of suspects."

"What do we do now?"

"I'll head back over to Dr. Valburg's office and speak to his receptionist. Maybe other people threatened Valburg, people he didn't report. Plus I'll get that patient list."

"I'll go fishing around in the drug scene tonight," Chandu told him, "and see who tries swimming away. Could take a few days, but if this Dr. Valburg was up to any funny business, I'll find it."

Jan gave Chandu a warm pat on the shoulder. "Thanks for your help."

"Don't mention it."

"We'll see each other tomorrow evening. Your place."

Chandu nodded. "Till then, happy hunting."

•   •   •

When Jan returned to Dr. Valburg's office, Vanessa Ziegler was struggling through a stack of files.

"I'm almost finished. I have your list too."

"Perfect," Jan said and handed her his card. "Could you send the documents to this e-mail address?"

She pocketed the card. "Will do."

"I was just at Dr. Aaron Ewers's office."

"That's too bad."

"You don't like him?"

"No one does. He's a vain, smug douchebag and only half as good as he thinks."

"Did Dr. Valburg butt heads with him a lot?"

She nodded. "The two of them knew each other from university. I was always warning my boss to take it easy. Talking to a man like Dr. Ewers about medical ethics is pointless."

"But he tried anyway?"

"Dr. Valburg was an idealist, sacrificing everything to care for his patients. That's why I liked working for him."

"That mean we should rule out any of his patients as a potential murderer?" Jan asked.

"I'm a doctor's assistant, not Sherlock Holmes. Of course there was trouble with some patients. Some weren't satisfied with their recovery process; others couldn't understand it when insurance didn't cover all the costs."

"About how many unhappy patients were there?"

"Tough to say. Three or four a month."

"That adds up to quite a lot over the years."

"Compared to other practices, it's a ridiculously small number."

"Were there patients who were especially unhappy? Say, someone who threatened Dr. Valburg?"

"A quibble over extra fees here, a door slammed there. Nothing that would justify a murder."

"Was there ever a misdiagnosis that harmed a patient?"

Vanessa narrowed her eyes in anger. Nothing a casual observer would notice, but it was exactly the type of thing Jan was looking for. He'd hit a sore spot.

"Medicine is not mathematics," she told him. "Of course, in over twenty years of practicing as a doctor, you occasionally don't recognize an illness or give the wrong diagnosis. But Dr. Valburg was a conscientious pulmonologist."

Jan was careful here. He didn't want to further anger the woman. He asked, "How severe were these erroneous assessments of his?"

"What do you mean by 'severe'?"

"Did anyone die because of a wrong diagnosis?"

"No." She sounded certain of it.

"So none of Dr. Valburg's patients ever died?"

"My dear Herr Tommen," Vanessa began as if speaking to a three-year-old. "A lung specialist doesn't just treat asthma patients and cure bouts of bronchitis. Many people come to us severely ill. In the case of, say, an advanced bronchial carcinoma or pulmonary arterial hypertension, there's not much more you can do to help. Of course some patients die."

"Let's move away from patients to other individuals Dr. Valburg dealt with."

"What kind of other individuals?"

"Friends, neighbors, pharmaceutical reps, or other caring colleagues like our Dr. Ewers. Especially anyone Dr. Valburg might have had a dispute with."

Vanessa rubbed at her lips in thought. Her forehead wrinkled up as if she was trying hard to think. "Maybe there was someone."

"Who?"

"I don't know him," Vanessa explained. "He wasn't a patient. It was evening; the office was closed. Dr. Valburg had just left, and I was tidying up the waiting room. When I went to lock up the door, the doctor was still standing out in the parking lot. He was arguing with a man."

"Could you hear what it was about?"

"No. They finished arguing. The man screamed, 'Quit bothering me!' and took off down a side street. Dr. Valburg got into his car and drove off."

"How long ago was this?"

"Four weeks."

"You know the man?"

"That was the first time I saw him. And I haven't seen him since."

"What did he look like?"

"About five foot eleven. Slender. Short dark hair."

"A fellow doctor?"

Vanessa shook her head. "I know most of Dr. Valburg's colleagues. Plus, he was too seedy-looking to be a doctor."

"Too seedy-looking?"

"He was wearing worn-out jeans and a leather jacket. His nose was crooked, and he had a scar running above his eyebrows."

"You can remember that so clearly?"

"My passion is portrait painting. I can size up a person's looks quickly, and I have an eye for small details."

"Would you be able to sit down with a police sketch artist? Using your skills, we're sure to get a good picture of the man."

Vanessa nodded. "As good as any photo."

Jan Tommen smiled at that. He had his first suspect.

Chapter Three

Jan jolted awake screaming. His heart was racing, and he was panting as if he'd run a marathon. It took a moment for him to recognize his surroundings. The light from the hallway shone faintly on his bedroom—the large wardrobe, the bed, and the dresser. He closed his eyes and buried his face in his hands. With every breath, his beating heart slowed, his panting calmed, and his hands relaxed. Sometimes when this happened, in an effort to forget the nightmare, he'd try to recall the latest soccer scores or even take a cold shower—but when the nightmare was this intense, not even that shock to his system made a difference.

Jan's weapon lay next to the bed on the nightstand, not securely stored like it should be at home, flouting regulations. The gun was dark and heavy. A constant reminder of the day he had shot his girlfriend dead.

A hundred times he had entertained the thought of throwing the thing out the window, but he was terrified of what the person who found it might do with it. As a cop, he was supposed to carry his duty weapon on him when it wasn't locked up for safekeeping. Always. No exceptions.

He used to like to practice at the shooting range, but today he felt sick just looking at the gun. So he took the pistol off the night table, yanked out the magazine, and removed each cartridge. Carrying his weapon without ammo was a severe breach of regulations as well, but as long as the pistol was in his holster, no one would know. Besides, he couldn't imagine shooting anyone again, even if life depended on it.

He tucked the cartridges inside the drawer. Then he lay back down, pulled up the covers, and closed his eyes. Maybe he could sleep a little now. He had so much to do before they all gathered at Chandu's that evening.

He left the light on in the hallway, just in case the nightmare returned.

• • •

It was a weird feeling for Jan, being back in Chandu's apartment. He had hidden out here for several weeks when he was wanted for murder. It had been his safe harbor, and he had felt at home immediately.

Nothing had changed since he'd moved out. He recognized the sharp aroma of incense that greeted him as he walked in the front door. The leather couch—Jan's ad hoc bed—shone as if polished. The flat-screen was set to the sports channel.

Chandu was toiling away in the kitchen. He opened the oven, and a whiff of Alsatian tart wafted through the room, a wave of pure delight. Jan closed his eyes and inhaled the aroma of the thin, pizza-like delicacy. His friend's culinary talents never ceased to surprise him.

"Just about done," Chandu called over to him. "Sit yourself down."

Jan smiled back, feeling a rare contentment. It was so much better to meet here than in the conference room at the station. He was about to sit down at the table when someone knocked on the door and rang the bell aggressively at the same time.

"One brief moment of bliss," Jan muttered. He took a deep breath, then went to open the door.

"Well, finally," Zoe said, stepping inside.

"And a good evening to you too."

Zoe replied with a grouchy grunt and lit up a cigarette. Max followed her in and shrugged as if to say, *It's not my fault.*

Zoe went into the kitchen and bent over the tart, eyeing it critically. She stayed there a moment and then sat down at the table, scowling and silent.

While she blew smoke rings at the ceiling, Jan helped set the table.

Chandu turned to Jan as he cut his masterpiece into wedges. "Did you find out anything else?"

"Not much at first. I spoke to the assistant, Vanessa Ziegler. She only had good things to say about her former boss. I questioned her about unhappy patients or colleagues, but Dr. Valburg appears to have been a well-liked and respected physician."

He bit into a piece of tart. "Then it got more interesting. Vanessa Ziegler told me about an argument the doctor had with an unknown man. Four weeks ago. There was a violent exchange of words, and the two of them did not part amicably."

"Could she describe the man?" Chandu asked.

"Better than that. Vanessa Ziegler is a portrait painter. She and our sketch artist got together and produced an amazingly good picture of the man—crooked nose, scar over his eyebrows, and all."

"So?" Zoe asked, sighing impatiently. "Who is the guy?"

"No idea," Jan said. "Not yet. We're comparing the picture with suitable Berlin-area offenders, but we don't have any hits yet. We've distributed it to all bureaus, informed patrols."

"Do you have the picture on you?" Zoe asked.

"I'll show you after we eat."

"Any idea what this dude's turf is, what scene? Drug smuggling? Prostitution?" Chandu asked.

"Unfortunately, I don't have anything apart from his appearance."

"I could probably help you there," Zoe said with her mouth full.

The three men's eyes turned to her.

"The good Dr. Valburg was taking drugs."

Jan started. "What? His assistant never told me any of that."

"Maybe you're not as irresistible as you think."

"What was he taking?"

"Coke."

"Was he on drugs the day he died?" Jan asked.

"No. I only discovered it when I was testing his hair. His blood had nothing. From the amounts, I'm guessing casual user."

"What about knockout drops or some other narcotic?"

"Nope."

"How's it looking with any defense wounds? Did he try and defend himself?"

"Nope again. Nothing points to a struggle. He got one on the back of the head and was done for."

"And the eyes?"

"What about them?"

"Post- or premortem?"

"The former."

"That's interesting."

"In what way?" Chandu asked.

"Gouging out the eyes can mean a million things. One murderer doesn't want the victim looking at him, while another is scared of the eyes because they're the mirror of the soul. All that crap. A profiler could fill a book with the possible interpretations. Since the killer gouged out Dr. Valburg's eyes *after* he died, he's likely not the type of maniac who wanted to make his victim suffer. It was a quick death, remember, from the blow to the head—not some drawn-out torture."

"But why gouge out his eyes, then?" Max asked.

"That takes us back to where we started. It must have a meaning. What, I can't say."

"Maybe Dr. Valburg saw something that he wasn't supposed to see," Chandu said.

"Possibly," Jan said. "But this piece of evidence isn't helping us much right now."

"Let's keep an eye on it, though," Zoe added, chuckling.

Chandu and Max laughed along with her.

"Real grown-ups here," Jan said, rumpling his brow at them. "Murder weapon?"

"Just as I thought. A hammer."

"Hmm." Jan stared at his plate with its half-eaten slice of tart, deep in thought.

Chandu interrupted his musings. "O great thinker, enlighten us with your wisdom."

"I was just matching up the various reports in my head. The crime-scene investigators at Dr. Valburg's house didn't find any evidence of a break-in. So the perp is a capable intruder. That, or he had a key. What's still unclear is whether the murderer was waiting for his victim or let himself in after Valburg came home. In any case, he surprised Dr. Valburg and struck him dead from behind. Dead before he knew what was happening."

"How did the murderer get the body to the cemetery?" Chandu asked.

"We don't have much on that," Jan said. "Zoe already mentioned that you can't lift an over-two-hundred-pound man onto your shoulder and carry him out of the house like a sack of lawn fertilizer. One thing that sticks out is that we haven't found any traces of blood outside of the living room, so I'm guessing the murderer wrapped up the body somehow."

"There could also have been a case or a barrel," Chandu added. "If the killer couldn't carry the body out himself, he'd have some means to help him. A wheelbarrow, a handcart, something like that. Even a corpse wrapped in plastic would be noticeable because of its odd shape."

"The murderer struck at night," Zoe said. "You don't see anyone in a neighborhood like that at that hour."

"There's always someone heading somewhere," Chandu argued. "Street cleaners, newspaper carriers, bus drivers on the late-night route. But since we're assuming that the job was long in planning, the killer would have taken that into account."

"So he'd have chosen something inconspicuous for transport," Jan said.

Chandu nodded. "I'm betting it's an oil barrel or a large box or crate. The killer wraps up the corpse so as not to leave behind any more clues. Then he schleps the body to the back door and heaves it into this container. Using a wheelbarrow, it's easy enough to get the corpse to the car."

"So how does this help us?" Zoe asked.

"It does tell us something about the vehicle," Jan explained.

"Bingo." Chandu gave them two thumbs up. "A corpse wrapped in plastic? You can stuff that in any kind of car. A box that has to be big enough for a corpse? We're talking about a small van or SUV. Which narrows our search a lot, if you think about how few vehicles are on the road at that time of night. And he was certain to have a vehicle. It's not like he walked over a mile to Dorotheenstadt Cemetery."

"Did you check the property for tire tracks?"

"The area surrounding the house isn't exactly detective-friendly. Valburg had a wide flagstone path that led all the way up to both the front and rear exits. You can forget about footprints or anything of the sort." Jan sighed. "Just once, I'd like to have a murder take place in an apartment building with surveillance cameras."

"Maximal?" Zoe said. "Do you have anything to add?"

"Maximum," the young hacker said, correcting her. "Maximal is a major bullshitter from Nuremberg."

"Good to know."

Ignoring Zoe's taunting, Max rubbed the back of his hand across his mouth and cleared his throat as if he was about to give a speech. "Once I alerted Jan to the fact that Dr. Valburg ratted out Ewers, I scoured his personal computer. The victim didn't use his computer much. Barely twenty minutes a day. He checked his personal e-mail and browsed medical sites now and then to find an article. That was it. Nothing suspicious."

"What about the solo stuff?" Zoe asked.

"What solo stuff?"

"Oh, you know, the sites where desperate types like you go. Porn, online singles, Giantboobs.com. That kind of stuff."

"You have the wrong impression of 'types like me.'"

Zoe chuckled. "No, I don't. Those calluses on your hand do not lie."

"What calluses—"

"Can we just stick to the matter at hand," Chandu cut in. "I really don't need these images in my head while I'm eating."

Jan steered the conversation back to the case. "You find anything else, Max?"

"A few letters, of little interest to us. Otherwise, no hidden sectors or things like that to make me suspicious."

Jan turned to Zoe. "Did investigating the body's location turn up anything?"

"You're not going to like the answer."

"Tell me anyway."

"We didn't find anything we could use off the corpse. The rain did its usual magic. The investigators were concentrating on the cross with Dr. Valburg's date of death on it. But there wasn't a shred of DNA or so much as a fingerprint on that either. You can get wood and nails in any home-improvement store, in that same color too." Zoe slid two pieces of tart onto her plate and sprinkled them with chili powder. "So, nothing that gives us any leads."

"What about questioning the cemetery staff?" Chandu asked.

"We have two officers on it," Jan told him, "but no one was still on the premises at the time of the crime. We're looking for connections between cemetery employees and Dr. Valburg, but we haven't come up with anything. Our officers are questioning visitors too, but I'm not counting on anything coming of that." Jan took a swig of beer. "Goddamn it. That's not much."

"But you do have a suspect," Max said.

"Which is all we have. Even if we do find the man, we can't be certain he's the one who killed Valburg. A fingerprint, a surveillance tape, some DNA would have been nice."

"What about his taking drugs?" Zoe asked. "Maybe he was having a problem with his dealer."

"I doubt that. Dr. Valburg had enough money to procure his drugs."

"Plus a dealer doesn't go to all that trouble when he wants to bump someone off." Chandu stuck out his thumb and index finger. "Pull your piece, bang, done."

Jan absently twirled the beer bottle in his hand. These initial findings were dispiriting. There was no concrete proof pointing to a murderer and only one possible suspect. He knew neither the motive for the murder nor the significance of the grave.

"I'm going to go talk with Vanessa Ziegler again. Apparently our good doctor was no angel. She had to know about his taking drugs."

"I'll take this picture of the suspect and go ask around in the underworld," Chandu said.

"I'll check out Dr. Valburg's patient list," Max mumbled, his mouth full of food. "See if I can find a match on the police servers. Violent criminals have to see doctors too."

"I need a cigarette, to aid my digestion," Zoe said, getting up. "I'll talk to the cemetery crime team tomorrow. I'm not optimistic, but they haven't evaluated all the clues yet."

Jan raised his bottle. "We'd better enjoy our evening, because our manhunt starts up again first thing tomorrow morning."

•   •   •

Jan shuffled wearily up the stairs to his apartment. He got a strange feeling every time he passed Father Anberger's apartment. The priest had been the final victim of Jan's girlfriend, Betty. Jan missed their casual conversations in the stairway, the priest's unshakeable optimism, his faith in Good.

The apartment door opened, and Jan leapt aside as if expecting the deceased father to greet him. Instead, a small young woman came out. She had short dark hair, a dark complexion, and lovely almond-shaped eyes. Jan guessed she was in her early twenties. She carried two books under one arm and had a cloth tote bag hanging off the other shoulder.

She came over to Jan and held out a hand. "Hello. My name is Lan."

Jan shook her hand. After a stupid-sounding "Hello," nothing more came out of his mouth. He hadn't realized Father Anberger's apartment had already been rented.

"So do you have a name?" she asked.

"Tommen. Jan, I mean. Tommen is my last name. You can just call me Jan." He was still holding on to her hand.

He pulled back his fingers as if he'd burned himself and stole a glance over the young woman's shoulder into the apartment, still half expecting the priest to come out.

His new neighbor caught him looking in the apartment and furrowed her brow.

"Sorry about that, Frau Lan," he muttered.

"Lan is my first name."

"Oh—then, sorry, Lan. Speaking of which: what kind of name is that?"

"Vietnamese."

"Ah. You're from Vietnam."

"No. Potsdam."

"Oh," Jan said, and added, by way of apology, "I only thought, because you're so . . . I meant, you look like you—"

"My dad's Vietnamese."

"Ah." Jan squeezed out a tortured smile. "Vietnam is awesome. I could die for some *bami goreng.*"

"That's Indonesian. Maybe you mean some *bánh mì?*"

"Right." Jan coughed in embarrassment and changed the subject. "Anyway, sorry for peeking into your apartment—it's just that I knew the renter who lived there before you."

"The priest who was murdered?"

"You know about that?" Jan was surprised. The tenants' association had asked the residents to keep it quiet so as not to scare away potential renters.

"Sure I do. That's the reason I got the apartment so easily."

"I didn't think anyone knew about it."

"The Internet helped. I followed the case online, Herr Detective," she said with a wink. "I posted in apartment-seekers' forums that the victim had lived here. Once I did that? All the potential renters bailed. Apart from me." She shrugged. "Made up a few extra-bloody details, and the pad went down two hundred euros."

Jan had to cough again. His new neighbor was nobody's fool. Plus, it was pretty ballsy admitting to a detective that you'd run what basically sounded like a con.

"Well, have a good night, Jan. A little sleep would do you good," she said, gazing into his eyes.

"Thanks." Jan wasn't sure what he was thanking her for.

"I have to go to my study group." She held up her books. "Number theory." She smiled at him, shut the door behind her, and went down the stairs.

"Good night," Jan said, still confused, and waved after her.

Today was just not his day.

· · ·

Jan had lain awake thinking about the case half the night and only fell asleep around two a.m. Now he sat at his desk in the police department, rubbing at his eyes, exhausted. He was badly in need of caffeine, and he could read up on the facts just as well over in the police department's coffee lounge. As he was leaving his office with his notes, he nearly collided into Bergman, the head of detectives.

"I was looking for you."

Jan sighed. Those words were never a good sign.

Bergman pointed a thumb at the woman next to him. "Let me introduce you to Dr. Kerima Elmas. Clinical psychologist."

Jan shook her hand. She was a petite woman with a friendly smile. Her brown locks matched her dark eyes. Only her large nose and old-fashioned glasses detracted from her attractiveness. Jan put her in her late thirties.

"Kerima will be spending the next hour with you."

"I thought we agreed I'd be spared all that."

"We did?"

"You gave me your word."

"Then I must have been lying." Bergman flashed his radiant smile.

"Nothing to be afraid of, Herr Tommen," Kerima said. "So far? No deaths or injuries have resulted from my little conversations."

"It's not that. I'm in the middle of an investigation, and I don't have the time to talk about my childhood or my relationship with my mother."

"You must not have a very high opinion of psychologists."

Jan stuttered, "Well, I wouldn't put it like that—"

"In any case," Kerima went on, "we always hold these conversations during work time. Possible post-traumatic stress disorder occurs during situations of stress, not while golfing."

"What post-traumatic stress disorder?"

Kerima briefly glanced behind them, down the hall. Some of Jan's fellow cops just happened to be leaning in doorways, trying to look busy. "I'm not sure we should be discussing this here."

Jan turned to Bergman. "I have to get over to Dr. Valburg's office."

"You'll have to take a short detour first."

"There's a murderer on the loose out there."

"He'll still be there in half an hour."

"I'm really not up for this."

"Tough luck. I'm the Chief of Detectives. So you're going with Dr. Elmas right here and now. Don't come back out until a half hour's up."

The psychologist turned to Bergman. "Afterward, we should talk about your management style."

"Hey, I'm not the patient here, Jan is."

"It's no problem," Kerima said. "I don't have anything else scheduled for this morning."

"Yeah, you should definitely talk to Herr Bergman here about his management style," Jan added, grinning. He might just get to like this woman yet.

"Shut it, Jan, or I'll use your Christmas bonus to bet on horses. And as far as you're concerned, Dr. Elmas? When I feel the need to interpret inkblots, I'll give you a call."

"Doesn't work that way—in my position, I can suggest a consultation and all the staff have to comply." She allowed herself a smile.

Bergman looked at his watch. "Oops, got a meeting." He turned and left them standing in the hallway.

"He does that a lot," Jan told Kerima.

"Does what, exactly? Insults, threats, appears unwilling to learn?"

"All of that."

Max came around the corner. He was riding a chrome kick-scooter, leaning into it like a race driver in an aerodynamic stance. He pushed off with his right foot to gain speed and whooshed by them. "Morn-eeeng," he called out in a childlike voice, drawing out the *ee* until he reached the end of the corridor.

Kerima peered after him. "Maybe I should set up a permanent office right here in the station," she muttered. "Lots of work to be had here." She steered Jan into to the conference room and shut the door behind them.

"What do you want to hear?" Jan grumbled.

"I'm interested in how you're doing."

"Me? Pretty well."

"You'll have to be more specific than that."

"What makes you think I'm having any problems?"

Kerima took a file folder from her bag. "Let me go over it. In your last case—just a few weeks ago—you were suspected of murder, were hunted by your colleagues, and had to go underground. It was finally revealed that your girlfriend was the murderer and she was using you as the fall guy. She tried to kill you, so you had no choice but to shoot her dead." The psychologist folded her hands in her lap. "Even if you're the toughest cop in Berlin, Herr Tommen, no one recovers from all that in just a few weeks."

"What was I supposed to do, take time off, go into a monastery and meditate?"

"I want to know how your life has changed since this case. How you're getting through the day, if you're having trouble sleeping, things like that."

"I have nightmares. I had to get rid of all photos of Betty and me, and yet I drive by all the places in Berlin that remind me of her."

Kerima nodded. "I've never heard anyone be so open the first time we talk."

"What do you expect? Of course it's stayed with me. But the worst thing I can be doing is nothing at all. Working helps. Hanging out with friends helps. Sitting in front of the TV watching a good soccer game helps too. What doesn't help is always having to think about it."

"Talking about it helps too."

"Who am I supposed to talk to? My buddy? He was there. He saw my girlfriend pointing a shotgun at my head. He saw me putting a bullet in her, her life flowing out of her. He nearly bought it too, that day."

"You can talk to me."

"But you don't understand," Jan said. "You might well be a capable psychologist, but you don't know a thing about everyday life as a cop. You've never aimed a weapon at someone, and I highly doubt that you've shot your lover."

"If I don't know how all that feels, then why not try and explain it to me?"

"What is there to explain? Betty had a shotgun in her hand and was about to blow my head off. If I hadn't shot back, I'd be dead now."

"So you had no choice."

"You might have that impression, but it's cold comfort. I live through that moment again and again and keep asking myself whether I handled it right. If I had just wounded Betty, she'd still be alive."

"She wasn't the first person you'd ever killed."

"The other ones deserved it."

"You don't think that a serial killer who tried to murder you deserved it?"

"It might look that way when you describe it like that. But she was my girlfriend and I loved her. In my dreams I saw us as an old married couple, sitting together on a veranda, watching the sun go down." Jan looked at the floor. "I might have acted according to protocol, and I probably had no other choice, but I still won't ever forgive myself for killing her."

Kerima observed Jan a moment as if hoping he would continue. Then she paged through a folder. "Has your relationship to your colleagues changed in any way?"

"What do you mean?"

"To the Berlin police, you were the main suspect in the George Holoch murder case for several days. Your colleagues, one Herr Patrick Stein in particular, basically became your worst enemies overnight."

Jan leaned back in his chair. "It's complicated."

"Try to untangle it."

"Patrick and I could never stand each other. I thought he was a conformist, always going by the book. He categorized me as this trigger-happy maniac who didn't care about the rules. Not the best conditions for working together. But with this last case, it was different. Patrick was downright obsessed with catching me, ignoring all clues pointing to other suspects and focusing entirely on the evidence that incriminated me. Only after our little encounter did he finally start to have doubts."

"And this impressed you?"

"To understand what I'm telling you, you'd have to know Patrick better. For him there was only the proper, by-the-book way of doing things. He ignored anything outside the box. He was obstinate and refused to learn and got stuck on the completely wrong track in pursuing George Holoch's killer. But eventually, Patrick's intellect won out over his obsession with getting one over on me. He was man enough to own up to his mistakes and apologize. That's when I understood that for Patrick, it's not about his ego but about the cause. I hadn't thought him capable of operating like that."

"So you're good friends now?"

"That might be taking it a bit far. But we respect each other and are learning to work together. I appreciate his preoccupation with details and precision work, and he admires my unconventional methods." Jan shrugged. "If anything good came out of the last case, that was it."

Kerima eyed him, then stowed the folder in her bag. "Thanks a lot for your time, Herr Tommen."

Jan blinked at this abrupt end to the conversation. "That was it?"

She nodded. "I just wanted to talk with you."

"So what's your evaluation? Can I go back to work?"

"You misunderstand my role. I'm not here to make a decision about you. You should simply be sharing your thoughts and worries with someone. Even if you don't think a psychologist is useful, I'm sure that it'll help you feel better. And if it has a positive effect on your work, then it's in everyone's best interests."

"Am I crazy?"

She smiled. "No. But you do have a ways to go before you've worked through all this."

"Are you saying that things will eventually return to normal, that I'll feel like myself again?"

Kerima pulled off her glasses. "This incident will stay with you for the rest of your life. You'll just learn to live with it."

"I thought time healed all wounds."

"It's a nice thought, but unfortunately just that. Most scars are for life." Kerima was biting her lower lip. Jan had the impression that she knew what she was talking about.

She set down her card. "If you ever need to talk, call me. Doesn't matter how late." And with that, she left the conference room.

Once Kerima was gone, Jan leaned back in his chair. He didn't want to admit it, but he really did feel better. Maybe all this psycho hocus-pocus made some sense. He pocketed her card, stood, and went out to his car. It was time to go see about a killer.

•   •   •

When Jan returned to the doctor's office, Vanessa Ziegler was outside, loading a box of tchotchkes into her car—corny little figurines from vacations, decorative picture frames with fading photos. Jan noticed a deformed little plastic Eiffel Tower.

Vanessa looked tired. Her eyes were red, her face devoid of makeup.

"Good morning, Frau Ziegler," Jan said.

Vanessa turned to him and flashed a fake smile.

"Do you have a moment to talk to me?" he said.

She shrugged. "I'm unemployed. I have all the time in the world."

"It's about a serious matter, unfortunately."

"More serious than the murder of Dr. Valburg?"

Jan hated revealing unpleasant things about a murder victim, but he had to pursue every clue. "We found cocaine in his system."

Vanessa pursed her lips. Jan had expected a fit of fury or at least an outraged denial. But she only lowered her head in shame.

"You have to understand," she said, nearly whispering. "It all started when his wife was diagnosed with cancer, five years ago. Countless operations followed, X-rays, chemotherapy, the works. Annika saw the best doctors, but she couldn't get rid of it. Dr. Valburg spent every free second with his wife, went on vacations with her when they had a break from treatments, and even bought a new house without stairs just to make her days easier. But nothing worked. Annika died sixteen months ago. And Dr. Valburg's will to live died with her. If he hadn't been a faithful Christian, I'm sure he would've committed suicide."

She paused, then continued. "His patients didn't notice the change, but I knew him better. After work he'd go into his empty house and just vegetate. One evening, he seemed so out of it that I followed him and watched him from out in the yard. He took off his coat, sat on a chair, and stared at the empty wall. His eyes blinking were the only sign that he was still alive. After a while he buried his face in his hands and started to cry."

"Why is his house so empty?" Jan asked.

Vanessa lifted her head. "What do you mean?"

"He bought the house over a year ago, yet the moving boxes haven't been unpacked, cabinets not put up, no ceiling fixtures installed."

"That had to do with his wife dying. He bought that house for Annika. They wanted to spend the rest of their lives together there. The house kept reminding him of her. To him, it wasn't a home, it was a grave."

"So he turned to drugs."

"Dr. Valburg's happiness was deeply intertwined with his wife's. The cancer diagnosis threw him off course. The drugs helped him."

"Taking cocaine helped?"

"Dr. Valburg was barely sleeping after the cancer diagnosis. Some mornings he could scarcely keep his eyes open. But after lunch break, he'd be full of pep and wide awake, as if he'd drunk too much coffee."

"And that's how you knew he was doing cocaine?"

"I nearly lost a brother to drugs," Vanessa said. "I know the symptoms, unfortunately."

"What kind of symptoms?"

"Most noticeable was how his productivity would change. In the mornings, I was scared that he'd fall asleep right in his chair—but in the afternoons, as I said, he couldn't be stopped. And his entire mood changed too—he was always in great spirits after lunch. I didn't need to know any more than that."

"How addicted was he?"

"He struggled whenever he wasn't taking stimulants."

"How often did he take them?"

"Once a week."

"Where did he get the drugs?"

"That I don't know."

"Cocaine is still being used in medicine."

Vanessa nodded. "In cranial surgery."

"Could he have procured his drugs that way?"

"No! The medical profession was sacred to him. It might sound funny, but he never would have exploited his position for such a thing."

"Through a dealer, then?"

"I'm guessing, yes."

"Maybe a patient?"

"It's possible." Vanessa sounded unsure. "But I can't supply you with a suspect."

"Our computer geeks will do that," Jan told her. "They'll compare the patient list with any drug-related offenses in the database. Maybe we'll get a hit." He noted that down for Max.

"Could that man who was arguing with Dr. Valburg have been the dealer?" Vanessa asked.

"Maybe. We'll put out a search for him." Jan put away his notepad. "Thanks for your time." He shook Vanessa's hand. "I'll be in touch if I learn anything new."

Vanessa nodded, then went back inside the office.

On the way to his car, Jan took out his phone and called Chandu. It was time to stir things up in Berlin's underground.

•   •   •

It was late afternoon as Chandu strolled through the old hood. He'd spent most of his time here collecting on debts and roughing up borrowers who hadn't paid, people who'd been dumb enough to borrow money from underworld kingpins. They had all deserved it—dealers, fences, pimps, and other pillars of the community.

As he turned a corner, he noticed the street coming to life. Nothing that a normal citizen would notice. Up on the second floor of a tenement building, a face turned away from the window. A group of kids dispersed down below and disappeared into a back courtyard. A man on a park bench discreetly pulled his cell phone out of his pocket. It was more than enough warning.

Chandu had switched overlords. He had no friends here anymore, but more than enough new enemies. He could handle these gung-ho kiddies, but it wouldn't be long before the tough boys came marching in. Debt collectors taking his place, bodyguards wanting to protect their investment—whether it was a lucrative hooker or some little drug hideout. No one knew why he was here, but they would all assume that it wasn't for nostalgic reasons. And they would be right.

It was hard to predict how fast this network operated, but he was giving it ten minutes, tops. He might not be able to get back out after that.

It wasn't much time, but he couldn't reveal the slightest panic. He had worked hard for his rep as one rough thug. Any show of haste would give him away. Then those little hyenas would pounce on him even before the big lions arrived.

Chandu hated these ugly prefab tenement buildings. The gray walls were cracking and washed out, and the glass of one building's front door was shattered. A cheap satellite dish hung at every window. The place reeked of piss and vomit. Chandu stepped over a man propped up next to the door. He was holding a bottle of rotgut and muttering nonsense to himself.

Chandu headed to the fifth floor. Taking the elevator was too dangerous; he might get stuck there, unable to move. So he walked slowly up the stairs. There was neither a fire escape nor a second stairwell. The ideal conditions for a hunter. And he was still the hunter—but that would be changing soon.

Nine minutes, tops.

On the fifth floor, Chandu stopped in front of a door made of cheap pressboard, but he knew it was reinforced with extra deadbolts, a steel bar, and metal plating. At any rate, you couldn't just walk on in. Chandu was hoping his old trick still worked; otherwise he was going to lose valuable time.

He knocked three times, waited a moment, and then knocked twice. On the other side, a key turned and a chain pulled back. A clicking sound.

A little man with unusually thick glasses opened the door. His unwashed dark hair gleamed in the corridor's fluorescent light. His protruding teeth were more rodent-like than human. A tattered T-shirt hung off his scrawny shoulders.

Chandu landed a straight punch to the nose. Man and glasses flew, arcing backward, into the apartment.

"You should change your secret knock, Rat." Chandu stepped in and shut the door behind him.

He had three minutes—max. He'd need the rest of the time to clear out of the hood. So as not to give away his sense of urgency, he sat on an old armchair, crossing his legs. *Never be in a hurry; never show weakness.*

Tim's apartment hadn't changed in the last few years. Dark curtains kept the light out, though a small hole in the fabric gave him a sneaky glance onto the street. The kitchen consisted of little more than a sink with a dripping faucet and a microwave oven. Enough for Tim to warm up his dearly beloved ready-made tortellini, which had to be the only food in the droning fridge next to his folding camp table. There was no TV, much less flowers, photos on the walls, or any sort of decoration at all. At odds with the scant, rickety furnishings, a high-tech coffee machine stood on a stool next to the broken-down bed in the corner. Tim's second love—caffeine.

"You broke my nose," Tim shouted, pulling himself up. He felt around for his glasses with one hand while the other found his bloodied face.

"That beak of yours always was crooked. Can't be any worse than before."

"You know I hate that nickname."

"Your problem."

"My name is Tim."

"Can I get you anything else? Maybe some dessert?"

"What do you want? I don't have any debts."

"If you did, I wouldn't be treating you so nicely right now."

Tim picked up his glasses off the floor. The bridge was busted, the glasses in two pieces. He tried setting one piece on an ear while holding his nose with the other hand.

"You broke my glasses," he whined.

Chandu sighed. "Sometimes I ask myself how you survive in a hood like this."

"Why'd you have to hit me?"

"For old time's sake."

Tim stared at the blood streaming down his hand and forearm and pressed his lips together. He looked like he might start bawling.

"I don't keep any stuff at my place and no money here. If you want to rob someone, try the seventh floor. That pimp, he—"

"Spare me your bitching. Give me some info, and I'll be on my way."

"What's in it for me?" Tim's expression switched from sniveling to all business. He straightened up, his broken nose apparently forgotten.

"I won't rip your ears off, that's what."

"I'm not doing jobs anymore," Tim began. "So it's hardly like I'd—"

"I'm not here to chat." Chandu rose from the chair. He positioned himself before the little man, whose head only reached Chandu's chest. The threat did the trick. Tim's gaze found the floor.

Chandu pulled the police sketch from his pocket and thrust it at him. "I want to know who this is."

Tim squinted with one eye and stared at the picture with the other. "Why come to me?"

"You know every cockroach in Berlin. If you don't disappoint me, I'll send you a teddy bear for Christmas. Maybe stuff it with a few bucks—if the info's any good."

Tim grumbled to himself.

"I'll take that as a yes." Chandu lifted a threatening finger. "I'm expecting results within the next thirty-six hours. That'll spare you another visit. You know how to reach me."

Chandu left the apartment without turning around. He'd put the Rat on the scent. Hardly anyone in Berlin knew its seedy underbelly better. If the man in the picture was involved in any dirty business, this little snoop would find him.

Chandu closed the door and glanced at his watch. He had to hurry.

As he headed down the stairs, he heard tires screeching outside. A man was shouting something in a foreign language. He thought he heard a gun being cocked.

He cursed to himself. Time was up.

．　　　．　　　．

Chandu ran to the second floor, rammed a door open with his shoulder, and rushed inside. The apartment stank of grease and cheap schnapps. An old man sat on a shabby couch. He wore a stained undershirt and wagged a beer bottle at Chandu's face.

"Get outta here!" the man hollered.

"Gladly," Chandu replied, crossing the room. He opened a window, positioned himself on the window frame, hung down, and let go. The ground wasn't too far, about ten feet. He rolled away, hauled himself up, and ran into the building's rear courtyard. With any luck, the thugs would search the building first before they were on to his trail.

He headed deeper into the tenement blocks. Three more buildings and he'd reach the safety fence at the train overpass. The area beyond that was vast and offered little cover. His only chance was along the fence line to the neighboring buildings and through their backyards.

Chandu came to a run-down playground. The swings were torn off, and the wood on the jungle gym all weather-beaten. A teen boy rode up on a dirt bike. He wore faded jeans, an old jacket. Chandu could tell at a glance he wasn't carrying a gun. Maybe a concealed knife, but Chandu wasn't worried about that.

The kid brought his motorbike to a stop two yards from Chandu, straightened up, and shouted, "Here he is!"

Chandu overcame the distance to the kid and connected a solid haymaker to his temple. The kid flew from the motorbike and landed next to the jungle gym.

"Always wear a helmet, kid."

Chandu pulled up the motorbike, got it in gear, and rode off. A shot rang out. He ducked and revved the engine.

Another shot. Dust sprayed up next to him.

He raced on across the footpath and yanked the motorbike hard to the right. A bicycle rider appeared and saved himself by veering into the bushes. Earth and pebbles filled the air as Chandu raced toward the street. He laughed as the wind rushed past his face.

Maybe being an informant wasn't so bad after all.

•   •   •

Jan paced back and forth in the investigations room. His conversation with Vanessa Ziegler hadn't told him anything new. Zoe was still analyzing the last of the evidence, Max was comparing the patient list with the police database, and Chandu was out looking for the possible perp from the sketch.

An image of Dr. Valburg was starting to emerge, however. The better Jan knew a victim, the easier he arrived at his killer. But he had not yet found the decisive clue.

The way the murder had been carried out remained unclear. The grave, the cross, announcing the victim's death in advance—it all had to mean something. He could rule out that testy Dr. Ewers, along with the possibility of a dealer. Neither of them would go to so much trouble. It was something personal. Someone who knew and hated Bernhard Valburg.

Jan's phone rang, jolting him out of his thoughts. He looked at the screen. Bergman. Jan moaned.

"Jan Tommen here."

"Get your ass in my office," Bergman said. "We have a new grave."

Chapter Four

The man in Bergman's office was visibly upset. He'd rumpled the jacket of his dark suit, unbuttoned his shirt, and loosened his tacky paisley tie. He sat hunched over a cup of coffee, staring into the dark brew like he was trying to read his fortune in it. His brown hair was damp with sweat, as if he'd run all the way to the police department.

Bergman rose from his chair. "Herr Quast, allow me to introduce you. This is Jan Tommen. He's my lead investigator."

Jan shook the man's hand. It was moist and frail. "What happened?" Jan asked.

"This morning I went to visit my parents' grave, as I do every Wednesday. Stahnsdorf Cemetery. When I got there, I discovered that a pit had been dug next to it."

"Dug next to it?"

"There's a patch of grass to the right of the grave site. No graves are supposed to go there. You can imagine my surprise when I saw a wooden cross planted there too—with my name on it."

"With the date of death?"

"Tomorrow. June twenty-seventh." He took a slug of coffee. "I would've thought it some kind of sick joke if I hadn't heard about that doctor being murdered. He was standing at his grave too."

"Did you know Dr. Bernhard Valburg?"

"Never heard of him."

"Are you certain?"

"He sure wasn't my doctor. I'll go through my customer list, though, to see if maybe he bought a car from me."

"You're a car salesman?"

"If you're into roomy Toyota wagons, I'm your man."

"Could you provide me with a list of potential customers, or is there some sort of privacy issue?"

"I value my life more than anyone's privacy. You'll have more than my customer list; I'll get you my personal contacts list too. You can even go through my underwear drawer if it'll save my ass."

"That won't be necessary." Jan pulled out his notepad. "Can you think of anyone who would want to kill you?"

"A couple years ago? I would have guessed my ex-wife. But she's taken off with her fitness trainer to Majorca and is now trying to become one with the universe. Plus she always hated gardening, so a grave wouldn't be her thing."

"Anyone else? Unhappy customers, envious colleagues, angry neighbors?"

"You're occasionally going to have arguments with neighbors or coworkers. Things can always come up with a car sale, but it's all harmless stuff."

"Have you recently received any threatening phone calls or nasty letters, had your car keyed?"

"Nothing like that."

"Maybe persons from some other period in your life?"

"What period would that be?"

"Have you ever had gambling debts or any problems with drugs?"

"Come again?"

"Herr Quast," Jan said coolly. "If we're lucky, we'll find out that Dr. Valburg's murder inspired some idiot to play a cruel joke. Until then we have to take this death threat seriously. So you really should be telling us everything, even things you're not too proud of."

The man hesitated. Too long, Jan thought.

"I have nothing to tell!" he said finally, sounding offended.

Jan wasn't getting anywhere this way. He shut his notepad. "That'll do for now. Please do send us your customer list and contacts. We'll take a look at the grave and check out your background."

"You'll receive police protection, of course," Bergman added. "I'm recommending that you not go to work today or tomorrow and stay locked in at home. We'll post a patrol car outside your house. It might well prove to be a sick joke, but for now we have no choice but to take this kind of action."

The man sighed in relief. "Thank you."

"Stay there a moment, drink your coffee. I'm going to have a quick chat with Herr Tommen."

Bergman led Jan into the hallway and shut the door behind him. "How's it looking in the Valburg case?"

"Could be better," Jan said. "We have a possible suspect, but the killer left no clues behind. No fingerprints, no DNA."

"Is this the same offender?"

"Could well be. Now that we have two potential victims, we just might find a connection that'll give us some new leads."

"Between a doctor and a car salesman?"

"Dr. Valburg was going through a good deal of turmoil. Maybe the cocaine was just the tip of the iceberg. I do know one thing: our new victim, Moritz Quast, was hiding something from me."

"What?"

"No idea. First I have to make sure Herr Quast survives the night. I'll take it up with him again tomorrow morning."

"Maybe it really is a coincidence?"

"I doubt that. There has to be some kind of connection between the doctor and our car salesman, and it's going to lead us to the murderer."

•   •   •

Dusk was approaching as Moritz Quast lowered the shades in the living room. He had hardly any furniture. No books or CDs. No flowers to add a touch of color to the room. No framed family photos. Just an oversized poster of Pamela Anderson on one wall. The room did sport a flat-screen standing amid assorted game consoles. A little fridge abutted a daybed. Bottle caps and beer stains decorated the battered throw rug in front of it.

Only missing the bearskin rug and porn collection, Jan thought as he checked the windows.

Lowering the shades wasn't strictly necessary, but Jan wanted to show Quast that things were secure. The car salesman was still jumpy. On the way home, even with Jan accompanying him, he had peered nervously around at every intersection. Quast had practically sprinted up the short path leading from the street to his house, and he'd barely managed to get the key in the lock with his hand shaking so badly. If Jan hadn't been there, the guy probably would have hidden under that daybed.

"What now?" asked Quast.

Jan was hoping the man would start to calm down now that he was home, but no such luck. His eyes were those of a cornered animal, and his blue shirt was soaked with sweat. He clawed at the inside of his jacket with his right hand.

"Let's go through the routine one more time." Jan said, doing his best to sound composed. The whole way over, he had explained how Quast should conduct himself while under police protection, but a second go couldn't hurt. Otherwise the man might flip out at the slightest sound. "We secured the windows and pulled down all the shades. Front and back doors are locked up. You do not let anyone in. No friends. No relatives. Not even pizza delivery. At the front door are two of my colleagues, who'll be watching out for you the whole night. Their names are David Fleck and Fabian Gisker. Both are reliable men with experience."

Jan handed Quast a police radio. "This is how you reach the officers out there. Press the button on the left here and speak. That saves you having to call. My colleagues have a key to your house. If you need help, they'll be in here in the blink of an eye."

Quast took the portable radio in his hand and pressed it to his chest as if his life depended on it.

"If anything strikes you as unusual, just report it over the portable. You also have the police number and my cell."

Jan placed a hand on the car salesman's shoulder. He was surprised at how much the man was shaking.

He pointed to the flat-screen. "Watch some TV. Try to relax and enjoy your evening. I'll come back by tomorrow morning and give you the latest on the investigation."

Quast nodded and sat down on the daybed. He turned on the TV with the remote and began surfing through the channels. The man would do a handstand if Jan asked him to.

There wasn't any more to be done there. The house was well secured, and his colleagues watching the door were reliable. Jan had searched all the rooms twice, so the killer couldn't already be in the house. Unless he was some master break-in artist, no way was he getting in.

"See you tomorrow," Jan said and left the house. Moritz Quast raised a hand without looking away from the screen.

Jan went through the front yard to the street. A patrol car was parked in front of the house. At first glance, it differed little from other cop cars, but if you looked more closely, you could recognize the driver's distinctive character. The rear window prominently displayed a Hertha Berlin soccer club sticker. The backseat served as clothes closet. Jackets, pants, and gloves were piled up next to shoes. On the middle console, a glittery little Elvis swiveled, and the cup holder was just as against-the-regs as the cell-phone tray next to it. And those were only what a passerby could see.

Jan knew the driver from his own days in training. Fabian Gisker was a legend. He didn't have great arrest stats, hadn't solved any big cases, was a miserable shot and even worse behind the wheel. But there was no shortage of anecdotes about him. Jan's favorite story involved an official reception where Fabian had barfed into his potato salad during the mayor's speech. Back then, Jan was still wet behind the ears and had just been assigned to Fabian. It proved to be the most exciting year of his police training. Fabian had shown him the darkest corners of Berlin and explained the rules of the street. He removed any illusions Jan held that the police were always respected wherever they went. It was a tough time, but he never forgot Fabian's favorite line: "Training with me isn't supposed to be fun, kid, it's supposed to help keep your ass out of the firing line." Jan had counted the days until he was assigned away from Fabian, and yet he had never learned as much as he had during that year.

Since the last time they'd seen each other, at the big police party, Fabian had gained some weight, and he now sported a full head of gray hair. His addiction to sweets was unchanged. On the floor of his car, Jan could see an empty six-pack of sticky buns, and a package on his lap still held one chocolate croissant. Only the family-size bag of gummy bears on the dashboard shelf was untouched. Five years from now, Jan predicted, Fabian's stomach would have grown so much that his hands probably wouldn't reach the steering wheel.

"Nothing like healthy eating," Jan said.

"Janni," Fabian greeted him enthusiastically. The cop wiped a coating of glaze off his mouth and reached through the open window to squeeze Jan's hand.

"Kid, this is Detective Jan Tommen," Fabian said to David, the young cop in the passenger's seat. "A pain in the butt and a wiseass you might just want to smack sooner rather than later, but he can drink a Russian polar bear under the table and is one of the few among us to make it all the way to the homicide squad."

"How's your side job as billboard going?" Jan said.

Fabian roared with laughter, resting a hand on Jan's shoulder. "Ah, Janni, I've missed you. Want a sticky bun?"

"There's some left?"

"No. I'll have the kid go fetch some. Then it'll just be us adults here and you can tell me about the case."

Next to him, David grumbled something. Jan was surprised by how young the other cop was—a smattering of stubble on a pimply face.

"Save your money," Jan said, waving Fabian's offer aside. He would've liked to accept, but he didn't want young David to be any more tormented than he already was. Training under Fabian was hard enough. "Not a lot to tell about the case. Our man Moritz Quast got a death threat. Someone dug a grave for him at the cemetery and wrote his name and date of death on a wooden cross next to it. Tomorrow this should all be over. Might have been a sick joke, except for the fact that we had the same incident three days ago—and now we have a corpse on our hands."

"I could smell how scared shitless this Quast was just walking in the front door," David said.

"Shut it, kid. Only the big dogs get to say the big lines," Fabian replied. He turned back to Jan.

"You thinking there'll be trouble?"

"I'm not sure. If it's the same murderer? He's going to try something tonight. Or it could be a copycat situation."

"You guys on his trail, though?"

"There's a few clues, nothing concrete."

"There's no maniac you don't nab."

"There's always a first time."

Fabian waved the notion aside. "Don't worry that fine head of yours. I'll see to it that our Nervous Nellie in there stays alive and you get your killer."

"Sounds good," Jan said and shook Fabian's hand again. "I've got to press on. Watch yourself and the freshman here, while you're at it. We can't underestimate this situation. The murderer, he's clever. He's not going to come knocking on the front door first."

"I may be fat and slow," Fabian said, "but I've got a gun. And the little one here can do the running."

Jan went back to his own car. He was trying to keep calm, but he couldn't help feeling uneasy about this. Fabian was a dependable officer, but it seemed to Jan that he was treating this case too casually. The guy knew his way around junkies, pimps, and drunk thugs, but he had never had to deal with a cunning serial killer, possibly psychotic. If they were assessing the perp correctly, nothing would stop him.

Jan suddenly got the feeling that he was seeing Fabian for the last time. Then he brushed the thought aside, started up the car, and headed out to see Chandu.

• • •

Jan bounded into the apartment. He was at least twenty minutes late, and he hated not being punctual. Chandu waved him in. Judging from the strong smell of smoke, Zoe had already been here a while. Max was sitting in an armchair working his phone, his body tensed up and his forehead furrowed in concentration. He was probably busy with his favorite game—something to do with zombies and plants.

"Sorry," Jan told them. "I had to help our potential victim calm down a bit—he's out of his mind with fear that he's going to end up a dead man tomorrow."

"How did you do that?" Zoe asked. "Stroke his head, feed him a little bedtime snack?"

"I secured his house and put a patrol car out front."

"Good people?"

"You know Fabian Gisker?"

"The fat one? Threw up on the buffet at the mayor's reception?"

"The very one."

"That's just great," Zoe grumbled. "I'd better be ready to work tomorrow."

"He's an experienced police officer," Jan shot back, defending his call.

Zoe sucked on her cigarette and exhaled, on edge. "We going to get started or just keep yapping all night for no reason?"

"I like yapping for no reason," Max remarked without looking up from his phone.

"Can it, Maximum Moron. Start up that projector."

Max put down his phone and turned to Chandu, standing over in the kitchen. "Would you, please?"

The light went out. With the shades pulled down it was pitch-black.

Zoe's voice rang out in the darkness. "Look here. Whatever you guys got planned, I have a scalpel in my pocket and no scruples about using it."

Flickers of light came from the kitchen. Chandu carried in a cake with candles. Jan, Max, and Chandu sang "Happy Birthday." And Chandu set down the cake at Zoe's place. The light came on again.

"How did you . . ." Zoe was clearly speechless.

"Our good man Maximum here just happened to be in the staff database and stumbled upon your birthdate," Jan explained. "So we thought you'd like a little something."

"Cherry cheesecake." Chandu gestured to it. "I overheard that you liked the combo."

"Is that thirty-two candles?" Max whispered in Jan's ear.

"Are you insane? I told Chandu to do twenty-seven. She realizes you know how old she is? She'll perform a dissection on you right here. Alive."

Chandu leaned down to Zoe and gave her a kiss on the cheek. "With love, my little charmer. You can blow out the candles now."

Zoe shut her eyes, took a deep breath, and blew out the flames. Her eyes sparkled with childlike excitement. It was the first time that Jan had ever seen Zoe smile. For a brief moment her armor had weakened, and she seemed something like happy.

Chandu handed her a cake knife. "Here. Since you do know a thing or two about cutting things into pieces."

Zoe raised her head, looking into Chandu's eyes. Her smile had vanished, but she didn't look grim. She acted as if she were seeing them all for the first time.

She jerked up, standing. "I have to go to the bathroom," she said and pushed past Jan. Surprised by her urgency, he took a step back and almost fell onto the coffee table.

"Cut the cake," she shouted at Chandu. "Be right back."

Jan thought he spied tears in her eyes as he watched her rush down the hallway in her high-heeled boots.

Then she disappeared into the bathroom and slammed the door.

•　　•　　•

Several minutes later, Zoe, Chandu, and Jan were sitting on the couch holding plates of cake. Jan was stealing glances at Zoe, who appeared to have recovered from her outbreak of actual emotion. Her expressionless mask was firmly back in place. Max stood next to the couch, adjusting the projector beam. His hands were stained with remnants of cherry. Two images appeared on the wall.

Max pushed a key on his laptop, and a little *ta-da* fanfare sounded.

"Allow me to introduce . . ." He made a sweeping gesture toward the wall. "Bernhard Valburg and Moritz Quast."

Both photos were formal. Each man was peering earnestly into the camera. Bernhard Valburg was wearing a doctor's coat and had a stethoscope hanging around his neck. Moritz Quast was dressed in a dark suit, looking like a serious car salesman with his red tie.

"A grave was dug for both men," Max continued. "Bernhard Valburg was murdered and dumped into his. Moritz Quast is still alive and is locked up in his home."

"This the same perpetrator?" Chandu asked, chewing.

"Officially, we're not certain," Jan said, "but internally we're going with the same perp."

"How come?"

"The crosses," Zoe said. "The type of wood is identical, as is the paint."

"Are there connections between the two men?"

"We haven't found any yet," Jan said.

"The first thing I did was compare the patient list with the car salesman's customer list, but I got no hits," Max added. "Moritz Quast was not a patient of Bernhard Valburg, nor did the doctor buy a car from Quast."

"Did the two know each other personally?"

"Not according to Quast," Jan said. "But our car salesman was quite rattled. It took him five minutes to tell us his address. We're not going to get anything significant out of him before tomorrow."

"If he's still alive tomorrow," Zoe said.

"We have a car outside his house; the doors are locked up and the shades down. I checked the rooms twice."

"It's still not impossible."

"He'll survive tonight, but I have no idea how we're going to keep watching over Moritz Quast indefinitely. We can't keep him locked up in his place forever."

"Then we'll have to find the killer." Chandu beamed, ever the optimist.

"I'm not seeing much progress as of now." Jan turned to Max. "Did you find any offenders among the doctor's patients?"

"Sort of," Max answered after hesitating a moment.

"So, no," Zoe said.

"I got one hundred and four hits. Most were petty offenses. There was one man in jail for aggravated assault, but he died of lung cancer five years ago."

"Like I said," Zoe added.

Max pursed his lips in anger. He was clearly frustrated not to have come up with better results.

"How's the search in the underworld?" Jan asked Chandu.

"I've persuaded my contact to cooperate, put the police sketch in his hand. He's keeping his ears open."

"Persuaded?" Zoe asked.

"I clocked him right on the nose."

"Oh, how creative."

Chandu shrugged. "It's a kind of a greeting ritual among us thugs. You don't get far by being polite."

"That might be a good way to motivate some of my lame-ass coworkers," Zoe said.

"I'm meeting up with him again tomorrow night. Maybe he'll have found out something by then," Chandu said.

"Can I come?" Zoe blurted.

"Where?"

"To meet the guy."

"Why would you want to?"

"To learn more about investigative work."

"It doesn't have much to do with investigating. Either the little rat has info or I bash him in the snout again."

"Sounds kind of fun, though."

"Fine by me. I'll call you with the when and where."

"I'm glad you two are having such a good time," Jan said. "But maybe we should be thinking more about our potential victim? The murderer didn't just pick these two out randomly."

Max's laptop let out a *ping*. The hacker pressed a few keys and stared at the screen, transfixed. Then a grin appeared on his face.

"I have something on our car salesman," Max said, wiping his sticky fingers on his pants. "Not exactly something a person can be proud of. But maybe it's the connection we're looking for."

•   •   •

Fabian rubbed wearily at his eyes. He had drunk three cups of coffee and still felt sleepy. It was barely past midnight. He turned to his young partner, who didn't look the least bit tired.

"Freshman, how do you do it?"

"What? Look so good?"

"Don't get cocky. All I mean is, how are you able to stay awake on the night shift?"

"Caffeine powder."

"Huh?"

"While you're chugging down one coffee after another, I go for a little caffeine powder." David raised a baggie containing what looked like a portion of sugar. "Got a half gram of caffeine in here. It's the equivalent of five liters of soda."

"I wouldn't be able to keep up with all the pissing."

"Thus the powder."

"Huh," Fabian said. The little dude was cleverer than he deserved to be. A boost of caffeine would fix Fabian right up—but then he'd have to admit that David was the smarter one. And that would endanger the hierarchy in the car. So coffee it was.

"What was that?" David asked with a start, pointing at the house.

"Where?" Fabian turned his head but couldn't make out anything unusual. The house was half in shadow. The porch light was on, illuminating the little front yard. Shrubs grew on the other side of the metal fencing, barely waist-high and too far apart for anyone to be able to hide behind. The path coming around from the little backyard door was laid out with stone pavers. The house itself was just as boring as the neighborhood it was in. Only the knee-high red garden gnome looked out of place at first glance. But if you got a little closer, you spotted its raised middle finger. Fabian saw no suspicious figures, no one lurking around or trying to mess with the premises.

"That a light that went on there?"

"Outside the house?"

"No, in it." David leaned toward the driver's-side window so that he was practically lying across Fabian's stomach."

"Easy, young 'un." Fabian pushed him back to the passenger's seat. "Our Moritz Quast was probably just going to the can."

"The last time, he reported it in over radio."

"True." Fabian looked annoyed. "And when he made a sandwich, and brushed his teeth, and went to bed. So nice of him not to be a pain in our balls." He raised his coffee cup to his ear and did a slick-talking car-salesman voice: *"Hey there. Going to fart any second. Just wanted you to know."* The cop lowered his window and spat on the sidewalk. "Pussy."

"It wasn't the can, it was the kitchen."

"Good God, David. Haven't you ever hit the fridge during the night, eaten up yesterday's leftovers?"

David frowned. "No."

"Which is why I'm asking," Fabian muttered and took a gulp of coffee. "Little proposal for you: we take that portable radio there and ask the owner of this house if he's doing okay or if maybe the killer's hiding in the fridge and just slaughtered him."

"But if he's just been slaughtered, he can't exactly answer—"

"Shut it!" Fabian interrupted. "Don't always take me so literally." He picked up the portable radio and pressed the "Talk" button.

"Herr Quast, Fabian Gisker here. You receiving me?"

Static.

"Herr Quast? You awake?"

"But if he's asleep, then—"

Fabian's irritated glance, with its unspoken threat of violence, silenced the younger man.

"Herr Quast?"

Static.

"Something's not right," David whispered. He stared at the portable radio, tensing up. His eyes widened as if he'd just seen Martians landing.

"Batteries could be dead."

"These ones hold for twenty four hours. Even with constant use."

"Then it's a bad battery."

"Not likely. That portable radio is brand-new. I tested it out myself."

Fabian held up his hands to pacify David. "Okay, okay. We'll call in over the phone network." He pointed at David's cell phone on the dash. "Call."

The young cop grabbed his cell, pressed a couple of keys, and turned on speaker mode.

It rang. Once, twice. Then came a brief pause. The voice-mail message started in, and they heard the car salesman: *You've reached the number for Moritz. Leave a message.* He sounded happy, relaxed, completely unlike the man they'd been guarding for hours.

"Huh," Fabian said. It was weird that the Nervous Nellie hadn't reported in. Twice he had emphasized to Quast that he should keep his portable radio as well as his phone next to his bed. He should even take the radio in the can with him. And if he was sound asleep, there was no explanation for why the light had gone on in the kitchen.

"Maybe he's a sleepwalker," Fabian said, trying to ease the tension.

"I read an article on that," David began. "You wouldn't believe all that sleepwalkers are capable of—"

"Shut it! I'm trying to think here."

Fabian absently took a sip of coffee. This death threat was a serious matter, above all because they already had one victim. They had to go see what was happening inside the house. If it was a false alarm, he'd use the opportunity to take a piss. Better a guest can than a tree.

"Well, then, young 'un. Let's do this." Fabian opened the door and stepped out. With his massive stomach, this took him longer than it took his more slender fellow cop, but he managed the extra girth just fine.

"Shouldn't we call for backup?" David said, sounding nervous now as he came around the car.

"We are backup. Now stop your blabbering and listen." Fabian pulled out a key from his pocket and held it up. "I'm going in the front. You stay by the rear entrance in case someone tries to bolt; wait there until I let you in. Then we'll search the house."

David nodded and drew his weapon.

"Put that thing away! I don't want you getting all gung ho and blowing away the homeowner. Use the pepper spray."

David holstered his pistol and started to head around to the back of the house.

Fabian held him back by the arm.

"Stay loose, young 'un. Don't get scared." He smiled confidently.

"I'm not scared," David replied, but his trembling hands suggested otherwise.

"I'll be sure to watch your ass." Fabian placed a fatherly hand on the young cop's shoulder. "Now go get around back."

Fabian headed through the yard to the porch, inserted the key in the front door, and opened up. The main floor was dark. Only the kitchen was showing some light. No sign of the homeowner.

"Crap," Fabian muttered and went on in.

•   •   •

Meanwhile, David headed to the rear of the house. *This case has been creepy from the start,* he thought. *What kind of sick bastard digs out a grave to bury his victim in?* The path's paving stones were so sloppily placed, David had to watch that he didn't stumble. It was noticeably darker here than out front. The branches of the beech trees separating Moritz Quast's property from his neighbors' hung menacingly over the path, as though trying to prevent the moonlight from revealing David's way. The rear of the house was lit by only one small spotlight, the one they normally used to help cordon off traffic accidents—planted here so they wouldn't have to use flashlights every time they came around the back. But the light wasn't all that bright and barely reached the edge of the property. David would've given anything for two super-bright halogen spots.

He wished that Moritz Quast's house was located on a busy street. The silence of these rows of single-family homes had been making him crazy the whole night. He was a city kid. He'd seen a lot in his two years as a cop. Drunks on a rampage, mass brawls, domestic violence. One time he had to help pull a critically injured person from a car wreck. He was no scaredy-cat, but a murder was something else. He had trained plenty for entering a house, but in training, the worst abuse came from your instructor. A real murderer was a different story.

David peered in the kitchen window, which had no shades. The light was on, but he couldn't see anyone. He tried the lever on the rear door leading to the kitchen, but the door was locked.

"Herr Quast . . ."

He heard Fabian's voice but only faintly. The light in the living room came on. David tried to make out his partner, but the door from there into the kitchen was only partially open and he couldn't see much. He'd have to wait till Fabian passed through the house. Then he heard a grunt and something falling to the floor. The light in the living room went out.

"Fabian!" David shouted. He shook the door lever. "Fabian, stop this shit."

He pressed his face to the window. The kitchen light was still on. No sign of his partner. A carton of milk stood on the kitchen table next to scraps of white bread. A jacket hung on a chair; dishes were piled up next to the sink. He thought he smelled burnt scrambled eggs—probably the homeowner's sorry attempt at cooking himself something warm that evening.

David cursed under his breath. The back door was all there was back here. No other windows to see through besides the one in the kitchen. To locate Fabian, he'd have to leave his post and go around to the front.

Maybe he was wrong and his mind was playing tricks on him. Fabian had probably just gone upstairs to check in on Moritz Quast and, in the process, had knocked over a vase or whatever.

David paced back and forth at his spot. He wouldn't be surprised if this was just one of Fabian's stupid jokes. The murderer could not be inside the house. Detective Tommen had checked all the rooms. The back door was locked and there were no signs of a break-in. All the windows were closed, and they'd been keeping an eye on the front entrance this whole time.

But if the murderer was inside, every second would count. Maybe Fabian was injured and needed help. Or Moritz Quast.

David banged on the window frame in frustration. He had to get inside. He instinctively reached for his weapon but then remembered his partner's words of warning. He grabbed hold of the pepper spray instead and went around to the front entrance.

The door was open. Slightly ajar. Practically an invitation.

He pushed the door wider with his foot, waiting on the porch. Feeling his heart thumping. He really should be running over to the car and calling for backup—but then he might be in big trouble with Fabian, and for good reason. Fabian would call him a gutless little girl, and the whole department would know about it by first thing tomorrow.

The living room was dark. Some light was coming through the gap of the kitchen door, but there was no sign of Fabian. David took a step inside and hit the switch. It clicked, but the light didn't come on.

"Fuck." Something wasn't right here. David wanted to scream.

"Fabian?" he called into the shadows. "Herr Quast?"

No reply.

His flashlight was back in the car. Of course. David fought the urge to draw his weapon and fire into the air. But that might wake the whole neighborhood.

He moved toward the kitchen in hopes of finding a light switch or a lamp.

Then Moritz Quast stepped out of the kitchen. David instinctively jumped back a step.

"God, you scared me." David sighed in relief. "We were getting worried. You all right?"

Moritz Quast was looking down at the living-room floor. David saw tears on his cheeks. His left hand trembled. His right was concealed behind his back. David took a step closer to the car salesman. Within the shadowy light coming from the kitchen, he now saw Fabian slumped on the living-room floor, lying against a chest of drawers, his flabby chin pressed to his chest. His eyes seemed to be closed, but David couldn't quite tell in the near darkness.

"What's going on here?"

"I'm sorry." Quast pulled a stun gun from behind his back and pressed it to David's neck.

A sharp pain seared through David's insides and he screamed. The pepper spray fell from his fingers. He wanted to reach for his weapon, but he couldn't control his hand anymore.

His legs buckled, and he fell to the floor. Then everything went black.

•　　•　　•

"O Saint Hacker Maximum, do share your wisdom with us," Zoe teased.

Max was leaning back on the couch, enjoying his moment of triumph. "Moritz Quast worked for a health insurer before his stint as a car salesman."

"And?" Chandu asked after a moment of silence.

"He was let go because he did something crooked."

"Maybe give us something a little more concrete?" Jan asked.

"Moritz Quast was mixed up in an accounting scandal. A few others were in on it with him—including some doctors. They billed for expensive meds without ever prescribing them."

"How much money are we talking about here?" Jan asked.

"A few thousand euros per man. Their little racket was blown because one of the medications wasn't approved in Germany. As a result, one of the doctors got banned from practicing and three received suspended sentences—along with Moritz Quast. After that, he started working as a car salesman."

"Nice little story," Zoe said. "How does it get us anywhere?"

"The exciting part's still to come, you see," Max said, grinning. He loved these moments, when a case started coming together. "Twelve doctors were investigated. One of them was Bernhard Valburg."

"Was he involved?" Jan asked.

"He was not. They couldn't prove he had actually prescribed any of the meds, so they let him go."

"But now we have a connection," Chandu said.

"It's too thin for me," Jan said. "Sure, the health insurer lost some money, but that doesn't turn anyone into a murderer. And Bernhard Valburg didn't even take part."

"Sure, but a connection between a doctor and a health-insurance employee is far easier to imagine than one between a doctor and a car salesman."

"Good point," Jan agreed. "I'll pay the insurer a little visit tomorrow. See what I can dig up—"

Jan's cell phone rang. He looked at the screen and raised his eyebrows, his voice conveying his surprise as he answered the call. "Jan Tommen."

The caller was shouting into the receiver.

"What? There's no way, how—" Jan got cut off. "I'm on my way!" He hung up, pocketed his phone. "Come on," he said to Chandu as he grabbed his jacket.

"You two remain on standby," he said to Zoe and Max. Running out the door, he fumbled for his car keys. Max had never seen him so frantic. "I'll call in from the car!"

Chandu ran out behind him. As the door slammed shut, Max was left scratching his head. He had no idea what had just happened, but it did not bode well.

Chapter Five

Spotlights illuminated Moritz Quast's grave. The site was completely cordoned off with police tape. Crime-scene investigators searched the paths around the spot where the corpse had been found. It was shortly after two a.m.

Jan observed the dead man as he was being lifted out of the grave. Moritz Quast's face was crusted over with dried blood and earth. His eyes were closed. He wore only pajama pants. No shirt, no shoes. The murderer had caught him sleeping.

The cause of death was obvious. Moritz Quast's head had been bashed in. Jan could see pieces of his skull. Not a pretty sight.

Fabian sat on a bench not far from the grave. The cop's head was down and he stared at the ground. He'd thrown up when he'd laid eyes on the corpse. Even in the most gruesome situations, he had always had a casual remark at the ready. But the death of Moritz Quast had silenced him. Beneath his macho facade, the fast-food binges and sexist comments, Jan's former partner was a dependable cop. He would never have risked the life of an innocent man through simple negligence.

Jan sat down next to Fabian on the bench. Under other circumstances this would have been a nice spot, on a green, surrounded by big chestnut trees.

Jan said nothing. He would leave it to Fabian to do the talking whenever he was ready. Meanwhile, the search of the site continued full bore. Flashing cameras made the night flicker. Footprints were secured and possible clues marked around the grave.

Chandu had gone over to Moritz Quast's house and was speaking with the investigators there. Zoe was sharpening her knives over at Forensics, and Max was trying to find out more about the billing-fraud incident. It was going to be a long night.

"I don't know how the bastard got into the house," Fabian began without lifting his head. "We couldn't reach Quast—not on the radio, not on the phone. So I had the young 'un go cover the back door and I went in the front using my key. I turned on the light and called for Quast, but got no answer." He paused. "Before searching the house, I wanted to let David in. I was going through to the kitchen when that bastard got me with the stun gun."

"Did you see him?"

"No, zilch." Fabian lifted his head and threw his hands up in despair. "There was not the slightest sign of an intruder breaking in. The doors were locked, no footprints in the apartment. Nothing suggested we weren't alone. Maybe Moritz Quast took a sleeping pill. I woulda in his position. No sign of imminent danger, so I went to the kitchen. That son of a bitch knew exactly where he had to stand so I couldn't see him."

"What happened then?"

"The kid had must have heard me hit the floor. He got suspicious, went around the house, and came through the front. The bastard caught him with one there too. David hit his head against the coffee table going down."

"Did he see him?"

"That hit he took on the head had to be nasty. He kept stammering about how Quast was saying he was sorry."

"Sorry for what?"

"No idea. He could have been imagining Quast when he was unconscious." Fabian shrugged. "Don't know any more than that. Ask him yourself when he's back on his feet."

"Where is he now?"

"In the hospital. They sewed him up with twenty stitches and examined his head." Fabian exhaled loudly. "When I woke up and saw that blood on his face, I almost had a heart attack. Thank God it's not so bad."

He shook his head, stared at the ground again. The pain of his failure was etched in his face. Serving with that young kid wasn't easy, but Fabian would have thrown himself in front of any bullet fired at his trainee. He would've died rather than put David in danger.

"I only woke up about twenty minutes later, so I'm told," Fabian went on. "The fucker had tied us up with zip ties. It took us another twenty minutes to get the goddamn things off. We sounded the alarm. But Moritz Quast was nowhere to be found. Later we got the radio call that they'd found his body in the grave. No sign of the murderer."

Jan placed a hand on Fabian's shoulder, one friend to another. Nothing he could say would help his former partner. But Jan wanted him to know that he was on Fabian's side.

Fabian would never forgive himself—for the death of Moritz Quast or for letting David get wounded. Whether the department pronounced him free of fault was irrelevant. The only thing that could help Fabian was seeing the murderer behind bars.

So Jan would see to that.

•　　•　　•

After three hours of detective work at the cemetery, Jan arrived back at Homicide. The sun was coming up, and he looked as tired as he felt after a night of no sleep. He yawned, stretching his arms above his head. He headed for his office, where Bergman was already waiting for him, leaning against a column. Even at this hour he was neatly dressed, his hair perfect and his shoes shining.

Jan, on the other hand, looked like a man sorely needing a shower. His clothes were filthy, and he had what felt like three feet of earth caked to the soles of his sneakers.

Bergman lifted up a printout from a website. "The Grave Killer Strikes Again!" he read out loud. Under the lurid headline was an image of an old-style cross standing at an empty grave.

"I haven't told the reporters a thing," Jan protested.

"I know. But the days of calm are over. Once again," he added, referring to their previous case. "Meaning, in plain language: I'm going to have the police chief, the mayor, the attorney general, and God knows who else calling me within the hour. So what do we have?"

"Not much," Jan said reluctantly.

"We have two dead bodies," Bergman corrected him. "And one was under police protection."

"Fabian, he was trying to—"

"I know," Bergman snapped, cutting Jan off. "I talked to Gisker. Nevertheless, he won't get around an internal-affairs investigation. Plus I'm assigning him a few days' leave of absence."

"I don't think that—"

"It's got nothing to do with fairness. A man under police protection was murdered. We can't carry on as if nothing happened. Find the murderer, and Gisker gets back in the game."

"What do you think I've been doing this whole—"

"I'm assigning you more people."

"More people?"

"Don't question me," Bergman snapped again, sounding offended. "I'm giving you Patrick Stein and his team. I want you to lay all your findings on the table for them. I want you all on the same page by the end of the day. Maybe you overlooked something. You're still the lead. But a special team of four people with only one criminal detective? No way I can sell that."

Jan grumbled, but he was secretly glad for the support. What had initially looked like a bizarre homicide by a maniac was fast developing into a serial-homicide situation. And the way the murderer had neutralized Fabian and David pointed to one clever and extremely dangerous killer.

"What's next for you?" Bergman continued.

"I'll go take a look at Moritz Quast's house. It's most likely the scene of the crime."

"I want a report on my desk every evening at seven p.m." Bergman ended their conversation with a curt nod and started back for his office. "I hope you don't have any vacations planned," he shouted back Jan's way.

Jan sighed and pulled out his cell phone. The initial autopsy report should be ready by now. Hopefully the second victim would give them more to go on.

•   •   •

Bergman opened his office door. "Stein!" he roared down the hallway and slammed the door shut again.

Thirty seconds later, Patrick Stein came inside and sat down in the chair across from Bergman's desk.

"This grave-killer case is turning into a major problem. We have two dead and no leads." His displeasure was clear. "Now I have to put more people on the case. Thus my first question: you have any problem working under Jan?"

"No," Patrick said.

"No? Your animosity was known well beyond the walls of Homicide. A little birdy told me that you two get along now, but to be honest, it's tough for me to believe."

"We talked things out. Didn't happen overnight. But we did." Patrick shrugged. "Maybe it took an extreme case, like the last one, for us to resolve our differences."

Bergman scrutinized Patrick. His pomaded hair, his perfectly fitting suit. Smart. Correct down to the tips of his no-doubt-manicured toenails. Yet without instincts and as stubborn as a mule. "Jan is our best detective—but to put it tactfully, he isn't very systematic in his approach. Writing reports, reading documents, and studying lists of suspects are not his strong suit. So I need someone who likes to do those things." Bergman looked Patrick in the eye.

"I'd have no problem with that."

"Just so we don't misunderstand one another, Stein: you really screwed things up in that last case. What I really should do is have you directing traffic all day, out on the city bypass. But the thing is, detectives don't exactly grow on trees. This grave-killer case is your chance to redeem yourself. Jan needs someone like you, but it remains his case. You'll have to take a subordinate role."

Bergman folded his hands across his chest. "We have no more resources, so I phoned around a little this morning. A former colleague is giving us a few men from security services, and we're getting interns from various departments, plus trainees from Admin and even a few academy students. Your task will be to build a team from this motley crew. Most have no clue about police work, but they'll do for making calls and combing through documents. Throw yourself into it. And we'll forget the past."

Patrick stood and nodded to his boss. "You can depend on me."

"Don't screw this up," Bergman said.

Once Patrick was gone, Bergman leafed through Jan's report on Dr. Valburg's death. He would never have tolerated such slipshod style from anyone else. It was yet more proof that Jan was still not his old self. His scars were still too raw. Patrick was the last thing Bergman would be able to give Jan. He just hoped it would prove to be enough.

•   •   •

Moritz Quast's corpse lay uncovered on the dissecting table. His eyes were closed, and his face had been cleaned of dried blood after the crime-scene analysis was completed. His whole body had been shaved and washed. Chest and abdominal cavities were opened.

The formalities had been taken care of. Height, weight, body temp, scars, tattoos—Zoe had duly recorded it all.

Now the real fun began: the internal inspection. Zoe bent over the corpse. One glance at liver and lungs showed her that Moritz had been no slouch when it came to enjoying himself.

"Additional info on topic of poisoning," Zoe said into a dictating machine she operated with a foot pedal. "No visible evidence from the external inquest. No dilated pupils as from atropine or cyanide, no contracted pupils as with opiates. No visible signs of injection to be found. The coloring of *livor mortis* normal. No foaming around the mouth is visible, also no blisters suggesting intoxication. Stomach and intestines are being analyzed for traces of poison. Regarding the internal inquest, no unusual discoloration or internal burning to be seen. Liquor, vitreous fluid, venous blood, and hair have already been taken to lab, as well as blood from heart and the urine. Tests on liver, brain, and kidneys to follow, along with those of stomach contents. This concludes analysis findings as of June twenty-seventh, eleven sixteen a.m."

She stopped recording and was reaching for a scalpel when her phone rang. She went over to the storage table and then groaned when she saw the screen. Jan always knew just the wrong time to call. Since her gloves were smeared with blood, she turned on speaker mode by tapping with her scalpel. "Not done yet," she said, and went back over to the corpse. "I have both hands down inside his organs."

"I don't want to take up a lot of your time. I just need the most important stuff. How Moritz Quast was murdered, if it was the same perpetrator."

Jan sounded like he was calling from a car.

"His head got smashed in after midnight. I haven't analyzed the wound yet, but I'm guessing it's a hammer. Could be the same murder weapon used on the first victim." With a flick of her hand, Zoe sliced off a piece of the liver and held it up with tweezers. "But there is one other little thing."

"What?"

"His tongue was cut out." She placed the sample in the petri dish.

"Why?"

"What am I, some shaman who can ask the dead?" She frowned. "You should probably go question the lead detective. Name of Tommen or something like that."

"Postmortem again?"

"Yep. We only noticed it here in autopsy on account of no blood in his mouth."

"Self-defense wounds?"

"Nothing I can see." She took a glass lid and covered the sample. She'd wipe her bloody fingerprints off the glass later.

"Signs of being tied up?"

"Nope."

"Was he killed while sleeping?"

"Possibly. The perp might have surprised him—that or drugged or poisoned him. Even if there are no signs of a poisoning, I'll run the whole gamut."

"Signs of being dragged?"

"No."

"So the murderer packed up Moritz Quast like he did before and got him to the cemetery. Are there pressure marks?"

"Huh?"

"If Moritz Quast was carried in, say, a crate or box, there might be pressure marks proving that."

"You watch too much TV," Zoe said. "That's how it works on bad crime shows. Reality is different."

"How about any residue from packing materials?"

"I can tell you more about that once we've analyzed the clothing under a microscope. That will take a couple days." Zoe leaned back over the corpse. "A little more brain and the stomach contents, then I'll get started on my jigsaw puzzle," she said.

"Puzzle?"

"You do not want to know."

"Oh," Jan said. He always did upset easily. "Till next time," he said and hung up.

Zoe pushed the big magnifying glass into position over the head and, using her scalpel, excised a portion of brain. The back of the head was smashed something awful. It would take hours for her to piece it all back together and make an impression of it. But then she'd know if a hammer had been used as the murder weapon again. Humming happily, she placed the sample in the petri dish and grabbed a large container for the stomach contents.

·   ·   ·

Moritz Quast's house had been cordoned off. A few photographers and rubberneckers stood behind the police tape. The media had gotten wind that the cemetery was where the body had been found. There was little for them to see here at the house.

Chandu was holding a cup of coffee, waiting for Jan at the backyard gate.

"How's the crime scene?" Jan asked.

"You're not going to like it."

"I was afraid of that."

"No one knows how the murderer got inside," Chandu said. "There are no signs of a break-in, and the surveillance car had an eye on the front door the whole time. He likely had a key to the back door."

"Where from? Moritz Quast and I counted all the keys last night. None were missing."

"That's a cheap lock. The key's easy to copy. Making an impression would work."

"Damn it," Jan said. It was starting to get to him, how screwed up this was. "So he knew the murderer?"

"That or he was able to come up with some other way. But days ago. As a handyman or gardener, maybe."

"Clues?"

"They found fingerprints and DNA everywhere. The evaluation is still ongoing, but we could very well strike out, just like with the first murder."

"Where was Quast murdered?"

"That's our next problem," said Chandu. "There's no evidence that he was killed in the house."

"What?"

"The crime-scene guys couldn't believe it themselves, so they went through the place twice. No murder weapon. No blood. A few dried semen stains on the living-room sofa. Since Moritz Quast subscribed to a porn channel, they probably came from him."

"So he was still alive when Fabian and David went in?"

"Seems so. What are those two saying?"

"Fabian didn't see anything. David took a hit on the head, he's no help. I'll just have to wait till he's recovered."

"Maybe Quast was tied up?"

"Zoe says he wasn't."

"Drugs? Narcotic to knock him out?"

"They're still running tests. We'll have to wait it out till this evening."

"Maybe the killer was holding a gun to Quast's head?"

"While taking out Fabian and David at the same time? Hard to imagine." Jan shook his head. "We're overlooking something."

"Just have to wait till the tests are done. Can I do something for you, meantime?"

"Go home and get some sleep. I'll question the neighbors and take a look around the neighborhood. Tell the others that we're meeting again this evening. We got a lot to talk about."

"Sleep sounds good."

"Thanks for the help."

"Don't mention it."

Once his friend was gone, Jan leaned against the fence and took a good look at the house. The murderer had not come from the front. There was no rear exit leading from the premises out to any road. So he had come through the neighbors' yards. The fences were low, and there were no guard dogs in the neighborhood. The crime-scene investigators had examined only Moritz Quast's property.

It was time to expand the search radius.

•   •   •

The murderer must have come with a vehicle. The cemetery in Stahnsdorf was too far for strolling over to. He had checked the street in front of Moritz Quast's house. Every car there belonged to a neighbor. It was unlikely that the murderer had parked his vehicle there; Fabian and David would've noticed. So he had gotten out on a neighboring street.

To the left of Quast's house there were ten more houses until the next cross street. Single-family homes with yards not much bigger than the smallest scale caged-in play court. Enough for a barbecue, a flower bed, and a garden shed. Maybe a patio. They all had that same off-white rear facade with its evenly spaced upstairs windows. Idyllic and boring.

To the right of Quast's property, Jan made out only three homes. The properties ended at a green area with bushes and trees, likely a type of noise buffer separating the next street over. The shorter the way, the better, he figured. Jan jumped over the fence to the neighbor's backyard and took a look around.

The guy living here obviously loved to barbecue. The yard consisted mainly of a patio with a gas grill two yards wide. Next to it stood a table with a stone top and a little outdoor fridge. The grill was covered with clear plastic, and the windows looking out on the patio were shuttered. The owner was probably on vacation.

Jan looked out over the next house's yard. Half of the property consisted of lawn. A garden of precisely placed vegetables on the farthest side was an eco-geek's dream. Jan recognized tomatoes, zucchini, and lettuce next to other greens he didn't know. In the middle of the garden rows, an older man with a hose was watering the bushes separating his property from that of his neighbor's on the other side. The man was working so hard not to look in Jan's direction he was surely going to cramp up. Watering was clearly just an excuse that let him follow the crime-scene investigation going on two houses over. Good thing, too. A neighbor nosy at just the right time could provide that decisive clue.

"Good morning." Jan showed his badge from his stance on the empty patio. "My name is Detective Tommen. Berlin Police. Could I ask you a few questions?"

The man turned off the water, came over to the fence, and shook Jan's hand. "Anton Möller. Nice to meet you."

His eyes lit up. He looked really excited to be questioned.

"You know what happened here last night?"

"Someone killed Moritz Quast." Anton Möller ran a thumb across his neck, rolled his eyes, and made a sound like someone slashing his throat open.

Jan refrained from remarking on the man's bizarre sense of humor.

"You knew Herr Quast?" he asked.

"Only from Florian's barbecues."

"Florian?"

"Florian Uland. The one with the huge grill. You're standing on his property."

"He's not home?"

"Florian has been on vacation for a week now. Trip through the US. Won't be back till next month."

"What was your impression of Moritz Quast?"

"Didn't fit the neighborhood. Mostly families with kids live around here. He was the young bachelor type—used to get worked up about the noise of the kids playing. He drove a flashy car. Often came home late, probably from some bar crawl. I didn't much care for him."

"I see." Jan noted something down.

"I didn't mean it that way," Anton hastened to add. "I may not have liked him, but I didn't want to kill him."

Jan showed him a wide smile. "He get visits from people who seemed suspicious to you?"

"Suspicious in what way?"

"Other people who didn't fit a neighborhood like this. Late-night meetings with sketchy figures. Heated arguments."

"Most of his visitors were coworkers from the car dealership."

"You know any of them?"

"Barely. For the World Cup, Moritz set up a projector in front of his house and showed every Germany game on his garage door. He invited all the neighbors over and a few coworkers. It was constant pandemonium. His driveway was filled with empty beer bottles for days. Being the good neighbor that I am, I did head over and help drain his beer supply."

"Was Moritz Quast the careless type?"

"Careless?"

"Left the door open when he popped out for bread? Gave keys to guys working on the house? That kind of thing."

"He left his windows open when he left for work."

"Open?"

"Well, not all the way. But cracked." Anton shook his head. "One time I told him how easily an intruder could pry open the window and climb into the house. He just laughed. Fresh air was more important to him."

"Anything else?"

"The delivery people."

"Delivery people?"

"Moritz wrote notes for delivery people, saying that his packages shouldn't be delivered to the neighbors but rather left at the back door. He got deliveries a couple of times a week. People were constantly coming and going."

Jan shook his head. If that was true, it would have been a piece of cake for the murderer to get inside.

"Let's go back to last night. Were you at home?"

"Yes. I went to bed after *Heute Journal*, the nightly news. My wife was already asleep."

"What time was this?"

"After ten."

"Did you notice anything unusual?"

"I didn't, sorry. I'm a deep sleeper." Anton stepped closer. "I heard that Moritz is the second victim," he whispered, as if anyone were listening. "Is there a serial killer in Berlin?"

"I'm not allowed to say anything about that."

Anton was clearly put off by Jan's defensive stance. He pursed his lips like a child who'd just had his toy shovel taken from him.

Jan put his notepad away. "Could I come over and inspect your yard? We might find traces of the murderer there."

A smile appeared on Anton's lips. "You really think so?"

The prospect that a murderer might have traversed his yard seemed to spark a macabre fascination in him. He turned and eyed the yard as if the blood-smeared murder weapon itself might be lying there.

Jan hopped over the waist-high fence. He checked out the lawn but saw no sign of footprints.

"This here's a sports turf, got the *Poa supina* seed," Anton explained like a pro landscaper. "They use it for soccer fields. Sturdy and indestructible. Pops right back up again."

"Terrific."

Anton nodded proudly, missing the sarcasm in Jan's voice. First that patio, now this supergrass. Jan was hoping the last property would offer up something, anything. He crossed Anton's yard and came to a dark wood fence.

"Simon Illgen lives there with his wife and three kids," Anton said.

The Illgen yard was a hodgepodge of toys and furniture. The swings hung crooked, hazardously so. The outdoor table and chairs looked like they had been pulled out of a Dumpster, and the little barbecue was a pockmarked heap of rust with only three legs. The patchy, weed-covered lawn looked no better, but it might provide him with a clue.

"Is anyone home?" Jan asked Anton.

"The kids are in school at this hour, Simon's working, and his wife's hanging out with her yoga teacher." Anton winked at Jan suggestively.

Jan hopped the fence. He landed on a yellow plastic thing that must have once been a rubber ducky. It didn't even release a final peep of despair. "What chaos," he muttered.

He moved along the fence and came to a spot free of grass. There he found what he was looking for. Footprints. He knelt down, rolled a rubber ball to the side, and took a good look at the prints.

One could have come from military or hiking boots. The other appeared to be sizes bigger and was from a bare foot.

"Did you find something?" Anton asked from over the fence.

"I did," Jan said, taking his cell phone out and calling the crime-scene techs. "Riddle solved."

· · ·

Ten minutes later, the Illgen family's backyard was besieged by crime-scene techs. Next door, Anton had pulled up a lawn chair and observed the techs deploying, his eyes twinkling as if expecting them to find a corpse any minute now. Leaning on the fence, Jan watched them make an impression of the footprints. One of the techs came over to him, holding up a baggie with a pebble in it.

"Found these in the barefoot print. The pebble bored into skin, made a little wound. Enough blood to check DNA."

"Compare that sample with Moritz Quast's DNA. It has to be a match."

The man nodded. "If I had to deduce height and weight from the footprint? It could fit Moritz Quast."

"And the perpetrator?"

"Judging by the foot length, I'm guessing he's about five feet eight. The depth points to a slim man. Both men planted their whole feet, so they weren't running. Otherwise the steps would be farther apart, and the impressions up front would be deeper than from the heel."

"Thanks."

Anton came over to the fence. Jan put on his friendly face. He would have to ask the man a few more questions after all.

"Find something there?"

"The murderer might have left behind a footprint."

"So he ran through my yard?" Anton gasped with excitement as if he'd just learned that aliens had used his flower bed as a landing pad.

"Possibly," Jan said, wanting this nosy neighbor to stay that way. "From this we can deduce that the murderer parked his vehicle on the side street. Did you notice anything there after ten, when you went to bed?"

"No, unfortunately," Anton lamented. "For noise protection, the city planted bushes and birch trees between the street and the Illgens' property. It's all sprouted up like weeds in the last few years. I wouldn't even have seen a truck parked there. Not even from my balcony."

Jan noted something down. The only thing left to do was the grinding slog of questioning all the neighbors in the area. He put his pad and pen away. "Thanks a ton for your help." He shook Anton's hand and turned to follow the path the murderer took, when Anton grabbed him by the arm.

"You don't have a card?" he said.

"Don't have what?"

"You know, one of those business cards with your number on it, in case a person finds out anything more. Maybe the murderer will return to the scene."

Jan reached into his jacket and handed him a card. Anton stared at the piece of cardstock as if it had been consecrated by the pope.

"Thanks, Herr Tommen. You'll be hearing from me."

"That's what I'm afraid of," Jan muttered under his breath. He followed the marked tracks through the yard, out to the street. He could only hope the murderer had left behind a few more clues.

•   •   •

Three hours later, Jan wearily sat down on a bench next to a bus stop. He had questioned all the neighbors, but no one had seen a thing. No suspicious car, no unusual characters, no Moritz Quast running around barefoot. Adding to his bad luck, the light on the side street had gone out, right where the murderer's vehicle had likely been parked. He pointed that out to the crime-scene techs, certain that they would find the power cut or some other sabotage. And, of course, no fingerprints.

They were dealing with a master planner. Insane, to be sure, but well organized and not easily unnerved. Psychopaths like this were the toughest to catch.

Jan's phone rang, interrupting his brooding.

"Herr Tommen, Johannes Arnold here. I'm one of the managers at Stahnsdorf Cemetery. I was asked to call you." The man's voice sounded anxious. He had probably never dealt with the police before.

"Thanks for your call," Jan began, keeping it casual. He normally preferred to have conversations like this face-to-face. A person's body language said much more than his words.

"I'm a little confused here, because one of your fellow officers already questioned me about the case."

"In especially volatile cases we do two rounds of questioning, to play it safe," Jan lied. He had no desire to wait for the report, and he wanted to get the lay of the land himself.

Jan wedged his cell phone against his shoulder and pulled out his notepad. "It's just general stuff. Did you or a coworker see anything suspicious? This would be during the time from midnight till two in the morning."

"I called the staff together this morning to get you the answers. The last man left the cemetery yesterday at seven fourteen in the evening. The first employee today arrived at three minutes after six a.m. No one noticed anything during his shift, and we can't say for sure what time the grave was dug. The grounds cover nearly five hundred acres, so it's impossible to monitor every grave site."

"Do you have an idea how the grave was dug? Could the murderer have used some of the cemetery equipment?"

"We use an excavator. It sits locked away in an equipment hangar. It wasn't used during the night between Tuesday and Wednesday."

"And your shovels and axes?"

"Those are kept in a shed that's locked up at night. The lock looks untouched, and as far as I can tell, none of the tools were taken or used."

Jan noted down that the murderer brought his own tools. On the one hand, a man like this wouldn't leave something like that to chance; on the other hand, it could look conspicuous to be seen heading into a cemetery with axe and shovel.

"What kind of clothing do you and your staff wear?"

"Typical gardening gear. Either green overalls in a cotton-polyester blend, with a short jacket in winter, or gray work trousers without suspenders. Some of us swear by safety shoes; for others they're too clunky."

"You wear any insignia on your clothing?"

"Insignia?"

"Emblems, patches, stickers. Something that identifies you as Stahnsdorf Cemetery staff?"

"Not much. Our work clothes wear out sooner than I have the resources to replace them. The other thing is, some of the cemetery care has been awarded to outside firms."

"So a man in simple work clothes without patches wouldn't look conspicuous?"

"Perhaps to me or a few of my coworkers. Certainly not to a visitor."

Jan sighed. Now he was certain that the murderer had brought his own tools. But questioning Wednesday-night visitors to the cemetery wouldn't tell him much. No one would give a second thought to a man wearing work clothes.

"We see," Jan said, "that the grave was only dug out about a foot and half deep . . ."

"That's still quite a lot. Normally, the deceased are interred at least six and a half feet down. But that can't be done in one night with axe and shovel."

"Why didn't anyone notice that a grave was being dug at that hour?"

"No one goes to the cemetery at night, apart from a few whacked-out freaks. You won't find a quieter place in all of Berlin."

"Had a grave plot been assigned there?"

"No. No graves were supposed to be dug there, actually."

"Did Moritz Quast acquire some other burial spot?"

"Herr Quast paid the fees for his parents' grave site. We've had no other contact with him."

Jan rapped on his pad with his pen. This was starting to drive him nuts. Either the murderer was a genius at improvising, or these homicides had been planned precisely and well in advance. Just like with Bernhard Valburg, the cemetery wasn't going to offer any revelations.

"Thank you for your time, Herr Arnold. If I have any further questions, I'll be in touch."

"Glad to help."

Jan hung up, leaned back on the bench, and closed his eyes. The leads were scant. Even the traces still to be analyzed weren't going to bring them any closer to the murderer. Jan would have to rely on his own three investigators. They were meeting again at Chandu's that night. Before that he had to finish another report, one that Bergman was not going to like.

He was just getting up from the bench when his phone rang a second time. He looked at the screen but couldn't place the number. He hoped it wasn't his new friend, Anton.

"Jan Tommen," he answered.

"It's David here. Fabian Gisker's partner."

"Hello there, David." It was good to hear from the young man. One corpse was enough. He didn't even want to think about a cop being murdered. "How's your head?"

"It's no big deal."

"What about that stun you took from the murderer?"

"That wasn't the murderer."

"What?" Jan's weariness vanished.

"You're going to think I'm nuts. But I didn't just imagine what I'm about to tell you."

• • •

Jan was the last one to get to Chandu's, his report having taken more time than he'd expected. He grabbed a beer off the table and sat down on the couch.

"Salami with extra cheese and pepperoni," Chandu said, handing him a personal pizza box.

"You're not cooking?"

"No time. I caught up on sleep and then had to take care of some business."

"This works." Jan took a slice from the box and sank his teeth into it.

"Find out anything?" Zoe asked with her mouth full. She managed to smoke, drink beer, and eat pizza all at the same time. Luckily her pizza was covered with garlic, which helped offset the cigarette smell.

"The fog is slowly lifting," Jan replied. "The murderer got to Moritz Quast's house by coming through the neighbors' yards. No signs of a break-in were found, so he must have had a key to the back door. Moritz Quast was not into security, kept his windows open, and liked to throw parties, all of which made it easy for the murderer to get a key."

"No one noticed it missing?" Max asked. He'd moved on from pizza to ice cream.

"The rear entrance is fitted with a standard pin lock," Chandu said. "The murderer would only have needed an impression to make a duplicate."

"Talking from experience?" Zoe asked.

"You bet."

Jan continued: "Our perpetrator entered the home around eleven p.m. Then he woke Moritz Quast, went into the kitchen, flicked on the light. Which, in turn, made our patrol suspicious. Fabian went in the front and got the stun-gun treatment. David, who was supposed to be covering the rear door, heard a thud and ran around to the front entrance."

"Didn't that warn him, make him all the more wary?" Max asked.

"It did, actually. But now for the freaky part. Inside? He didn't encounter the murderer, but rather Moritz Quast. *He* put David down with the stun gun."

"The victim himself?" Zoe asked. "Was he crazy, or maybe in cahoots with the killer?"

"I'm guessing the killer forced him to do it. According to David, Quast was near tears."

"But if Quast knew that he was going to die," Max said, "why didn't he defend himself?"

"If someone has a gun in your back, you do anything," Chandu replied.

"Even attack the very people protecting me?"

"Anything. Believe me."

"Clever," Zoe said. "No one's counting on the victim attacking."

"That neutralized Quast's guards," Jan continued. "The killer tied both up and then had enough time to do the deed."

"Moritz Quast was beaten to death at the cemetery," Zoe remarked. "How did he get him out of there?"

"On foot. We found footprints in one of the neighbors' yards matching Moritz Quast. Then, on a side street, they got in a vehicle and drove to the cemetery. By the time Fabian and David freed themselves? It was too late."

"Speaking of cemeteries," Zoe said, pulling out her cell phone. "I want to check in with evidence analysis, get the latest results."

She dialed a number, switched the phone to speaker, and set it on the table. On the third ring, a woman answered: "Berlin Police, Evidence Analysis, Franziska Niklas."

"Aloha," Zoe said. "Dr Diek here from the medical examiner's. I need the results on the Moritz Quast case."

"Other team did that one. Who you want to speak to?"

"Any of them will do," Zoe grumbled.

"Who exactly?"

"That Robert one."

"There's no Robert here."

Zoe moaned. "That young whippersnapper. Black hair, little tummy going, smells like Clearasil and has never had to shave."

"Ah, you mean Romir?"

"Like I was saying."

"Just a sec."

The phone was set down. A moment later, footsteps could be heard approaching.

"Romir Hannim," the young man answered.

"Well, finally," Zoe said. "It's Dr. Diek from the medical examiner's. Remember me?"

"Sure. You're the bossy chain-smoker with the charm of a power saw."

"How about I come right over there and—"

Jan yanked the phone off the table and turned to the side. He needed those results from the cemetery and didn't want to go spoiling things with the crime-scene techs. "Hi, Robert, it's Detective Tommen here from Homicide."

"Romir."

"I'm running the investigation on the Valburg and Quast cases. You secure any evidence from the cemetery?"

"We're still analyzing, but we have most of it." Romir cleared his throat. "So. The cemetery was the crime scene for this case. The murderer had Moritz Quast kneel down at the grave and killed him with a blow from behind. Quast had pajamas on and was barefoot."

Jan turned to Zoe. "You confirm the blow to the back of his head was the cause of death?"

"I did," she replied grumpily. She was leaning back on the couch and blowing streams of smoke up toward the ceiling.

"So was it the same murder weapon used on Bernhard Valburg?"

"Most likely."

"Most likely?"

"Ninety-nine-percent match."

"Which is nearly a hundred percent," Max remarked.

"You don't say, Maximum Wiseass," Zoe snapped.

Jan turned back to the phone. "You find any other clues?"

"We found footprints and boot prints. They match the ones from the yard of Simon Illgen, that neighbor of Moritz Quast."

"And the DNA sample from the blood on that pebble?"

"We compared it to Moritz Quast's DNA. The match is ninety-nine point nine percent."

"Which is nearly a hundred percent," Zoe remarked.

"Thanks for the pro tip," Romir added over the phone.

Chandu whispered to Zoe, "I think he likes you."

"Shut it, Mr. T. Why don't you go make me some coffee."

Chandu grinned and saluted her, then went into the kitchen.

"Any fingerprints or DNA from the murderer?"

"We combed the area around the grave millimeter by millimeter. The rain didn't wash anything away this time, but we still found nothing."

"And the cross?"

"Identical material as Bernhard Valburg's. Same wood, same nails, same paint. Mass goods, get 'em at any home-improvement store. Can't be traced back."

"How could he make that cross without leaving any fingerprints? He wearing gloves?"

"Didn't have to," Romir explained. "He nailed the cross together and smeared a thick coat of paint on it. That will cover any fingerprint. We also found traces of bleach. The murderer thought of everything."

Jan sighed. "I guess it would've been too easy, finding something."

"Searching for clues is a dead end," Romir said. "You'll have to get the murderer some other way."

"Okay. Thank you very much."

"Anytime. If we do find anything else, I'll be in touch." He hung up.

"Well, that's my cue," Max said. He turned the projector on, and a photo of Moritz Quast appeared on the wall.

"To recap," he said, pointing at the picture with the last slice of pizza. "Moritz Quast worked for a big health insurer and helped doctors fake bills for expensive meds. He got a suspended sentence and became a car salesman."

Max pressed some keys, and a photo of Bernhard Valburg appeared next to Moritz Quast. "Dr. Valburg was suspected of conspiring to commit insurance fraud but was acquitted of all charges."

"We know this," Zoe said. "This undermines our one possible link between the two victims."

"What if the charges against Dr. Valburg were justified, though?"

"Huh?"

"Did you find evidence?" Jan asked.

"The records don't tell the whole story," Max said. "But maybe the cops didn't find out everything."

"Not a bad thought," Chandu said. "Say Dr. Valburg was more clever than his colleagues. He profits just like they do, but he doesn't get caught."

"It might connect the two men," Jan said, "but it's too weak for me. Which brings me back to my original take. A few thousand euros in damages doesn't turn you into a double murderer."

"You had me convinced of that too," Max interjected. "So I got in touch with an official in CID Three, crime analysis. A Bettina Arns, with Department Thirty-Two, responsible for white-collar crime. She worked the case back then and was happy to give me some details.

"She couldn't tell me much, but one thing she said really got me listening. Moritz Quast was the puppet master in the whole operation. He actually should've landed in prison, but he engaged in a little horse trading and provided the police with evidence on a man they'd been after for quite some time, a man who'd made a tidy sum importing meds not approved in Germany. This deal spared Moritz Quast a prison sentence."

"So he narked and sold out to save his ass," Chandu said. "Which would explain the cut-out tongue."

Max tapped around on his keyboard, and a third picture appeared on the wall, accompanied by the *ta-da* sound. "Allow me to introduce . . ." He made a sweeping gesture toward the wall. "Robin Cordes. The man Moritz Quast sent to prison. Herr Cordes just happens to have been set free from prison six weeks ago."

"Well, fuck me," Zoe said, standing up from the couch.

Chandu came running out of the kitchen as Jan stared at the photo, his eyes widening. The hair, that crooked nose, and the scar above his eyebrows. It all looked familiar.

They had found the man in the police sketch.

Chapter Six

Jan pounded on the door, waited a moment, then pounded again with a flat hand.

"Robin Cordes!" he shouted. "Berlin Police. Open the door."

Jan preferred to make a dramatic entrance in such situations. Anyone with enough marks against them panicked when the cops hammered on the door. Some tried stupid moves or got violent, but the chances of catching a criminal were still better than with the polite approach. Politeness was generally just a waste of time.

Jan kicked at the door. He unclasped his holster and stood to the side of the doorway.

"All right!" a woman roared back. "I'm coming!"

The lock turned. The door opened, and a young woman stared at him with sleepy eyes. She held her bathrobe closed over her chest; she had only a black slip on underneath.

"Detective Tommen." Jan showed his badge. "Can I come in?" He pushed the door open and headed for the hallway. "Thanks."

"Are you crazy? I didn't say you could—"

"Is Robin here?" Jan bounded down the hallway. To the left was a dimly lit bathroom. Empty.

"I'm filing a complaint," the woman snapped.

"No problem. My name is Tommen with two m's." Jan shoved the next door open. The bedroom had two mattresses and a large wardrobe. Jan lifted the bedcovers and opened the wardrobe. A mess of clothes and shoes, but no one was hiding there.

"Robin's not here." She grabbed Jan's arm.

Jan shook himself free. "Best not interfere with a police investigation. And you should put something on. You're going down to the station with me. We'll see how you like the cells there."

The woman jerked back as if Jan had just hit her. She'd leave him alone now.

"I didn't do anything . . ."

Jan exited the bedroom, crossed through the hallway, and entered a small kitchen. Barely bigger than a rabbit hutch.

"We'll see about that." Intimidation was part of the game.

He followed the hallway down to the end. The living room. A blue couch in front of a large TV. Case of beer on the floor. A cheesy picture of a naked woman on a Harley. But no Robin Cordes.

Jan looked out the window. No balcony. They were on the fifth floor. He whipped around to face the woman.

"Where's Robin?" He took a step closer.

She shrunk back. "He's not here."

"I can see that. I want to know where he is."

"I don't know." She was close to tears.

"Who are you?"

"I'm Robin's girlfriend."

"So you have a name?"

"Friederike Roth."

"You live here?"

"Most of the time, I still have a place over in Wedding. We want to move in together soon."

"Robin is your boyfriend, you want to move in together, and yet you don't know where he is?"

She sank to the floor. "He's gone underground. Ever since that murder."

"What murder?"

"Of that car salesman."

"Moritz Quast?"

"Yes. That's his name."

"Could you be more specific? Did he pack a bag and book a flight to Australia, what?"

"I came back from my morning shift and he was gone."

"How could you tell he was gone and not just out for a stroll?"

"Because of his father's picture."

"What?"

Friederike pointed at the TV. "His father and mother left him when he was two years old, so he has no family pictures. He has just one single photo of his father, from a park. He framed it, put it on top of the TV, dusted it every day. He even took the stupid thing along with him when we went on vacation." She shrugged. "No idea what the deal was with him and his old man, but that photo was everything to him."

"And that's how you're sure that he's bolted?"

"Not bolted. Gone underground," Friederike corrected him.

"Is there a difference?"

"He likes this apartment. Most of his things are still here. He'll come back. He packed a duffel bag, stuffed some clothes in, went underground. Even his weird cable box for receiving Bundesliga games is still here.

She wiped at her runny nose.

"Maybe he wanted away from you?"

"If he wasn't into me anymore he would just throw me out. Robin's enough of an asshole for that."

Jan sat down on the couch. "What did Moritz Quast dying have to do with his disappearing?"

"No idea. I didn't know who Moritz Quast was until today."

"Did he mention it?"

"He was completely freaking out at breakfast. Kept pacing around the living room like some crazy dude and babbling something about a Moritz. 'Him too,' he kept saying. I didn't know what was wrong. I've never seen him so worked up, but I was running late and had to get to work. When I heard the news about that murdered car salesman, I knew for sure."

"And then?"

"There was no 'then.' When I came back home, he was gone."

"Did he mention a Dr. Bernhard Valburg?"

"No."

Jan leaned back on the couch, observing Friederike. She was staring hard at the floor and clutching the bathrobe as if it was the only thing she had left in her whole bleak life. The woman didn't seem to have anything to do with any of it.

"Put something on, please," Jan said gently. "We'll talk more about this later."

Friederike nodded and shuffled into the bedroom.

Robin Cordes knew both victims. No surprise there. Dr. Valburg's receptionist had identified him, and Moritz Quast had sent him to prison. Robin was obviously the perfect suspect, but his girlfriend's story was making Jan doubt it. Either she was a great liar and Robin was the perpetrator, or she was telling the truth—in which case Robin got spooked and headed underground.

One thing seemed clear: if Robin wasn't the killer, he knew the killer.

.   .   .

"The work hours used to be better," Zoe grumbled as she stepped out of the car. "I didn't have to hang around cemeteries in the middle of the night or drive to Berlin at all hours just to question some mouse."

"Quit your whining, Princess," Chandu said. "You were the one who wanted to come with me. Plus, his nickname is *Rat*. Not *Mouse*. Has to do with his looks—that and his last name is Ratinger."

"Couldn't we have done this tomorrow at lunchtime?"

"Nine thirty p.m. is early. Most people in this world have just eaten breakfast."

Zoe took a look around. "What's so special about this place? The buildings all look like a thousand others. Shops, a few pubs, no flashy cars on the street. Not even any hookers or drug dealers. It all looks pretty boring."

"That's exactly why we're meeting here. A boring neighborhood with boring residents."

"I don't get it."

"Tim is paranoid. Which is precisely why he's survived as long as he has. Meeting with me in public is not without its dangers. I associate with people who don't get along with certain other people. Someone sees us, he'll be associated with my people, something that could cause problems for his business."

"God, so complicated. Why not just send you an e-mail?"

Chandu laughed. "I suppose it would spare me some bumps and bruises, but sometimes the old tried-and-true methods are still the best."

"You mean slugging a guy in the nose, stuff like that?"

"Exactly."

Zoe looked at her watch. "Being punctual is evidently not a strength of this Rat of yours."

"Oh, he's been here a while now. He likes to probe his surroundings and study who he's going to be talking to. If you weren't here, he'd already have surfaced."

"I look that dangerous?"

"In the age of automatic firearms, everyone is dangerous."

"I prefer a knife. Firearms are too vulgar for me."

"Here he comes," Chandu said, gesturing toward the other side of the street.

A short, skinny man was moving along the parked cars. His head darted from side to side as if he expected an attack from every angle. Every few steps, he pivoted as if he were being followed. He looked down the street, waited until a car went by, and ran across. He slowed his steps as he approached them.

Zoe finally got a better look at the man. He had unkempt black hair streaked with gray and really needed a trip to the barber. He was unshaven and wore a faded black pullover. His front teeth protruded noticeably, but the most distinctive thing about him was his glasses, which were far too big for his haggard face, with lenses that looked about two inches thick.

Chandu shifted his weight. With his legs spread apart and shoulders flexed back, he looked like a boxer before the bell sounded. This was his stance for intimidation.

"Tim," he said, his voice grave.

Their contact raised a hand and was about to respond when Zoe landed a powerful blow right on his nose. Glasses and man flew backward.

"What are you doing?" Chandu yelled. "You can't hit him!"

"I thought this was our way of greeting him."

"It's not. Well, okay, in my case it's different."

"Ah, you get to give him one and I don't?"

"We've known each other a long time."

"You only slug people you've known a long time?"

"Normally I don't slug anyone."

"Apart from Tim."

"Yes. But only sometimes."

"Then don't get all worked up. I just wanted to take some work off your hands."

Chandu balled his fists and smacked at his own temples. "You're going to drive me crazy before this is all over. I've knocked around with plenty of nut jobs in my time, but you? You beat them all."

"Oh, thanks a lot." Zoe threw her head back, running fingers through her hair. "You really know how to charm a girl."

"What was that for?" Tim howled, holding his bleeding nose.

"A misunderstanding," Chandu said to smooth things over.

Zoe came closer to have a look at his nose. "Not a big deal. A clean break. Won't hurt by tomorrow."

"Thanks!" Tim shouted at her. "Makes me feel better already."

"Your glasses." Chandu set the broken frame and cracked glass in Tim's hand.

"You know what a custom-made pair like this costs?" he said, waving the remains of his spectacles in Zoe's face.

"Two euros?"

"Ah, she's funny too. What rock did you find her under?"

"She's assisting with my investigation."

"Well, maybe you should start looking for a new partner."

"Tim, just calm down." Chandu placed an arm around the little man. "Give me something good, and then you can head right over to the optician with your reward."

"What about my nose?"

"That'll need a doctor," Zoe said.

"A doctor? You really think I have health insurance?"

"No big deal." Zoe pushed up her sleeves. "I can set that beak of yours right here and now—"

"No!" Chandu and Tim said in unison.

"It's fine like it is," Chandu added.

Zoe held up her hands. "Hey, I only wanted to help."

Chandu turned to Tim. "So. What do you have for us?"

"Your call was a little short-notice. I take it you already know who the guy is in the police sketch?"

"We do now. It's a certain Robin Cordes."

"What do you know about him?"

"He was caught up in a billing scandal. When it all blew up, one of the people involved sold him down the river. Robin ended up in the joint."

"That business with the billing," Tim said, "that was only one of his gigs. Robin did whatever shady job brought in the dough. Push drugs, sell stolen goods, break into cars. Nothing huge. He always swam clear of the big sharks."

"You heard about any connection to a Dr. Valburg?"

"Doesn't ring a bell, but I haven't had much time to ask around."

"How did Robin do in the slammer?"

"Not too bad, the way I hear it. He's changed, apparently."

"Changed?"

"Broke off all his old connections. No dirty dealings anymore. No drugs, nothing. Even declined an invite on one real lucrative job."

"How does he earn his dough? Collecting bottles?"

"Word is, it's poker games."

"Robin's rigging poker games?"

"No idea. The games could be bogus, or he could just be running no-limit games, or maybe he's just a good player. But the man's a ghost of his former self."

"You got any idea where he could be holing up?"

"That brings us back to the problem of his avoiding all his old contacts. He's withdrawn. Three years ago? I could've told you his favorite pub. But he hasn't shown up there in a while. He still lives at the same place, though. Try there."

"It was a dead end. He's apparently gone underground."

"In that case, it'll be tough. Robin grew up on the street, knows his way around. If I hear anything, I'll be in touch, but if he doesn't want to be found? He'll stay invisible."

Chandu reached in his pocket and pulled out two hundred-euro bills. "Consider it a down payment," he said, pressing them into Tim's hand. "When we nab Robin, there'll be a bonus."

"Well, I should hope so," Tim muttered.

Chandu slapped him on the shoulder like a pal, which made Tim's knees buckle. "Thanks, old buddy." Then he grabbed Zoe by an arm and dragged her toward the car.

"What was that for?" she said, trying to shake free.

"I don't want you kicking him in the nuts good-bye or whatever enters that mind of yours."

"I wasn't planning to."

"I don't buy it." Chandu unlocked the car. He turned around, but the little man was nowhere to be seen. Only then did he release Zoe.

"Maybe just a little kick," she muttered as she climbed in.

• • •

Max had booted up all his computers, grabbed the rest of the anchovy pizza from the fridge, and left *Pinky and the Brain* cartoons running on the TV. Armed with his favorite drink—Ovaltine and cola—he was now ready for battle.

He logged in to the police server, started up the search program, and entered Robin Cordes's cell-phone number. After a few seconds, a dialogue window appeared: *No location found.*

"Damn it."

His phone rang.

"Hi, Jan."

"Robin Cordes has gone underground," Jan said. "Can you locate his cell phone?"

"I'm striking out. Either he turned it off or he pulled out the SIM card."

"Will you get him back if he turns it on again?"

"I'll fire a stealth text at him."

"What kind of text?"

"I send a text to Robin's cell number. It won't display and won't chime—he won't even notice he's getting a message. But the text still arrives there and I get connection data about where the message went. But his phone has to be turned on for that. When he does, I got him."

"So you'll know his whereabouts?"

"More or less," Max said. "If he has a GPS in his phone, it's real precise. If not, it goes over the mobile network. In that case, I can only give you the nearest cell tower."

"And what if he never turns on his phone?"

"We can forget about real-time locating."

"Which means what, we wouldn't have him?"

"Well, there's something else I'll try." Max took a big bite of pizza. "I'll look up any connection data from Robin over the last few days," he said, chewing. "I'll use that to build a profile of his routes. Maybe we'll see other clusters apart from his home."

"Clusters?"

"Places he's visited more than once."

"How long will that take?"

"Depends on the amount of data. There's a difference between taking a stroll now and then and driving around Berlin for ten hours. I'll have more for you by tomorrow morning."

"Sounds good."

"Not a problem. I'll be in touch."

Before Jan had even hung up, Max was tapping into the mobile provider's database. He'd had this specific Trojan up and running before getting his internship with the cops. He could still hear his annoying neighbor's shriek when he got a cell-phone bill for €12,427. Some things were just priceless.

Max entered Robin's cell-phone number and started downloading the data. Meanwhile he'd have to write a program that overlaid the cell phone's points of contact on a map.

A few hours later, he knew Robin's favorite pub, where he liked to shop for groceries, and who his friends were. They would find him out there somewhere.

•　　•　　•

A loud pounding ripped Jan out of his slumber. He turned to his alarm clock and realized he wasn't lying in bed. The surroundings looked suspiciously like his living room, which meant he'd fallen asleep on the couch again. The harsh light of a floor lamp burned his eyes, and he was still dressed. Crime-scene photos were scattered across his stomach, and coffee had spilled all over the upholstery.

"Excellent," he grumbled. He rubbed at his temples to drive away his throbbing headache, but to no avail. He'd wanted to work through the night but fell asleep, despite the coffee. The last time he'd looked at his watch, it was two in the morning. He turned his head toward the kitchen. The digital clock flashed 4:57 a.m.

Jan thought he'd been imagining the pounding, but it turned out someone was actually hammering on the door.

"Jan, Jan!" Max's voice echoed down the stairwell. "Are you awake?"

"Yeah," he muttered wearily. "Along with the rest of the building." He heaved himself off the couch and opened the door. "Come on in."

"I got something." Max ran over to the couch and slammed a stack of printouts down on the coffee table. "My breakdown, it's done."

He sat on the couch and turned on his laptop. "Our route profile for Robin Cordes."

Then he sprang back up.

"It took me several hours."

He paced back and forth.

"But the work, it was so worth it."

He sat back down on the couch. "We have clusters."

He turned the laptop toward Jan, sprang back up.

"Max, just . . ." Jan rubbed at his eyes. He was barely awake. Three hours of sleep was nowhere near enough. "Have you been sucking down energy drinks again?"

The young hacker stopped abruptly. He didn't seem to have an answer. After a few moments, he said, "No."

"Max," Jan insisted. "Tell me the truth."

"Okay, maybe one or two." He stared at the floor.

"You're a terrible liar."

"But they had this deal going," Max said. "Buy a six-pack, get a second free."

Jan moaned. Twelve energy drinks. His young friend would be hopping around like a Mexican jumping bean for the next three days.

"The stuff helps," Max protested. "I worked straight through the night, and I'm not the least bit tired."

"I can see that." Jan shuffled into the kitchen and turned on the coffeemaker. "How did you get in?"

"Paper delivery guy was in the building. I waited till he was done and I slipped right in."

Jan pulled a mug from the cabinet, wondering whether a person could sleep standing up. "Okay. Give it to me."

"What I did was, I marked all of Robin Cordes's routes." Max turned his laptop toward Jan again. On the screen was a city map covered with red lines.

"Fascinating." Jan turned back to his coffeemaker.

"I thought so too," Max replied, even more fired up now. "So I made a program that bolds the red lines for places Robin visited multiple times."

"Awesome." Jan stretched, yawned.

"That's what I thought." Max pointed to a spot on the screen. "Robin's building is deep red. Other deep reds are the subway station, supermarket, and a newsstand."

"No surprises there." Jan closed his eyes, inhaling the aroma of coffee. He was slowly returning to the world of the living.

"Not really. But there are two unusual hits I'm seeing."

"And they are?"

"Robin Cordes visited Dr. Valburg's office—three days before the doctor died."

"Not bad." It didn't tell them anything about where Robin might be now, but it did reinforce the connection between him and Dr. Valburg. "The second hit?"

"Now, this second one is weird." Max zoomed in on the map. "Robin spent a lot of time near the old Tempelhof rail yards."

"What's a lot?"

"Three times a week."

"Always at the same time?"

"Different days and different times."

"Nights too?"

"Daytime only."

Jan took his coffee mug into the living room. "Anything unique about the rail yards?"

"You know the nature park there, Schöneberger Südgelände?"

"Never heard of it."

"The switchyards there are now a kind of nature reserve slash open-air museum. There's an old water tower, a steam locomotive, engine turntables. Everything to get a train fanatic's heart racing."

"So a railroad museum?"

"Something like that."

"What's Robin Cordes doing at an open-air railroad museum?"

Max shrugged. "Maybe he's an old-time locomotive freak?"

Jan shook his head. "Not one thing in Robin's apartment pointed to that. He had no model trains or train pictures or any other of that railway-buff stuff."

"Well, I can't tell you any more than that. This nature park is the only unusual thing on his route profile. His cell phone is still off; the last data is from the night before last."

"Are your dummy texts still active?"

"Stealth texts," Max corrected him. "And yes, they are. He turns on his phone, I'll know."

Jan sighed. Couldn't a suspect just once hide out in a kebab joint, a nice coffee shop, maybe even a strip club? Nope. It had to be railway museum.

"A stroll through this nature railway park will do me good," he said. Lies like that crossed his lips with such surprising ease. He emptied his coffee cup in one gulp. "Maybe I'll even trip over a murder suspect."

•   •   •

The huge rusty tower rose high in the sky. Jan stood next to a group of schoolkids and followed their fascinated gazes upward. He had no clue what was so exciting about the decrepit old thing. It was a metal monstrosity that had once pumped water into steam locomotives.

Jan shrugged and continued on.

He had been strolling around the grounds for two hours now, but he'd found no trace of Robin Cordes. He had been playing the engrossed tourist, holding a map and taking photos with his phone. He kept attaching himself to this or that little tour group so his meandering didn't look conspicuous. He now knew that the construction of the railway yards had been completed in 1889, but they lost significance after Berlin was divided and were eventually abandoned. Forty-nine species of birds nested here and even more spiders, and over three hundred varieties of flowering plants grew on the grounds. People were not supposed to leave the paths so as not to disturb the wildlife.

There was hardly a worse place to hide out. Jan had no idea what Robin Cordes could possibly have been doing here. He dialed Max's number.

"Yo!" Max answered. Obviously the energy drinks were still going strong.

"I've just wasted two whole hours walking around this park—and found nothing. Can you tell me anything more about where Robin Cordes was hanging around here?"

"Unfortunately not. I only get a bearing from two cell towers in the area. It keeps jumping around, which means he was there and he walked through the park."

"But why? There's nothing here."

"Were you over near the garden plot?"

"Where's that?"

"West of you," Max said. "Cross over the tracks."

"The light-rail tracks?"

"Exactly. Don't get run over."

A garden plot was the perfect hideout. Tough to make out. Scarce security. Most of the garden sheds had only padlocks on the doors. Yet they had water and electricity.

"How many plots are there?" Jan asked Max.

"Two thousand six hundred."

"*How* many?"

"Schöneberger Südgelände is one of the largest continuous garden plots in Berlin."

Jan groaned. There was no way he could check out all those tracts. "I'll take a look around. Thanks for the info."

"Welcome." Max hung up.

With twenty-six hundred plots, random spot checks would have to do.

Jan followed a path that led to a quieter part of the nature park. Once he'd determined that no one was around, he hurried into the forest and headed west. Soon he reached two rail lines. An S-Bahn light-rail train whooshed by him. He looked left and right but didn't see another train. He tiptoed over the tracks, went down a little embankment, and found a concrete path. A man strolling with a Rottweiler eyed Jan suspiciously as he came bounding out from between two trees. The dog jerked back in fright and hid behind its master. This Rottweiler was clearly not trained as a guard dog.

Jan smiled. "Nice day today." He pointed at the gray sky, which was growing darker by the second.

The man walked past Jan without taking his eyes off him, as if expecting to be mugged at any moment. Jan kept smiling, which didn't seem to help matters. Once the dog owner had gotten a safe distance from Jan, he turned and continued on at a faster pace.

As a precaution, Jan chose to go in the opposite direction down the path. He saw a high fence surrounding the garden plots. A wall of bushes and trees blocked his view inside.

After a short walk, he came to an outdoor café. Tables filled a beer garden, inviting visitors to take a break, all surrounded by a little white fence. It was pretty quiet at this hour. A man was wiping down chairs with a rag while a young woman placed vases of wildflowers on the tables. It was clear the two were related, even though the man had an impressive beer belly and his daughter looked more like she belonged in a fitness studio.

Jan strolled through the open gate. "Good morning," he said.

"Good morning to you," the man replied and gestured at a table. "You looking for some breakfast or just something to drink?"

"Breakfast sounds great, but unfortunately I'm here on official business." Jan showed his badge. "My name is Detective Tommen. I'm looking for a suspect who's been spending time around here in the last few days. We don't know if he's been in the nature park or on a garden plot, but maybe you saw him?" Jan pulled a photo from his pocket and held it up.

"That's Robin," the man said.

"You know Robin Cordes?"

"We went to school together."

Jan was speechless—though he wasn't sure whether it was because of his stroke of luck or because of the casual way the man admitted he knew Robin.

"He in trouble again?" the man asked.

"He's wanted as a witness."

The man laughed. "Robin's wanted by the cops a lot, but this must be the first time he's wanted as the witness and not the offender."

"You know about his criminal past?"

"Sure. I've always warned him to stay away from shady stuff, but with that childhood of his and who he hung out with, he never had a chance. It was only a matter of time before he ended up in the joint."

"Which is what happened."

"Robin isn't a bad guy. Life just didn't give him a chance."

"No offense, but that's the excuse every criminal gives."

"Now, I'm not saying he didn't earn it." The café owner raised his hands in defense. "But jail was a lucky break for him in the end."

"You call that luck?"

"Robin loved his freedom. Go wherever you want. Do whatever you want. With whoever. That kind of thing." The owner sat in a chair. "In jail he realized what freedom really is and what happens when it's taken away from you. No friends, no girlfriend, no phone calls, no Internet. Not to mention no live soccer games, pizza delivery, sitting at the bar with a vodka lemon."

Jan sat down across from the man.

"You know what he did when he got out of jail?" the man asked.

Jan shrugged.

"He came here for breakfast." The man nodded toward a table. "He sat over there, shut his eyes, let the sun shine on his face. Happy as a baby on Mommy's breast. Meanwhile, I got to work in the kitchen and served him up a nice big spread. Coffee, rolls, eggs with bacon, sausage, cheese, jam, Nutella. Whole nine yards. And when he drank the fresh-squeezed OJ? He cried." The man smiled. "I'd never seen Robin cry. Not even in school when he took all those knocks from the older boys. Never shed a tear. Robin is a badass. But that breakfast back in his newfound freedom, it made a different man out of him."

"In what way, exactly?"

"He left his old life behind. Moving stolen goods, the drugs, all that crap. He never, ever wanted to go back to jail."

"You believed him?"

"Like I said, I've known Robin since we were schoolkids together. So, yeah, I believe him."

"So what's he doing now?"

"Plays cards."

"Plays cards?"

"Robin was locked up with a poker pro for six months. The guy hadn't paid his taxes. They gambled all day long in jail. He got hooked on it."

"Gambling is illegal."

"Depends on where and with who," the owner answered. "I don't know the details, but Robin appears to be a good player. Not bringing in big money, but enough to survive on."

"When was the last time you saw him?"

"Four days ago."

"How was he doing?"

"What do you mean?"

"Was he worked up, or nervous?"

"Not that I saw."

"Did he say he was going underground?"

"Nope. Why should he do that?"

Jan looked around the beer garden. The owner's daughter had gone back inside. They were alone. It was always a delicate balance, knowing how much information to reveal in questioning. His position was stronger the less a person knew, but sometimes you had to give something up to keep the conversation going. If this man really was Robin's friend, he wouldn't be going to the media with it.

"Robin is connected to two murder cases."

The owner leaned back in his chair and folded his hands over his stomach. "I hope you're not talking about that grave murderer who's in all the papers?"

Jan simply lifted his eyebrows. Let the man infer what he liked.

"Oh, man." The owner rubbed at his forehead. "He really stepped in it this time."

"If it's any help, I still don't know if Robin Cordes is the perpetrator or just a witness."

The owner leaned over the table. "Robin's fouled up a lot in his life, but he's not a killer. And when I read in the papers what kind of sick shit this grave murderer is doing, well, you can rule out Robin three times over."

"Even if I did believe you, there is some connection between Robin Cordes and the two victims. He's involved somehow, and the sooner I figure out how, the faster we can leave him be. Tell me where he is," Jan urged. "The longer he stays on the lam, he's only making things worse for himself. If he's innocent, he's got nothing to fear."

"I have no idea where he's hiding," the owner replied. "I didn't even know he was on the lam till now."

"Did he mention anything the last time you talked?"

The owner shook his head. The news that his friend was a murder suspect had really hit him hard, Jan could see.

"Maybe you know of some secret hideout he uses?"

"Look, I want to help you," the owner insisted. "But if Robin's gone underground, you won't get to him. He's too clever for that."

"We'll find him eventually. If he really has become a different person, then he should turn himself in."

The man wiped at his brow, which was now damp with sweat. "You have to understand. The police were always the enemy to Robin. Changing his life and quitting his crooked ways, that's one thing. But trust the cops? No way. It's like a dog's reflex to bite. His survival instincts come into play."

"I'll leave you my number." Jan set down his card. "Call me if you see him. He can't hide out his whole life. If his freedom means anything to him, he should be talking to us. If he's innocent, then he's got nothing to be afraid of."

The owner took the card and stood. "I'll do my best."

Jan shook the man's hand. "Thanks for your help."

He left the outdoor café and headed back to the open-air museum.

He would leave checking out the garden plots to Patrick Stein's people, possibly helped out by patrol cops. He wasn't going to get very far covering twenty-six hundred parcels all on his own.

He hiked back up the embankment, waited till a light-rail train passed, and hurried across the tracks into the woods.

The café owner really seemed to care about his friend. Maybe he could convince Robin to talk to Jan. If Robin told them what he knew, they might get that decisive lead.

Jan was just about to head back on the path to the open-air museum when a man sprang out from behind a tree, wielding a pistol.

"Hey there," Robin said, aiming at Jan's forehead.

·   ·   ·

Jan had lost count of the number of times he'd been threatened with violence. Clubs and knives were dangerous, but a pistol was in another league altogether. Just a twitch was enough to unleash a round. You couldn't dodge a bullet, and your chances of dying were far too high.

Robin Cordes looked nervous, a sign that he wasn't used to threatening people with a pistol. Which only made him more dangerous.

Jan held up his hands and made no move to fight him. Robin was four yards away. It didn't matter how quick Jan was—Robin would be able to get off a shot.

"Get rid of the gun!" Robin shouted.

Jan carefully reached for his holster and pulled out his pistol, its safety on.

"Toss it in the woods."

The gun flew into the underbrush.

Robin kept pivoting around, as though fearful that some hiker would accidentally come strolling through the woods. He was trying to keep an eye on Jan at the same time, which made him spin his head frantically.

"What do you want?" Jan asked him. His pulse had begun to slow down after that initial shock. "If you were planning to kill me, you could have ambushed me. This spot was a good choice. A shot would be tough to locate with any precision. By the time someone found my body, you'd be long gone. You could have just stood behind a tree and I would have walked right on by without even seeing you." Jan shrugged, which was a bit awkward with his hands up. "So, you want something from me."

"You must be that wiseass cop."

Jan nodded.

"So, Herr Wiseass, why don't you tell me why you're all searching for me?"

"We have two dead. Bernhard Valburg and Moritz Quast. You had an argument with the first one, and the second put you in jail. A wiseass cop would call that a motive."

"I'm no murderer, goddamn it."

"So why did you go underground?"

"Because I don't trust fucking pigs."

"Don't trust how?"

"You're looking for a scapegoat because you're too stupid to find this grave murderer. So me with my jail time, it fits perfectly."

"Bullshit," Jan replied. "We don't want a scapegoat. We want the person who did it. And at the moment? You're the only suspect we got."

"That's what I'm saying." Robin came a step closer and waved the pistol in Jan's face. He was now maybe two yards away. Jan could've risked charging at him.

"You've as good as sentenced me," Robin said.

"Just because a person has a motive doesn't mean he committed a murder. But a motive gives us enough to question a guy."

"You have no clue what's going on here."

"Then fill me in. Why have it out with Bernhard Valburg?"

Robin lowered his pistol a little. It was the perfect moment to strike, but Jan kept his hands up. Wrestling over a gun was just too risky. Maybe he could get Robin to talk some more. It would spare the both of them.

"Shortly before I went into the slammer, I was supplying the doctor with drugs." Confessing this seemed to distress Robin. It was probably the first time he'd ever admitted committing an offense to a cop. "That's what they ran me in for. After I got released, I gave all the shit up. But Valburg, he wouldn't leave me alone. I kept telling him he needed to go find another dealer, that I was done with that scene. Eventually I went to his office and threatened to bash his brains in if he didn't stop."

"What about Moritz Quast? You certainly had a reason to bump him off."

"Sure did," Robin replied. "I actually did want to give it to him real good, but then they'd run me in again. That shithead just wasn't worth it."

Robin had lowered the pistol by now. Everything he was saying sounded sincere enough, but criminals like him, they lied for a living.

"I'm not into anything crooked anymore," he said as if trying to convince himself.

Jan wasn't buying his story of changing for good. No upright citizen went around carrying a gun. He said, "So that gun you got there's for shooting wild mushrooms?"

"It's for self-defense."

"Against who? Nosy cops?"

"Against the guy who put down Valburg and Quast."

"Who do you think it is?"

"Got no clue, man." Robin ran his hand nervously through his hair. Jan noticed that his shirt was damp with sweat and his hands were shaking. "Maybe it's some lunatic getting revenge on health insurers. Or Batman. I don't know and I don't care. Valburg and Quast are dead. I don't want to be next."

"Are you next?"

"I did some illegal shit with those two. Maybe we stepped on someone's toes and that someone is real pissed now. When I read what the killer did to Moritz? That's when I bolted. There's a maniac running around out there, and I'm not going to sit at home and wait for him to come for me."

"Then come with me," Jan urged him. "We'll help you."

Robin laughed. "You pigs made my life hell. I'd rather go it alone."

"We can protect you."

"Like you did Moritz Quast. I also read what the killer did to those guards you put on him." He shook his head. "No, I'll pass."

"Come down to the station. I'll show you the case files. Maybe you can help us catch the killer. Then you'll be able to sleep again at night."

"Nice try, pig." Robin raised the gun to Jan's head again. "Now turn around and walk toward the tracks. You turn back around, I shoot. I'm no killer, but I'm good for a bullet in your leg."

Jan turned around, keeping his arms raised. "Think about it," he said as he walked off. "In our hands you have a much better chance of surviving."

Right before reaching the tracks, Jan's phone rang. He glanced over his shoulder. Robin was gone.

His screen showed Bergman's number.

"Get down to the station right away," Jan's boss barked. "And use the back door."

Chapter Seven

"A state of siege" best described the situation outside the station. Jan had ignored Bergman's advice, which was proving to be a bad idea.

The front entrance was surrounded by a waist-high barricade. Four uniformed officers were trying to keep the premises off-limits, in spite of the pack of journalists pressing into them.

The chaos of cameras, cables, and microphones on long booms made for an impenetrable jungle of newsgathering. Photographers stood on ladders, TV reporters had their assistants dabbing their foreheads, and the print journalists jockeyed for the best position. Surrounding them all was a cluster of onlookers, rubberneckers, and people like Jan who didn't want to be standing there but could not get through the crowd. Ten yards away, a Mercedes driver was honking in anger at being stuck at a green light. No traffic would be getting through here for a good hour.

Jan stood atop a planter to get a better view of the entrance. On one step of the stairs was a podium sprouting several microphones. Judging from the logos on them, every broadcaster in Germany was present.

An operation like this would have been worthy of Barack Obama. Instead, Bergman came out the door. The police chief himself hurried out in front of Bergman. The chief wore a dark-blue uniform without much insignia. Only his epaulets and name badge indicated his position.

Jan had thought the chaos couldn't get any worse, but the appearance of the police chief set the group in motion once again. The uniformed cops at the barricade dug in their heels as the police chief stepped up to the microphone.

"Ladies and gentlemen of the media. Citizens of Berlin . . ."

The mob came to an abrupt halt. The cameras had been switched on and the voice recorders turned up; the photographers began shooting madly, their flashes creating a bizarre strobe effect. Reporters screamed questions as if the loudest voice would win a prize. The racket was deafening—but the police chief, unfazed, presided over it all as if over a class of obedient and curious schoolchildren hanging on his every word.

"We would like to bring you up to date on the latest in the case."

This launched a new round of questions, but the chief just ignored them.

"The so-called grave murderer, as he's described in the media, has not been apprehended. We are certain that this person is responsible for the homicide of Dr. Bernhard Valburg as well as that of Moritz Quast. This means we are dealing with the same sole perpetrator."

"Tell us something new!" a reporter roared.

"Our top investigators are on the case, and they're all working under enormous pressure. We're following more leads. Please understand that we cannot make the details public for fear of jeopardizing the case."

Jan glanced at Bergman. He knew how much the man hated reporters. It was looking mighty tough for him to keep calm, but as head of detectives he had to attend media events like this. He was a man to be avoided today. Jan didn't have a choice, though.

"In addition, we believe that these murders were of a personal nature. The grave murderer is no crazed serial killer choosing his victims at random."

"Is that supposed to comfort people?" the reporter yelled.

"We've postponed all officers' vacations and extended their shifts. Every cemetery is being watched by uniformed patrols and their fellow officers. All cemetery staff have been instructed to report any suspicious persons."

The police chief raised his eyes from his prepared remarks and looked directly into the cameras. "We are asking for the public's help in Berlin. If you knew either of the victims or witnessed anything during the nights of June twenty-third and twenty-seventh, please contact one of the police precincts."

The press conference was basically over. The police chief would answer a few questions in the same noncommittal way he'd done in his speech. The information would be enough for the news, but there was nothing truly new to report.

Jan climbed off the planter and worked his way out of the crowd. Hopefully the rear entrance was quieter. His boss surely hadn't called him in for a press conference.

Bergman had something new, something he was keeping from the press.

$\bullet \quad \bullet \quad \bullet$

Jan heard Bergman and his muffled cursing before he saw him. It would have been smarter to wait until his boss calmed down, but he didn't want to lose any time. He was going to get his ass kicked one way or another.

"There he is, our Super Detective," Bergman said.

"Mornin'," Jan said and smiled. It didn't matter what he said. Bergman's mood wasn't going to improve.

"You ever going to find the murderer, or should I just hope he dies of old age?"

Jan felt actual physical pain from not being able to strike back with a comment of his own. "Why am I here?" he grunted.

"You have a visitor."

Jan furrowed his brow. Patrick Stein and his crew were the ones responsible for questioning potential witnesses. If Bergman was calling Jan in too, it had to be someone important.

Bergman waved him into his office and slammed the door shut. A woman sat slumped in his armchair, her face buried in her hands. She looked so despondent that Jan fought an urge to go hide the scissors lying on the desk.

Bergman gestured at her and took his chair. "You already know Frau Roth."

Friederike raised her head. Her eyes were wet and swollen from crying, and her mascara had left black streaks down her cheeks. Robin Cordes's girlfriend had turned into a quivering mess.

Jan sat down across from her. Nothing could have happened to Robin. Jan had still been with the man when Bergman called.

Friederike held up a photo and placed it in Jan's lap.

In it, he saw an empty grave. On a wooden cross, it read: *Here Rests Robin Cordes. Born on March 12, 1972. Died on June 29, 2013.*

Jan tried not to swear.

"Where did it come from?" he asked.

"It was in my mailbox this morning."

Jan studied the photo more closely. Apart from the hole in the ground, he didn't detect much else. No buildings in the background and no other grave that would help them place it in a particular cemetery.

"Do you know where this is?"

Friederike shook her head.

Jan turned to Bergman. "Did Forensics get their hands on this yet?"

"That's a copy. Crime techs are on it."

Jan took the photo and stood up. "I'll be right back." He left the office, hustled down the hallway, and headed for the special unit's conference room. If there was one constant in the chaos of an investigation, it was Patrick. He arrived at work when most people were still asleep, and he was one of the last to leave. Sure, he was pedantic and humorless, but he was also dependable and exacting. The perfect man for this job.

Jan stormed into the room. "We have a new grave."

All heads turned his way. "So we've heard," Patrick said. "We're waiting on the crime techs' analysis."

"No time. Robin Cordes is supposed to die tomorrow. If it's the same murderer, we're not going to get any evidence off it anyway."

Jan laid the photo on the table. "This grave, it's somewhere in Berlin. The murderer left us no clues, so the only way to do this is the hard way. Call every cemetery, get all personnel back from lunch, whatever it takes. They'll have to search out this grave. No idea how the murderer is going to find his victim when he's gone into hiding, but if he does, we'll be waiting for him right here." Jan pointed at the photo.

"We should send all available patrols to the cemeteries to assist personnel there," Patrick suggested.

"Good idea. The more people searching, the better."

"What if the grave isn't at a cemetery?" Patrick said.

Jan hadn't considered that possibility. "It wouldn't fit the murderer's pattern up till now."

"But it's not inconceivable."

"We're hurting, in that case. We can't go turning all Berlin upside down in half a day."

"We'll just hope for the best," Patrick said. "I'll send a list of all the local cemeteries around. Everyone takes a few. It couldn't take more than an hour. Mark the addresses where we haven't reached anyone. We'll send a car there."

As if on some invisible signal, all the investigators turned to their computers and got to work.

Jan smiled. In less than two hours, he would know where this grave was. Then they'd set up a little greeting committee for the murderer.

· · ·

Friederike Roth was sitting on the visitors' bench outside the glass walls of Bergman's office, staring absently into her coffee cup.

Once Jan was back inside Bergman's office, Bergman asked him, "Did I understand correctly that you talked to Robin Cordes an hour ago?"

"Right before you called."

"So why didn't you bring him in to the station?"

"Because he had a gun in my face and wasn't exactly cooperating."

"So he's not the grave murderer?"

Jan shook his head. "He's all about escaping his own grave."

"But what if that was simply some clever chess move to throw us off?"

"The murderer doesn't need to do that. We're feeling around in the dark as it is."

"We know that, but the murderer doesn't."

"Robin Cordes was a small-time crook. Maybe he's changed, but such precise planning? It's not his thing."

"Did he say anything about his connection to Valburg or Quast?"

"Nothing new. Cordes was Valburg's dealer, and Quast put him in jail. He'd love to pay Quast back for that, but he didn't want to risk his probation."

"He wouldn't be the first," Bergman said.

"Cordes had the motive for Moritz Quast, but the way he died points to a more complicated relationship. Such a sophisticated production just isn't Cordes's style."

"So what's happening now?"

"Patrick's people are contacting all cemetery personnel in Berlin. Together with the patrols we have on it, we'll find that grave before sundown. If the murderer shows up there, we'll get him. Robin smelled a rat before we did, so I don't think he'll let himself be caught. I only stumbled upon him because he wanted me to."

"This would be simpler if we could keep an eye on him."

"He wouldn't do it. It's understandable from his perspective, considering how things went wrong with Moritz Quast."

"That's not a mistake we'll make a second time."

"Robin will stay underground. I'll talk to his girlfriend again and try to convince her to work with us. Maybe he'll get in touch with her. We might also locate him if he turns on his phone." He grinned briefly at the thought of Max's tech savvy.

"Good," Bergman said. "I'll put some pressure on Crime Tech." He reached for the phone.

•　　•　　•

Outside Bergman's office, Jan sat down on the bench next to Friederike Roth, who was still staring into her empty cup. He didn't want to pressure her, so he just sat there without saying a word.

"I flip through the paper every day," she eventually began in a low voice. "You read about muggings, accidents, sometimes even murder. But as soon as you put down the paper, you forget about all those headlines."

She turned the cup in her hand. "It's so bizarre being an actual part of one of these stories. In the blink of an eye, your whole life can change."

She turned to Jan. "Who is this grave murderer? Why come after Robin?"

"If I knew that, we wouldn't be sitting here and you wouldn't have to be afraid. The murderer is obviously deranged. The good news is, he's also arrogant and sticking to his pattern. He doesn't just want to kill his victims, he wants to make their death a ceremony. I don't know what's driving him to dig those graves, but it will be his Achilles' heel. He will return there."

"But only with Robin's corpse."

"I don't think so," Jan countered. "I'd rather your boyfriend was here right now, but not even the police have been able to catch him. And we have far more resources than the murderer."

"But why is he after Robin?"

"It has something to do with Dr. Valburg and Moritz Quast."

"The first two victims."

Jan nodded. "We can't ask them, and Robin isn't talking. He might know who the murderer is, possibly without even realizing it. There's some connection between those three."

"I wish I could help, but Robin never said a thing to me. And I guess I didn't want to know what he was up to."

Bergman came up to the glass from inside his office. He shook his head.

Jan sighed. Bergman must be referring to the analysis of the photo. So they hadn't found any leads this time either.

He turned back to Friederike. "You can help us—by persuading your boyfriend to talk to us."

"I've left hundreds of voice messages for Robin and I have no idea where he's hiding."

"He'll get in touch eventually. He might call you or be waiting for you somewhere." Jan handed her a card with his number. "I know he's had trouble with the cops all his life, but ask him to call this number. We can protect him. And when we've uncovered the exact connection between him, Dr. Valburg and Moritz Quast, then we'll have our man. Then your boyfriend can go home."

Friederike took the card. "Thank you." She raised her head and looked Jan in the eye for the first time. "If he contacts me, he'll call you. I promise."

• • •

After Friederike left, Jan allowed himself a stroll to his favorite kebab joint around the corner. He hadn't had any breakfast, and his stomach was growling. The lack of sleep was wearing on him, but he saw no chance of catching up on it in the next few days.

He liked being a cop, and getting assigned to Detectives had been his dream, but investigating homicide cases came at a heavy price. He missed the things so many people got to do every day. Knowing when he'd be home at night and not having to think about work until the next day. Enjoying the weekend with all its creature comforts. Sleeping in, a nice big breakfast, partying till any hour, or just channel surfing.

Jan didn't need a mansion, a swanky vacation, or a flashy sports car. But just to do nothing for a single day, with no responsibilities and without the knowledge that there was a maniac serial killer running around Berlin—he would give a full month's salary for that.

For now, he hoped to have at least ten minutes to get something to eat. Enjoy a cup of tea, some banter with Alkim, the restaurant's owner, and maybe one or two cubes of Turkish delight. Just ten minutes before his cell phone rang, before Patrick's team found the grave, before all the madness started closing in on him again.

"Just ten," he muttered as if it were a mantra, folding his hands and looking up to the sky. "All I ask."

Eight minutes was all he got. His phone rang. The Turkish delight would have to wait.

.   .   .

"We have the grave," Patrick said with pride. He bounded over to the map on the wall and pointed at a green area. "It's in a wooded cemetery in Charlottenburg."

"That's the big patch near Olympic Stadium?"

"Exactly. All thirty-seven acres of it."

Jan groaned. Conducting surveillance on all that was going to be a nightmare. Lots of exits, even more paths, and countless hiding places.

"How did you guys find the grave so fast?"

"The cemetery has plenty of famous people in it. Which means extra-attentive cemetery staff and more of them."

"We watching the spot?"

"Not yet. We have two patrols positioned nearby to observe the street, with instructions to remain inconspicuous."

"Then send two plainclothes officers out there too. They should water some flowers, pull some weeds, but stay back from the grave."

Patrick nodded.

"We have to stay under the radar. The murderer isn't counting on us finding the grave so quickly. We cannot lose our advantage. Maybe he's still in the vicinity or is checking it occasionally. Anything suspicious and he's going to clear out for good."

"Cameras?"

"They're essential. We'll mount them around the grave site. Park the surveillance van next to the grounds. On top of that I want plainclothes near all exits until dark. We'll look for somewhere to hide near the grave beforehand. We'll sit tight through the night. So far he's killed his victims right around midnight and then put them in sometime before dawn."

"I'll see to the plainclothes officers." Patrick went to a phone and was deep in a conversation a moment later.

Jan pulled his own phone from his pocket and pressed a number from his recent calls. "Max? Jan here."

"I see that," Max replied.

"Pack all you'd need for a night stakeout," Jan continued. "Above all, those cams that don't need any light."

"They call them infrared."

"Save the smart-ass quips. Move your butt and get over here. I want to be gone in twenty minutes."

Jan put away his phone. The special team's room was buzzing. In two hours, not even an ant would be able to pass through the cemetery without them spotting it.

They had been one step ahead of the murder the first time, and gotten behind the second time. They weren't going to miss this chance.

. . .

An hour after their find, the wooded cemetery was under the control of the Detectives Division. Fourteen plainclothes cops were strolling around: four along the cemetery walls, six near the exits, and four within the immediate vicinity of Robin Cordes's grave.

Jan had thrown on a cemetery-personnel jacket and was loosening up the soil of an overgrown planting bed with a hoe. After three minutes, he had the first blister on his thumb. Five minutes later, he needed a back massage. He had no idea how someone could do such work all day long without becoming totally disabled by age forty.

Since he'd been there, he'd seen no visitors. The area was off the beaten path. Surely no coincidence, Jan thought. The murderer had done his homework here too. But at the moment, the seclusion was working for Detectives. Max could set up the cams without being disturbed.

Jan looked over his shoulder at Max. The cemetery jacket was far too big for the scrawny geek. He'd had to roll up the sleeves so that at least his fingers would poke out. He was strapping a small cam to the branch of a big chestnut tree. He finished by covering the thumb-sized piece of tech with a leaf.

"That little thing's enough for watching the whole grave?" Jan whispered into his portable radio.

"With color and sound," Max replied. "It hardly needs any light for you to see razor-sharp images, even at night."

"There's no streetlights around here. Where's the light supposed to come from?"

"It's almost full moon. If the weather's clear tonight, that'll do. For safety's sake, I placed two little candles near enough."

"What about the paths to the grave?"

"As long as he doesn't come bushwhacking his way through the underbrush—there's only one path here. I installed a bigger camera in that holly. I can zoom it. When I'm done here I'll mount more of our little spies at the entrances. Then nothing gets by us." Max finished aligning the cam, grabbed his backpack, and went over to Jan. "You know where you're spending the night yet?"

"About ten yards from the grave there are these big shrubs about head high; luckily they don't have pointy leaves. A cemetery worker is cutting us out a hole in the middle and covering the rear part with bushes in pots. The hideaway is about as deep as my closet, but it will do."

"I'll set you up with a monitor. You can watch the grave and the path at the same time without having to get out. All that rustling could get conspicuous."

"Okay." Jan stood up and stretched. "I'm heading over to the briefing."

"I'll be at the main entrance." Max raised a hand. "See you soon."

Jan waved back. Still four more hours until it was dark. The trap was set.

. . .

Jan yawned as he left the conference room. He was going to have to either stock up on coffee for the night or steal some of Max's energy drinks, if he didn't want to fall asleep inside those shrubs. Still another hour until dusk. Robin's death wasn't scheduled until tomorrow, so Jan didn't believe the murderer would show up before midnight. But he might check in on the grave. Jan didn't want to spoil any chance of seizing him.

In a half hour, the plainclothes cops would withdraw. Visitors wandering around and caring for graves in the dark were just too conspicuous—but the cams were working and the paths weren't too long. An officer could be at an entrance or at the grave within twenty seconds. Worst case, they could lock down the cemetery. The canine team was on standby. They could even have a chopper over the area in a few minutes.

Wasn't more they could do. If the murderer were to enter the cemetery, he'd be leaving in handcuffs. The only unknown was Robin Cordes. Jan was hoping Robin really was as good as everyone was saying, Then at least they wouldn't be dealing with a fresh corpse.

Jan went to the coffee machine and pressed the "Coffee Black" button for what felt like the thousandth time. He closed his eyes and considered whether to go lie down for a half hour. This was going to be a long night, and he needed every trace of concentration he could summon.

His phone jolted him from his thoughts. The screen showed an unknown number.

"Detective Tommen," he answered.

"It's Robin here. You wanted to talk to me?"

Jan almost dropped his coffee.

"Herr Cordes. Nice of you to call."

Jan rushed over to the special team's office.

"You called me by my first name before," Robin said.

Jan pressed the door handle, closing the door with a shoulder. "Apologies. I'm normally a pretty polite guy, but with a gun in my face I forget my manners."

All his fellow officers turned his way.

"Wasn't anything personal."

Jan pointed to his phone using his free hand. "It's all right, Herr Cordes." Jan stressed the name with a special urgency and at the same time turned on the speaker undetected so that his colleagues could follow along.

Cordes's voice echoed through the room. "I'm not doing this because I feel guilty somehow or like you a whole lot. It's only out of love for my girlfriend."

Patrick lifted a phone off the table and dialed a number. A hand cupping his mouth, he urgently spoke to someone on the other end.

"Has your girlfriend told you about the latest developments?"

Patrick raised a thumb, pressing the phone to his chest.

"That motherfucker's photo, you mean."

At least ten sets of eyebrows stared at Jan, transfixed. No one moved. Jan wondered if anyone was even breathing, the room was so still.

"I do. The grave murderer has you in his sights."

"Just like I told you." Robin sounded amazingly calm. It was likely not the first time someone had threatened him.

"I'm sorry for doubting you."

Jan had to hold the speaker closer to his ear. The connection was bad. There was static and hissing and Robin's voice kept cutting out.

"What do you want? I'm not going to let myself fall in the cops' hands. So don't go telling me about protective custody."

"This is about the connection between the two victims and you."

"Like I said before. Valburg bought drugs from me, and I got special meds from Quast that I dealt."

"What kind of meds?"

"Mostly stuff you can't get in Germany. At first it was supplements for hair loss that are allowed in other countries but banned here. Later it got more rare. Experimental substances for cancer or HIV. Some of them were still in the testing phase."

"Where did Moritz Quast get them?"

"No idea. I was just the middleman between him and the customers."

"Who were your customers?"

"Regular people at first. The doctors and private clinics got in on it for the testing-phase stuff. They paid crazy prices. Made more profit off that than off coke."

"Did you sell bogus meds too?"

"Now and then."

"What exactly?"

"Hair-growth remedies and Viagra. But only when supplies were dwindling. Most were legit. The doctors would have noticed if we were peddling them sugar pills. And we did not want to lose those lucrative customers, believe me. Quast and I were earning tons. You had to know the right balance."

The person Patrick had called appeared to have reported back. Patrick scribbled something on a notepad and held it up. Robin's cell phone had been traced. An address in Charlottenburg. They'd managed to find it even without Max's help.

"Did anyone die from taking the meds?"

"One of our customers popped too much of the stuff and had a heart attack when he was with a prostitute."

Patrick pointed at two investigators and waved them out. They slipped out of the room.

"I mean the experimental substances."

"No idea. The doctors never told us what they did with the stuff. Why is that so important?"

"We're looking for the killer's motive."

"The guy is nuts, that's what."

"Possibly," Jan replied. Luckily Robin was in a chatty mood. A car would be at the address in a couple of minutes. Then they could get him into custody, even if it had to be against his will. He would survive the night that way. "But his choice of victims isn't random enough. You three are too connected for it to be coincidence."

"Hmm," Robin said. He seemed to be thinking about it.

"Reconsider our offer of protection."

"I can handle myself."

"I really do hope you can."

"If you promise not to bother my girlfriend anymore, I'll report back in."

Patrick came over holding up a finger. His mouth formed the words *one minute*.

"I promise. When will you call again?"

"I have something going on tonight. Tomorrow I'll keep a real low profile. If the day I die passes no problem, you'll be hearing from me again. I got your number."

"Take good care of yourself," Jan said. He didn't want to keep the call going unnecessarily long or he'd cause suspicion. The officers would be close enough to him by now.

"Thank you."

He hung up.

"We have two patrols in the area," Patrick said. "His bearings point to a public square with few options for hiding. Officers will call in as soon as they've picked him up."

He set his phone on the table. They all stared at it.

A minute passed. Patrick anxiously tapped his foot.

Two minutes.

No one said a word.

Three minutes.

"Goddamn it," Patrick said. "It shouldn't be taking this long."

Then, as if on cue, the phone began playing the theme song to *Bonanza*.

Patrick pressed speaker. "You have him?"

"He wasn't there."

"What? We had his phone pinpointed down to the yard with GPS."

"We found the cell phone. Just not Robin Cordes."

"He can't disappear that fast," Jan protested.

"He wasn't here. His phone was stuck to another phone."

Jan groaned. Thus the bad connection.

Patrick kicked at the table, furious. "This Cordes is clever," he said.

"Hopefully more clever than the grave murderer," Jan remarked.

He looked at the time. Dusk was approaching.

"Good luck, Robin. You're going to need it."

Chapter Eight

Jan was glad to have Patrick driving him to the wooded cemetery. He might be able to fit in a catnap while Patrick drove. He'd had no time to stock up on energy drinks.

Patrick didn't have to be doing this stakeout with him. But his colleague had packed bread, cheese, Vienna sausages, coffee, tea, and water. Plus bananas, grapes, and chocolate. It was enough for the whole unit.

Jan's window of peace and quiet came to an abrupt end when Patrick pulled into the cemetery parking lot. They crossed the street and passed the first plainclothes patrol. Jan nodded and entered the cemetery.

All units were in position. As planned, he and Patrick separated and took different routes to their hiding place. The cemetery had few visitors at this hour. Jan fished out some still-respectable flowers from the compost for disguise and strolled along the paths that skirted the grave site of Robin Cordes. He memorized possible escape routes and tried to note every spot a person could hide. Then he headed to his designated hiding place.

The shrub that had been prepared for them was every kid's dream. Dark and cramped like a robber's cave, it was the perfect hideout. Patrick had switched on the monitor showing the surveillance cams and set two tiny folding camping stools before it. There wasn't room for much more, but it would do. As long as it didn't rain, their bush wasn't much worse than most cars.

"Any activity at the grave?" Jan said into his portable radio.

"Negative," Max replied. "Three persons total have passed by. All were checked when exiting, but none were suspect."

"Thanks for the info," Jan said.

"Not much will happen before midnight," Patrick said. "Robin Cordes's date of death isn't until tomorrow, and so far our killer's been sticking to his word."

"He could check out the grave before the murder."

"So what happens when he doesn't get Robin?"

"Then he'll be tough to find. And he won't give up if we don't catch him tonight. Maybe Robin will play along eventually and let us tail him. When the murderer starts trailing Robin? We got him."

"I'll take the first watch." Patrick grabbed a thermos from their bag. "Sleep a bit if you can. I'll wake you up around midnight."

"Now there's an offer I can't refuse." Jan folded his arms at his chest and closed his eyes, content. He was asleep within seconds.

•　　•　　•

"Wake up." Someone was shaking his arm. Jan opened his eyes. It was pitch-black. Only the tiny monitor gave off any light.

"What is it?" Jan whispered, rubbing at his eyes.

"We have a visitor."

The right side of the monitor showed the feed of the cam in the holly bush. A man holding a bunch of flowers was heading toward the grave. He wore dark clothing with a hood up. Even with infrared it was tough to see him. "Not exactly visiting his grandma's grave," Patrick remarked.

"How late is it?"

"Just after one."

Jan picked up the portable radio. "You see him?"

"Yes," Max replied.

The man kept heading toward Robin's grave. He was only a few steps away when he halted and pivoted around, as though making sure no one was watching him.,

"He's mine." Jan shot out of their hiding spot and sprinted down the path. The man started, dropped the flowers, and tried to make a break for it, but Jan was too fast for him. Jan used his momentum to haul the man down and was rewarded with a loud groan. He flipped their nighttime visitor on his back, pressing an arm into his neck. Two plainclothes officers knelt next to Jan and bound the man's wrists with plastic cuffs, holding him down.

The man cursed in a foreign language.

"No weapons," Jan said after frisking him.

A plainclothes yanked the man's ID from a pocket and checked the photo. "A certain Martin Novak."

Jan had one officer keep the man on the ground. He stood, pulled out his flashlight, and shone it in the man's face. "What are you doing here?"

"I'm taking flowers to my mother's grave. What the hell is this about?"

Jan nodded to the officer keeping Novak down. He twisted Novak's wrist so painfully that Novak moaned.

"We're looking for a serial killer. You give me another stupid answer like that, I'll throw you in jail for double homicide."

"I steal flowers," Novak wailed. He appealed to them, still held down. "My sister-in-law has this nursery. It's not doing so well, see, so I hit the cemetery at night and clear out the new graves' flowers. I know nothing about any murder."

Patrick appeared by Jan's side. "His excuse is so dumb, it's probably true."

"We can't question him here," Jan said. "If he's not our man, all this pandemonium is going to scare off our grave murderer."

Jan turned to the other officers. "Take him down to the station. Check his story, see if he's got an alibi for the murders. If there's even the slightest link to the victims, keep him in custody. He'll have a nice long interrogation to look forward to."

The officers pulled up Novak and led him off, and they weren't gentle about it.

Patrick watched the man go. "What do you think?"

"Can't know for sure." Jan shook his head. "Depends if we can form any connections between him, Valburg, and Quast. We'll know more in a few hours, provided we even believe his story." He pointed at the flowers. "Let's get this cleaned up and back to our posts. The day of Robin's death is now one hour old."

. . .

At nine a.m., Jan leaned his hoe against a tree and sat down on a bench. They had given up on their hiding place a little after seven, thrown on some work clothes, and taken up their posts again. Martin Novak's story of being a flower thief had checked out. His sister-in-law had tearfully admitted to her shady swindle a little before dawn. Plus there was no connection to Bernhard Valburg, Moritz Quast, or Robin Cordes. To play it safe, they were keeping Novak in custody just the same.

Jan pulled his phone from a pocket and dialed Friederike Roth's number. She picked up on the first ring.

"You hear anything?" Her voice was a mix of anticipation and panic.

"Nothing yet, unfortunately. We staked out the cemetery all night, but Robin's grave is still empty. Did he check in with you?"

"No. I had my phone with me in bed all night."

"I'm going to hope that no news is good news. We'll stick it out here today. I'm optimistic that the grave will stay empty."

"Let's hope."

"Please let me know immediately if Robin calls."

"I will, right away."

"Thanks." Jan hung up and stashed his phone. He closed his eyes and enjoyed the rays of morning sun on his face. A few hours' sleep in their stakeout hole had staved off the worst of his weariness. And Patrick's catering job had supplied him with a nice breakfast, at least. Jan was losing himself in a daydream of mattresses and down pillows when his portable radio sounded.

"Someone's coming up the path." Max didn't sound the least bit weary, even though he hadn't slept for two nights now. Jan was going to have to get the brand of his energy drinks, and soon.

He positioned himself behind a tree so that he couldn't be seen from the path. "Who is it?"

"Two men from the cemetery."

"They really with the cemetery or they just wearing the gear?"

"They work here. Both were checked out."

"So why are you reporting in?"

"They're pushing a coffin your way."

Jan looked out from around the tree. It was just as Max described. He knew the two cemetery workers. He'd questioned one of them himself. They were pushing a cart with a wood coffin on it.

"Regular cemetery operations had to continue," Jan explained. "That was a condition of the management. They can't postpone burials or store the deceased."

Another officer's voice came over the radio. "There's no burial listed in this area for today, though."

Jan went up to the men pushing the cart. "Morning, gents." He showed his badge. "Can you tell me what you're doing with that coffin?"

"Ya know, burying the dead," one of the men said. He was looking at Jan as if the detective wasn't quite right in the head.

"Where?"

The man raised a clipboard. "D six-zero-four. Site B."

"What B?" the other man said. "We don't got no *B*s. First a letter, then the number. Never any *A*s or *B*s."

"See for yourself." The first man held up the clipboard for his coworker.

The second man shook his head. "Who filled that out?"

"What's the deceased's name?" Jan asked.

"Cordes, R."

"What?" Jan ripped the clipboard from the man's hand. Robin Cordes's name was there. "Open the coffin!"

"We . . . we're not supposed to—"

"Do it now!"

One of the men muttered something about disturbing the dead, but they finally did lift off the lid.

Inside the coffin lay the corpse of Robin Cordes.

• • •

At the cemetery, not even a celebrity funeral could have sparked as massive a police operation as the discovery of Robin Cordes's body. All visitors were inspected at the entrances. Two crime-tech teams searched for clues, and special patrols were checking out all cars parked in the vicinity.

Jan turned to Zoe. "How did he die?"

The medical examiner raised her eyebrows. "That hole in the back of his head interfered with his getting oxygen."

"So that was the cause of death?"

"Most likely."

"Murder weapon?"

"Egg spoon."

"Seriously?"

"Man, you'll believe anything." She lit up a cigarette with a windproof Zippo. "I'm going with a hammer again."

"What's with his fingers?"

"Cut off. But don't go asking me why again."

"Postmortem?"

Zoe nodded.

"With what?"

"Garden shears or something similarly crude." She beckoned a colleague over to her. With his sweater-vest, hair combed over a receding hairline, and orthopedic shoes, he couldn't have made a greater contrast to the always-stylish Zoe.

"Walter, pack up the dead guy and get him ready for autopsy. Put on coffee beforehand. I'll pick up something for breakfast on the way back and then I'll be in."

She turned back to Jan. "I saw Bergman earlier. Face all red and pinched up like one of those wrinkly Chinese dogs, gasping for breath. Wouldn't have thought he could be in an even fouler mood than usual." She pointed at the corpse. "Might have something to do with that one there."

"Thanks for the heads-up. I can use the encouragement right now."

"Always a pleasure." Zoe waved to go. "Tonight I'll know more."

The smoke from her cigarette had not yet cleared when Max came running up to Jan with his laptop under one arm.

"Find anything out?"

"I know how the murderer slipped us the corpse." He waved Jan over. "Let's go over to the administration offices."

On the way, Jan cut a wide swath around a group of cops with their gazes fixed at the ground. They were searching the path around the grave for clues. There was always a chance the murderer had lost something when he shoveled out the hole.

"The cemetery uses a computer program for scheduling the day's assignments." Outside the cemetery offices, Max flipped open his laptop and pointed at the screen. "Name, time, grave site, and all the other stuff are saved there. Every cemetery employee has a user account to view the log, but only four people are allowed to make entries."

"Who made the entry?"

"The cemetery manager—and early today, at one forty-one a.m., at that."

"Was he here?"

"No."

"So the murderer hacked his account."

"I wouldn't call it hacking. The manager can't remember passwords very well. He writes them down on a notepad in his desk drawer."

Jan groaned. "Doesn't get any easier than that."

"No one should ever write down their passwords, sure, but who'd be interested in messing around with a burial date?"

"So the murderer was here? Right under our eyes?"

Max pointed to a window of the administration building. A section of the glass was cut out.

"How could he get in here, though? All the cemetery entrances were supposed to be staked out."

"Which they were. He climbed over the wall somewhere, then cut out this side window here. The windows aren't barred on this side."

"He slipped right by our teams."

"You can't blame them. The cemetery is nearly thirty-seven acres. We would've needed the whole Berlin police department."

"So he knew that we were staking out the place?"

"We can safely assume that."

"But how did he bring the corpse in? He could hardly have just tossed it over the wall."

"We're still working on that one," Max said. "Honestly? I have no idea how, unless our killer is King Kong."

"Jan!" Bergman was coming down the path. His voice matched Zoe's earlier description.

"I'll, uh, just be on my way . . ." Max patted Jan on the shoulder for encouragement and disappeared inside the administration building.

Jan took a deep breath and prepared himself for the thrashing of a lifetime.

•   •   •

Jan couldn't have imagined that things could get any worse for the Berlin Police Department since the police chief's last public statement. But he quickly learned just how bad things could get. Some of his fellow officers were trying to keep the media from storming police headquarters while others directed traffic, which had come to a standstill. The reporters' loud, urgent demands drowned out clicking of the cameras, and the cops' instructions were lost amid the chaos. Only the angry honking of the frustrated drivers pierced the din.

Jan detoured around the throng of reporters and tried to enter the building from the back. But it was no better there. Sighing, he threw himself into battle. He propelled himself through the tightly packed mob, trying not to trip over a cable or get struck by a camera.

He was jostled and jolted, pushed to the sides, and grabbed by the shoulders. No one wanted to let him through—but he worked his way in to the crowd, which pressed forward toward the barricade like a horde of starving dissidents, as if police headquarters were the only place in Berlin they could find bread.

Five minutes and plenty of insults later, Jan reached the barricade. The uniformed officers behind the metal fencing helped him climb over.

He sat down on the stairs. His heart was racing and his T-shirt was soaked through with sweat. He was just about ready to order tear gas and water cannons himself.

"How did they find out so fast?" he asked a cop.

"There had to be an anonymous tip, minutes after the body was found."

Jan shook his head. The media would make investigating even tougher. Every person with a smartphone was going to follow along in the hope of shooting a photo they could sell to a tabloid.

"This is insane."

"The insanity's still to come," another cop said while pushing back an eager photographer who was trying to climb over the barricade. "Bergman ordered all our vacations canceled and shifts extended."

"My God. How many is that?"

"Over two hundred. Not counting the surrounding suburbs."

A reporter interrupted them. "Is this how the police update us? You're subverting freedom of the press. We have a right to more information."

Jan's training had prepared him for such situations. He had to remain calm, either not respond to the man or simply ignore him. No violence. Don't provoke.

But this was not a day for diplomacy.

He stood, showed the reporter both middle fingers, and under-
lined the gesture with a broad sneer. Bergman would freak out when
he heard about it, but Jan's personnel file was beyond redemption
anyway. Besides, it just felt good.

•   •   •

Chandu's apartment was an oasis of bliss. Instead of an uncomfort-
able camping stool, Jan sat on a soft sofa. His friend had prepared
in his wok a light meal of stir-fried veggies with rice, its spicy curry
leaving a pleasant aftertaste. There were no angry reporters in sight
and no Bergman on a tirade.

Jan fought a yawn. He had been reading reports all day, review-
ing crime-scene photos, and weighing evidence, yet the stack on
his desk was not getting smaller. Without Patrick's help, he would
have chucked it all. His colleague's troop of interns, trainees, and
freshmen, accompanied by experienced investigators, took a lot of
the work off of Jan. And yet he had left headquarters that evening
feeling like he'd accomplished nothing at all. Once again. Another
wasted day. Knowing that a crazed murderer was running around
out there, one who had already fooled them thrice—it didn't exactly
help him sleep. Add that to his regular nightmares, and he wasn't
going to be able to hold up much longer. Maybe he should finally
acknowledge that he wasn't the same old Jan anymore and just hand
the case over to Patrick.

"What's the deal with Max?" Zoe's words ripped him from his
thoughts. She was fishing a shitake mushroom out of the rice with
her chopsticks.

"He called me an hour ago, saying something about a visitor
and having to take care of some things," Jan explained. "He's coming after dinner."

"A visitor?" Zoe said. "Who would enter that apartment willingly?"

"He's not the only nerd on this earth."

"That's a scary thought."

"Well, I like him." Chandu brought more fresh rice from the kitchen. "He's still young and has a few quirks, sure, but without his help, I never would've gotten my surround sound installed right."

"A few quirks can be good," Zoe remarked.

Chandu winked at her. "He's not the only one."

Zoe showed him a broad smile. She was gobbling up rice when someone knocked on the door.

"Speak of the devil." Chandu opened the door. The big man had seen a lot of strange things in his time, but he was not prepared for what he saw now. His mouth hung open as Max strode into the apartment.

His normally wild hair was cut short and laced with streaks. He wore dark sneakers, slightly faded jeans, and a salmon-colored button-down with the sleeves rolled up. His digital watch had been replaced by a silver one with a dark face. His latest attempt to grow a beard had fallen victim to a razor. Chandu even caught a whiff of aftershave.

Max was all gussied up, his grumpy face the only thing not matching. He passed Chandu without saying hi and sat down in an armchair.

It was deadly still in the room. Chandu stayed over at the door, looking like he'd just gazed into the eyes of Medusa. Jan stared at the beer in his hand, unsure what to do. Only Zoe broke the silence—by dropping the rice bowl, which clattered onto the floor.

Jan spoke first. "Uh . . ."

"What . . ." Chandu added. His stare faded. He closed the door and sat down next to Zoe without letting Max out of his sight.

The medical examiner eyed the young man from top to bottom. Then she leaned back and began laughing. Chandu couldn't control himself a moment longer, so he buried his face in a sofa pillow. Zoe's laughter echoed through the living room; meanwhile, Chandu looked as if he were chomping at the pillow.

"Assholes," Max said, which only made Zoe laugh louder. She leaned into Chandu and slugged his shoulder as tears ran down her cheeks.

Her laughter was contagious. Jan was clearly having trouble controlling himself. He bit at his lip, balled his fists, and stared at the floor.

Zoe attempted to say something, but every time she looked Max's way, a new attack overcame her. Chandu's pillow would not survive the evening.

Max, his face pinched, stood and set the projector on the table and started up his laptop. He folded his arms across his chest and took his seat like a surly kid who wouldn't eat his vegetables.

Ten minutes later, Chandu had removed the pillow from his mouth and Zoe had stopped slugging the big man's shoulder. Jan wiped tears of laughter from his own face and became the first one capable of speaking again.

"Sorry," Jan said in an attempt to appease Max. "It was not nice of us to laugh. But your . . . transformation, it caught us by surprise."

"Oh? I didn't notice," Max snapped.

"Easy, my friend," Chandu said. "Just tell us what happened."

Zoe's laughing had ebbed to a giggle.

"My sister's in Berlin again," Max said.

"O-kaaay," Chandu replied, drawing out the vowels. "I might need one or two hints here."

Max abandoned his stubborn stance and grabbed a beer off the table. Things must have been pretty bad. He hated beer.

"Mira studies fashion at the University of the Arts. She also works for two designers and travels around the world most of the time. Whenever she visits me, she always has to play the older sibling and patronize me. She's worse than my mom. I had to air out the apartment, get rid of all the pizza cartons, and take back all the empty bottles."

Max took a gulp of beer and made a disgusted face. "I was standing at those goddamn return machines for a good hour."

Their conversation was interrupted by another of Zoe's giggling fits, which Max returned with a poisonous look.

"She schlepped me to a hair stylist who gave me this silly haircut. Then it was off to some trendy men's boutique and then a shoe store, till we eventually were in some vegan restaurant eating spaghetti made of zucchini." Max took another slug of beer. "That's why I look like this."

"You made a change for the better," Chandu said. "Your sister's visit paid off."

"You think so, huh? She even went through my underwear and got rid of my favorites. Some of them were downright antiques."

"TMI," Zoe said, taking out her cigarette case. She was almost herself again.

Jan changed the subject. "Back to our serial killer. Do we know how he snuck Robin Cordes's corpse into the cemetery?"

"Your colleagues found the answer." Max projected a photo of the cemetery administration building. "The murderer climbed over a tough-to-see stretch of the wall, worked his way through the bushes up to the admin building, and removed the glass with a cutter."

"How did he get in there?" Zoe asked. "I thought the cemetery was under full surveillance."

Max pressed a key on his laptop, bringing up an aerial photo. Most of the image consisted of trees.

"That the cemetery?" Chandu asked. "Looks more like a forest park with a big lake."

"That's why they call it Charlottenburg *Forest* Cemetery, which is exactly the problem," Max explained. "Not even the whole Berlin Police combined could keep watch over every inch of thirty-seven acres."

"Weren't they watching over the admin building?" Chandu asked.

"The front entrance, they were. There was no reason for much more. We were only looking at the building as just another way from which to enter the cemetery itself.

"The murderer got easy access to the computer system because the cemetery manager wrote down his password. And even if he hadn't, their system is ancient and *1234* isn't exactly a secure password." Max sighed, as if enduring such idiocy was almost too much for him. "During the night he typed in a burial assignment for Robin Cordes, so that the cemetery employees would look at their work queue in the morning and add it to the rest."

"It didn't occur to anyone that the name was Robin Cordes and that the site entered was the grave everyone was watching?" Zoe asked.

"Unfortunately not." Jan scratched at his head in embarrassment. "We had the grave blocked off and didn't let the cemetery workers near it. Plus we kept the name under wraps for fear that one of them might go blabbing it. Only a few were let in on it. The crews who usually do the burials weren't included."

"I wouldn't have done it any differently," Chandu said. "But how did he get the body itself into the cemetery if all the entrances were being watched?"

"He exploited a weak point," said Max, who now commanded their respectful attention.

"Which is?"

"The hearse."

Jan slapped his forehead. "Of course."

"Care to fill us in?" Chandu said. "I'm not following."

"So as not to arouse suspicion, regular cemetery business was allowed to continue as normal," Max explained. "The patrols recorded the hearse's plate and registration numbers and let it pass through."

"So he steals a hearse," Jan said.

Max pressed another key on the computer. The aerial shot zoomed in on the main entrance.

"According to the log, the front gate opened at one fourteen a.m., at which point a registered hearse left the premises. There's no surveillance video that makes out the driver. The hearse turned onto Trakehner Allee heading northwest and then took a left at Olympischer Platz. Thirty-one minutes later it returned the same way, passing the plainclothes officers near the admin building, and drove into the cemetery."

"With Robin Cordes's corpse aboard," Chandu added.

"It fits the time of death," Zoe said. "Around midnight."

"Did he break into the car?" Chandu asked. "Or did he get his hands on it some other way?"

"He broke into the key cabinet in the admin building. Then he could choose whatever. On top of that, the hearses have a gate opener inside for the driver. So he didn't have to get out when he came back with Robin's body. He left the car back in its spot, brought the body into the mortuary, and then disappeared."

Jan turned to Zoe. "Any evidence on the car?"

"Coworkers are still on it. Considering how meticulous the grave murderer's been up till now, I wouldn't be too hopeful."

"What about on the body?"

"Nothing. Robin Cordes was killed with the same hammer as his predecessors. No drugs, poison, or narcotics. He was fully conscious."

"His fingers?"

"Cut with garden or poultry shears, like I thought."

"This is starting to creep me out," Chandu said. "First it's eyes, then the tongue, now fingers. And you don't think that this person is insane?"

"Oh, he's definitely insane," Jan replied. "But he's no sadist. Otherwise he would've cut Robin's fingers off beforehand."

"So what does it mean?" Max asked.

"Cordes probably had his fingers in something that he shouldn't have," Zoe said. "So it was snip-snip."

"Any sign he was tied up?" Jan asked.

"Nope."

"Self-defense wounds?"

"Struck out again."

"I just can't believe this." Jan fought the urge to hurl his bottle against the wall. "Robin Cordes was underground and alert, cautious. How did the murderer know where he was?"

"Where was he killed?" Chandu asked.

"Not at home. I was there this afternoon," Jan said, sounding downcast, "and had to deliver the sad news to Friederike Roth."

"The crime techs are still dismantling the hearse," Max said. "Maybe they'll find a clue as to where the car went. The killer didn't use the navigation system."

Jan leaned back in his chair. "Me, I'm all out of ideas. I'll go talk to Friederike Roth again in the morning and ask her more about her boyfriend's illegal activities before he went to prison."

"I'll see what the city's speed cameras and surveillance cams have," Max said. "Maybe our hearse is in the footage."

"I'm toast, actually," Zoe said. "There are no more analyses to do, but I'll send any results coming in to a coworker who's nearly as good as me. Maybe he's got some idea."

"Hey, didn't you tell me that Robin Cordes organized poker games?" Chandu said to Jan.

Jan nodded.

"I have an old acquaintance who's a hard-core player."

"Who?"

"Becks."

"Becks?" Zoe raised her eyebrows. "Like the beer?"

"No idea how he arrived at that name."

"What kind of guy is he?"

"A pimp, and an aficionado of fine things. Drives a Maserati with a champagne cooler in it instead of a glove box."

"How modest," Zoe said.

"Not really my deal either."

"The Maserati?"

"The champagne cooler."

"Ah. Do you sock him in the face too, when you meet with him?"

Chandu eyed Zoe in disapproval. "That would not be good for my health. But whenever there's a big game going in Berlin, Becks is there. So if anyone knows poker king Robin Cordes, it's him."

Chapter Nine

The neighborhood had a bad rep, no doubt about it, but if a person didn't know what was going on behind the dark-red doors of the inconspicuous apartment building, they would just walk on by without giving it a second thought. The muscular man at the door might have been taking a smoke break, the cam over the entrance was well hidden, and drawing the curtains at such an hour was normal.

But there was a bordello behind those doors. Not the shabby, seedy kind for quick sex, but rather an exquisite establishment with exquisite rooms and just as exquisite prices.

Chandu had never worked for Becks. The loan business was not the pimp's game; his customers paid in advance. Still, they knew each other. New players came every year, but the core team stayed the same. You crossed paths at some point.

Chandu knew the rules. He stood before the door. Once his image registered on the cam, the door clicked open. Inside, Chandu gave the bouncers a friendly nod even as they were frisking him. He knew one of them—a former member of a British special unit.

Worked nights as a bouncer and taught self-defense by day in a gym. A tough dog with a soft spot for knives.

"Matt," Chandu greeted him, once the man was satisfied he was unarmed.

"Chandu." Matt tapped his forehead.

"Is Becks around?"

"'E's just there at the bar," Matt replied in a strong British accent.

Chandu entered the main room, which was full of comfy sofas, armchairs, and elegant little tables where clients could set down their glasses. The dark-brown polished wooden walls set off the brightly colored furniture. The women wore tasteful black dresses that looked designed more for some society ball than for a bordello. Each and every one of them was every man's dream in the flesh, tastefully made up and with perfect figures. They moved with a sensuous grace in their high heels, confident of their beauty. One night with one of them exceeded the monthly income of a wealthy executive, but from what Chandu had heard, it was worth every euro.

The establishment had none of the usual brothel clichés. The owner acted more like a top businessman than a pimp. His black hair was neatly trimmed. He wore a dark suit with a fashionable silk tie, and his shiny leather shoes reflected the soft glow from countless lamps. Becks could have easily passed himself off as a banker or lawyer.

When he saw Chandu, he waved and gestured to the stool next to him at the long bar.

"Chandu." He shook the big man's hand. His handshake was firm, assertive. "What brings you here? Work or pleasure?"

"I wish it was pleasure, but it's work."

Becks was drinking red wine. He signaled the barkeep, who immediately filled another glass with red and placed it before Chandu.

"I don't recall being in debt to any of your friends."

Chandu raised a hand to reassure him. "It's not about you, Becks. It's about someone you might know." He reached for his glass, toasted his host, and took a sip. He knew nothing about wine, but it did taste excellent. Whatever this was that Becks had served up, he wouldn't be finding it in a supermarket. Maybe the rumors were true—that he'd bought a major winery in France where he intended to spend his old age.

Chandu nodded in appreciation and set down the glass. "I'm looking for a small-time blowfly named Robin Cordes. Was dealing, then moving some goods, and ended up in the slammer for it. He's out again and keeps a low profile."

"I have nothing to do with small-time blowflies."

"Supposedly our small-time dealer changed his ways in the slammer and is now doing poker games."

"I see. Now I'm listening."

"Which is why I'm here. Robin owes a friend of mine a heap of money. It would spare me a lot of legwork if you'd seen him around."

"You have a photo of this Robin?"

Chandu pulled out his phone, selected a photo, and turned the screen to Becks.

"Ah, that Robin," Becks said. "I was just playing with him yesterday."

Chandu nearly dropped his phone. It was all he could do not to show his surprise. "Just not my lucky day, I guess." He was hoping that word had not gotten out about Robin dying. The media were reporting that the grave killer had a new victim but weren't releasing any names.

"It wasn't that big of a game. Seven people total. Robin had arranged the date, got the room, set it all up, and brought in the players."

"How did he know of you?"

"I went with a friend, on his recommendation."

"Where did you guys play?"

"In the Ochsen, not here."

"In a family pub?"

"In a back room. Was just a poker table in there. The owner brought the drinks. Was quaint but kind of nice."

"A setup?"

Becks shook his head. "Only beginners fall for that. It was a clean game."

"Who all was there?"

"My buddy Joe and I. Robin. There was a couple with too much dough, names I forget. A young snot name of Bernd, and some lawyer. Müller or something like that." Becks sipped his wine. "Why you interested in the game? I thought you were only after Robin."

Chandu wanted to swear out loud—the serial killer himself might have been sitting at that very table. But he couldn't let down his cover and admit he was investigating for the cops. The consequences would be nasty. Bouncers would be the least of his problems.

"What kind of money are we talking about here? The table had something, I'm guessing."

"I went home with five grand. It was just Bernd and I left at the end. The woman lost an all-in after a couple hours. The husband three hands later. The lawyer had played away all his cash by that point, since he was probably the worst poker player in the whole world. No idea what he was doing there. Joe's stomach wasn't taking the meat platter too well and he puked his guts out. That left only the young guy and me. A one-on-one is just too boring for me, so I took off."

"When?"

"Around eleven or so."

"What was Robin's take?"

"Hundred per person for arranging and dealing. A bonus from the owner, maybe. How much he owe your friend?"

"Over four," Chandu lied.

"Right. It'll work out."

Chandu kept up his cover. "You know when the next game is? I could go and have a talk with him."

"I gave him my number. When he calls, I'll let you know."

"Thank you." Chandu shook Becks's hand. "For the help and for the nice wine." He stood. "Anything I can ever do for you, just call."

Becks nodded. "Will do."

Chandu waved to Matt on the way out. Once outside, he went around the block, pulled out his phone, and punched in Jan's number. His friend picked up on the second ring.

"I think I have the crime scene," Chandu said. "Tell our chain-smoker she should pack her bags. Looks like a late dinner."

• • •

Jan lost no time. In a matter of minutes he had gathered a few people from Patrick's team—including four crime-scene investigators, two uniformed cops, and Zoe with her irresistible charm—and headed over to the Ochsen. The owner paled at the sight of the group, who threatened to shut down his business if he didn't cooperate. He gave investigators access to all the rooms, stopped all work in the kitchen, and began to confess all. He was gray-haired, with an ample belly and a red nose that suggested he liked to partake of the many varieties of schnapps lining the back wall of his bar.

"How do you know Robin Cordes?" Jan asked him.

"We have a friend in common who helped me get some kitchen equipment for cheap." The man was rubbing his hands on his apron as if he'd just reached into a foul-smelling trash can.

"Stolen goods, you mean?"

"I didn't say that," the owner protested. "It was all legal. Invoiced and all that. Just a real good deal."

Stolen ovens were of no interest to Jan. "Whose idea were these poker games?"

"Robin came to me about five weeks ago. Said he had a proposal for how I could use the old room in back. He would organize a poker game once a week for people who had dough."

"So what did you get out of it?"

"Robin said the players would be drinking a lot more than apple juice. I got whiskey, vodka, and champagne and marked it up three times cost. No one batted an eye. They soaked it up like sponges. On a single poker night I did more drink sales than a whole month from the bar."

"You do know that poker games like that are illegal?"

"It was all on the up and up. Robin swore to me that he wasn't using marked cards and he was dealing them himself."

"I don't mean the poker. I mean playing for real money. They call it gambling."

The owner stared at the floor in shame. "What was I supposed to do? Business was getting bad. People wanting more and more crazy things. Sushi, pizza, all that vegetarian stuff. Your standard meat platter isn't exactly drawing crowds these days."

"You know the people who took part in these poker games?"

"No one besides Robin. They wanted to be left alone. I took the orders, brought the drinks, cleared out again."

"Are there surveillance cameras here?"

"You making a joke? I pour the beers and serve liver dumplings. I empty the register every night. There's nothing to steal here. Why a camera?"

"Yeah, a camera would be way too easy," Jan muttered under his breath. "Could you describe the players for me if I sent a professional sketch artist by here?"

"I can try." The owner shrugged. "I do remember faces well."

Jan closed his notepad. "All right. That'll be it for now. Please keep yourself available for any further questions."

The owner nodded and shuffled into the kitchen.

Jan was heading over to the back room when Zoe's voice came echoing into the dining room. "Jan! Get your ass out here."

He sighed. He was the lead detective, but Zoe always made him feel like the gofer boy.

He went through the kitchen and out into the back lot. The medical examiner was standing next to an investigator who was taking photos of a spot on the ground. As Jan came closer, he realized it was a bloodstain.

"Crime scene?"

"Most likely." Zoe held up a test tube. "We found little bone splinters in the blood. They could have come from Robin's skull. Ralf is taking a blood sample we'll compare with the victim's DNA. Then we'll know more."

"My name is Romir," said a man down on the ground.

"What I said."

"That would be progress," Jan replied. "We know when the poker ended and we have the cemetery break-in time. With a crime scene, we can start building a route profile."

"Anything new on the perp?"

"The owner will help us come up with sketches. I think our murderer was at these card games. But a little more evidence would be nice."

"Maybe I can help," an investigator said as he climbed out of a Dumpster. His protective coveralls had food scraps stuck to them, which didn't seem to bother him. Jan saw fried potatoes, lettuce, liverwurst. The man was holding a cheap pocket-calendar notebook. "I believe this belongs to Robin Cordes," he announced proudly. "And it's full of telephone numbers."

Jan let himself smile. The murderer had committed his first mistake.

. . .

He was back in the kitchen, saw the altar lit up with candles, smelled the incense. Father Anberger was tied to the cross and a pool of blood was forming next to him. Jan called out for Chandu, but his friend was nowhere to be seen.

Betty came out from behind a column, a smile on her face, a shotgun in her hands. Jan raised his hands and wanted to give himself up, and yet his fingers were suddenly gripping his pistol. So he shot. Once, twice, three times. And Betty collapsed. The blood flowed from her body, and her eyes closed.

. . .

Jan started from his nightmare with a scream. His T-shirt was soaked with sweat, his head ached, and he was shivering as if in an ice bath. He had kicked the covers off the bed and was clawing at the pillow with his right hand.

He took deep breaths. He needed a moment to realize that he wasn't in that church anymore. Betty was dead. He had survived.

He stood up wearily. He trudged over to the closet and pulled on a dry T-shirt. In the bathroom, he let warm water run through his hair until the memory began to blur. He sat on the couch with

a washcloth on his forehead and turned on the TV. The third time
this week. He was barely getting any sleep. He wouldn't be able to
keep this up for much longer.

Lying on the coffee table was Kerima Elmas's business card. He
always used to be able to work things out for himself. Girl problems, trouble with his boss, a grisly homicide. When things got
really bad he'd go get drunk with a friend or maybe end up getting
in a fistfight. At some point the bad mood would be driven out.
But the last case had left him with scars that were too deep and raw
to leave behind. Five beers or a brawl weren't going to make the
nightmares disappear.

It was 5:14 in the morning. Too early for a phone call. Yet
Kerima had told him to try her anytime.

He picked up the phone and dialed her number.

"Hello?" The psychologist's voice sounded sleepy.

"Frau Elmas, Jan Tommen here." He was relieved she'd picked
up. "Apologies for the time, but you did encourage me to call whenever I'm having trouble."

"It's all right, Herr Tommen." It sounded like she was fighting
back a yawn. "I'm used to restless nights. How can I help you?"

"I was thinking that I was making progress and getting over
what happened with Betty dying, but lately it's been getting worse."

"My guess is, it has to do with this grave murderer. The stress
you're feeling about this case carries over to other matters." The weariness was receding from her voice. "Perhaps we should talk a little
bit about the period right after Betty's death. What did you do after
you realized your girlfriend was dead?"

"In those first few days after her death? I got rid of everything in
my apartment having to do with her. Photos of us together, clothes
she left here, and all those little things you give each other when
you're in a relationship. I tossed it all in a big garbage bag, got up
real early, and threw it into the trash can outside right before the

garbage truck came. So there'd be no way I could weaken and go fish it all back out of the trash."

"Did that help?"

"No. You can't forget a person for good just by throwing out their clothes and a few mementos. When that person is buried so deep in your heart, they're a part of you. Beyond salvaging." Jan's voice grew softer. "Sometimes I have nightmares and relive what went down in the church, again and again—but sometimes memories of better times surface. When that happens, I don't just see her face, I can *sense* her. I'm lying in bed, stroking her back, and feeling her soft skin under my fingertips. Her warm body touching mine makes me tremble. My fingers glide through her hair; it slides across the back of my hand like a warm breeze. I close my eyes and feel her with all my senses. Her scent surrounds us, like sunflowers, a little strong, with a hint of jasmine mixed in. These dreams are so intense," Jan added, sounding distraught, "it's as if she's still right here with me. When I wake up and turn on my side, I reach to pull her close, breathe in her scent, but then I realize that she's dead, and all the pain comes rushing back."

"What do you do then?"

"Cry, scream, tear at the bedcovers. Sometimes I head over to my punching bag in the living room and pummel it till my arms ache. But mostly I just get up, standing there groggy and blank, drag myself to work, and try to make it through the day." Jan's head sank. "Time heals all wounds, they say. Every day I keep hoping it will get a little better, that the memories fade, the pain will get more bearable. But every morning when I wake alone in my bed? It just gets worse."

"Worse in what way?"

"When Betty was still alive, the way she smelled was always with me. It was this perfume that permeated everything. She only had to sleep over for it to stay with me. A kiss or a brief hug was enough. Yet after I have a dream about her, her scent evaporates immediately and becomes only this distant memory. So one day I got up and went to one of the bigger perfume shops. I spent the whole morning there, sampled all the women's perfumes. I ended up with thirty of those samples, but I finally found it." Jan closed his eyes and inhaled as if he could smell the perfume just by the power of recall. "It's from Lancôme. La Vie Est Belle."

"Life is beautiful," Dr. Elmas translated.

"Yes. How ironic."

"Did you buy it?"

"No," Jan said. "It was too hard on me. Like actual physical pain."

"But why not, if you associate so many fond memories with it?"

"Maybe I had a moment of clarity, became conscious that the perfume would only make things worse. Something was telling me, Betty is dead, I would never get back my time with her. She wasn't a part of my life anymore."

"Oh, she is definitely part of your life," Dr. Elmas remarked.

"How so? She's lying in a cemetery."

"It doesn't matter that Betty is dead. You think of her when you go to bed and when you get up. You dream of her. There's a scent that reminds you of her. These are all things that form a strong connection to a person. This isn't necessarily a bad thing, since you can draw a certain strength from memories like that. You determine how you remember that person, whether it's good or bad, what you will carry with you, what you'd rather forget. You narrow your memories of Betty to the best moments you had with her. Again, it isn't a bad thing. But you also hate yourself for shooting her and ending your time on earth with her that way."

"I killed her. That's the truth."

"That's not the problem. You refuse to see that you *had* to shoot Betty. Consider what you did objectively, as if you never knew her. Then judge it from that angle."

"What if I arrive at the same conclusion?"

"Then you will never be free of it."

•   •   •

Bergman entered police headquarters with a stack of Sunday papers under his arm. Although the rest of the city was enjoying a typically slow Sunday morning, things were as busy as any normal workday in the Kripo. No one was taking time off until the grave murderer was caught. If Robin Cordes's notebook provided that decisive clue, then he'd be happy to push through all vacation requests.

On the way to his office, he ran into Kerima Elmas. He put on a smile that was rather friendly—by his standards, anyway. "Good morning, Dr. Elmas." He was in no mood for a conversation about managing the staff, so he hoped she was there for some other reason.

"Morning," she replied, yawning, a hand over her mouth.

"At least someone's had fun on a Saturday night," Bergman muttered as he headed into his office. He set down his papers, turned on the computer, and made his way to the coffee machine.

Out in the hallway, Bergman waved at a few colleagues. Jan was coming out of the break room, yawning, his cup half-full. He looked both exhausted and feebleminded. He seemed to have fallen asleep on his feet.

"Morning, boss," he said, shuffling by Bergman. When Jan saw Kerima in the hallway, he lifted his head and waved at her. His weariness vanished for a moment. He smiled at her.

The psychologist's face lit up at the sight of Jan. She waved back and then disappeared into an office. As soon as Kerima left his sight, Jan's head sank down again, his eyes nearly closed. He yawned again.

"Oh, man," Bergman muttered to himself. He really did not need the headache of those two getting together at a time like this.

. . .

Patrick stood up on the table and clapped his hands. The conversations silenced, all heads turning to him.

"Good morning," he greeted all present in a loud voice. "We have two critical things to get done today. We're going to split up into two teams. One team needs to track down a name for every telephone number in Robin's notebook. The prosecutor's office has promised us full support, meaning we can requisition phone providers' databases. Only abbreviations or first names were written down—I want to see a list with full names attached to each number. These can then be compared to our database so that we can see who's carrying any offenses. Get Max Kornecker on board for the computer search.

"The second team will deal with the six players at Robin's poker game. One of them might be the murderer. Thanks to an informant, we've been able to identify one player as coming from the red-light district. For all others, at present we only have the restaurant owner's descriptions and our initial sketches. They'll have to be matched against any relevant criminal records. It's likely all the poker players are in Robin's notebook, but we can't count on that." Patrick looked at his watch. "It's a little after eight. We'll regroup every two hours and compare notes, beginning at ten. I'm inviting Detective Tommen, so that he can know the latest."

He clapped his hands again. "Get cracking."

. . .

It had been one hard Sunday. Jan felt swamped by Patrick's reams of information, but that was an improvement over groping around in the dark like before. His once-despised colleague's teams were fast and precise. They were inching closer to the murderer by the hour. The only thing missing to round out such a perfect day was a good meal—and Chandu would see to that. He took his role as host quite seriously.

Seductive aromas wafted through his friend's apartment, and even Zoe's thick cigarette smoke couldn't dispel them. Jan waved at her as he headed for Chandu in the kitchen. He gave the big guy a heartfelt slap on the shoulder and dared to peek in the oven.

"Alsatian tart again?" Jan grabbed a beer. "Don't get me wrong. I like it, but normally that chef's pride of yours doesn't let you serve the same thing twice."

Chandu moved so close to Jan that their heads were almost touching. "Zoe called me this afternoon," he whispered. "She asked me to make the tart again. Because she liked it so much."

"Wait. You mean Zoe gave you a compliment?"

"Kind of creepy, isn't it?"

"Makes you worry. Are you sure you weren't dreaming it?"

"I wouldn't rule that out."

"We should tread carefully here."

"I was going to get my gun. Just to be safe."

The beep of a timer interrupted their talk.

"Food's ready," Chandu shouted out into the room. "Sit yourselves down. I'll slice it up and bring it out in a sec."

No one said a word over the next ten minutes as they turned their attention to the food. Jan didn't want to disturb the meal with the investigation's latest findings. They had the whole evening for that. Only when Chandu was pulling the first espresso from his machine did Max turn on the projector. A list of names appeared.

"These are our suspects," Jan began. "Thanks to Robin Cordes's notebook, we not only have the names of the poker players but also found phone numbers and e-mail addresses."

Jan wiped his fingers on a napkin. "Let's go through them. Number one is Hermann Wierend."

Max projected the pub owner's picture on the wall.

"Owner of the Ochsen, where the illegal poker games took place. We checked his alibi for the murder and found no connection to the previous victims, Bernhard Valburg and Moritz Quast. He had no reason to murder Robin, since the poker games were a lucrative source of income for him. In short: we crossed him off the list of suspects."

"Hartmut Beck, goes by Becks," Chandu said as he brought two espressos from the kitchen.

Max switched photos to the underworld big hitter.

"Upscale pimp, wine drinker, and avid poker player. Killing like this isn't his style," Chandu continued. "He's too clever for this, puts too high a value on discretion."

"Plus, we checked him out and reached the same conclusion as with the pub owner," Jan added. "His alibi for the first two murders is airtight, there's no connection to the first two victims, and we don't have any motive for why he would want to murder Robin Cordes."

Max pressed a key on the laptop, and a new picture appeared. The man in it had short dark hair, a dark complexion, and gapped teeth that could have been the result of either bad oral hygiene or barroom brawls.

"Joe Greber, goes by Alki Joe," Chandu said as he sat down on the couch. "Deals in smuggled booze. He only offers the real deal, nothing watered down. Depending on the amount, you can get a bottle of real champagne starting at ten euros. A guy like Becks sells them in his bordello for twenty times that. The underworld big hitters love Alki Joe and he's been doing big business for years. There's no reason why he'd suddenly mutate into a serial killer."

"Our colleagues in CID Four, organized crime and gang crimes, they've been after him for a long time," Jan added, "but they haven't been able to nail him because he's moved his camp to Brandenburg. They still watch his car and phone, though. So we can rule him out in the homicides of Bernhard Valburg and Moritz Quast. Not to mention he lacks a connection to them."

Jan nodded at Max. A new picture appeared. This man was not much older than the hacker. He wore his thin hair tied back in a ponytail and sunglasses that looked too big on his narrow face.

"Bernd Serad," Jan told them. "A tender twenty-one years old. Known in online poker circles as 'The Bernie.' Lives at home with his mommy, yet earns enough money in Internet poker games to own a Porsche Boxster."

"Not bad," Chandu remarked.

"Just about shit his pants when officers showed up at his door. After his mother slapped him around good and loud and threatened further smackings, he told all, starting from birth. Officers actually had to put the brakes on him. Like the others, we can rule him out as a murderer."

The next picture showed a couple. The man was suntanned and winking suggestively into the camera. His wife had bright bleach-blonde hair and flashy catlike eyes in a color that could not have been natural.

"Herr and Frau Nina and Paul Hauren on their last vacation. Childless and bored. He, a successful middle-class guy who puts his money into big poker games. Since his wife has nothing better to do, she goes along. Threatened us with lawyers and a wave of lawsuits of unimaginable proportions when we searched their place, which ended up proving a dead end. No motive, two more-or-less-certain alibis for murder one, two watertight ones for murder two."

"Not much left to go on," Zoe said.

"The big winner? We've saved him for last."

A police sketch depicted a man with thinning gray hair. His wide-framed glasses and thick mustache were reminiscent of the '80s.

"Maik Müller. Supposedly a lawyer and our final player in the card game."

"You don't have a proper photo?" Zoe asked.

"We would have if there really were a lawyer by the name of Maik Müller. The name is as fake as his job title."

"So how did he get in the card game?" Chandu asked. "I thought you only got in on Robin Cordes's invitation."

"This is where it gets good. Maik had Robin's number through Nina and Paul Hauren, who met him two weeks ago at a kind of charity tournament. The players had to pay in five hundred euros to start, all of which was to benefit a children's home. The winner got a fancy trophy. Now, according to the Haurens, Maik was looking for a high-jackpot game. They eventually gave him Robin Cordes's number, and our supposed lawyer called him."

"Could you trace the call?" Zoe asked.

"Better than that," Max replied. "Robin's cell phone has indeed disappeared, but using the Haurens' number and a few tricks, I've gotten full access to this phone via the provider."

"Are these tricks legal?" Jan asked.

"I won't answer that for safety's sake." Max turned back to the photo. "Maik called Robin a day before the card game at the Ochsen, using—get this—a second phone of Moritz Quast's. He hadn't used it for so long we'd overlooked it."

"Fuck," Zoe commented.

"I could not agree more," Jan said.

"It gets even better." Max opened a program. "Robin had the phone off at the time, so his voice mail recorded what Maik said."

The man's voice was gloomy and scratchy, almost a whisper. *"Herr Cordes, Maik Müller here. You don't know me, but I heard from a friend we have in common that you're holding no-limit poker games. I'll pay you two thousand euros for an invitation. Cash. You have my number."*

Jan leaned back on the couch, grinning. "Whoever this murderer is—that was his voice."

"We traced the phone," Max continued. "But the murderer only used it once, and that was to call Robin Cordes."

"Where from?"

"Somewhere in Friedrichshain Public Park. Too many tourists and too few cameras."

"Patrick's team is going through all the databases with our sketch. If our murderer has any criminal record, we'll find him."

"But you don't think you'll get any hits?" Chandu said.

"The killer must have reckoned on us finding the poker game and the other players being able to describe him. He's not going to make things that easy."

"So what next?"

"We have to find that one connection between all three victims."

"We already tried that with Dr. Valburg, with Moritz Quast," Zoe countered. "Without any result."

"Let's try it another way this time. In what areas, in what walks of life, do they have nothing in common?"

"We can rule out childhoods, school, higher ed, and training," Max began. "Moritz Quast wasn't born in Berlin, and Robin Cordes is from East Germany. Dr. Valburg went to university. Moritz and Robin didn't even finish high school."

"Hobbies, clubs, and all that kind of stuff too," Chandu said. "There's no overlap there."

"Neighborhoods and friends don't work either," Jan said. "We ran all of them through the computer without a hit. Business connections as well. At least on a legal level."

"The illegal stuff's all that's left," Zoe said. "It's definitely possible, given that Moritz Quast has a criminal record and Robin Cordes was in jail."

"And our supposed Herr Clean Dr. Valburg had his jones for cocaine." Chandu shrugged. "Could match up."

"Let's forget all we know up to now and just speculate—shots in the dark," Jan said. "What might a connection look like?"

"That's easy," Zoe said, releasing a swirl of smoke toward the ceiling. "Valburg procures a medication, he gives it to Quast, and Cordes sells it."

"So why would the murderer bump the men off?" Chandu asked.

"The meds were crap. There were side effects and someone died."

"But how did the murderer know about the supply chain?" Jan asked. "If he got the meds from Cordes, how did he know that Valburg and Quast were involved in it?"

"He was shaking them down?" Max said.

"Not likely," Chandu said. "Quast and Cordes would've told us if they were being blackmailed."

"So the murderer was in deeper. He knew the whole supply chain."

"We shouldn't forget the dismembering," Zoe said. "It's too specific not to mean anything."

"For Bernhard Valburg, we have gouged-out eyes," Jan began. "Then a tongue cut out for Moritz Quast and fingers cut off for Robin Cordes."

"The cause of death was identical. The only difference was the assault coming from the front versus the back. Otherwise, hit with a hammer, and out go the lights."

"Let's start with Dr. Valburg's eyes," Chandu said.

"Fine. What could the murderer—" Jan's ringing phone interrupted him.

"Bergman," Jan said, looking at the screen. "This is either really good or really bad."

Jan took the call and turned on the speaker.

"Get your ass out to Zehlendorf!"

"Why, what's there?"

"A posh wooded cemetery. And another grave."

Chapter Ten

Jan felt his hand holding the phone begin to tremble. There were three dead so far, and he had little to show for it. Now the grave murderer had a new target.

Jan was putting everything he had into this. The files were piling up on his desk in the office. Work on the case never let up. Without Patrick and his people, he would have broken down long ago. Jan used to be able to cope with it all, but the nightmares were still robbing him of sleep and wringing the last of his strength out of him.

"I can't do it anymore," he said into the phone. "It's too much for me. Let me go, give Patrick the case or find another cop for it. It's best for all concerned."

"I've had it with all this bullshit!" Bergman screamed.

Jan almost dropped the phone in shock. He could hear Chandu, Zoe, and Max cracking jokes in the living room.

"I've tried everything. Given you time to recover, lightened your workload at first, even handed you over to that psych nurse. And the first real case you get, you want to just throw in the towel?"

"I don't think I can apprehend the grave murderer, and I don't want him to get away, so it would probably be better if someone else—"

"Bullshit," Bergman cut him off. "Let me phrase this another way. In your other cases, did you ever catch the killer after just a few days?"

Jan didn't answer at first. He wasn't sure where Bergman was going with this. "Hardly ever."

"Have you ever hit a dead end in an investigation?"

"Lots of times."

"Did you still nab the bad guy in the end?"

"Almost always."

"So what's your problem? This case is no different from any of the others, and this dead end, it's no different from any other dead ends."

"In my previous case, I failed to notice that my girlfriend was a murderer and playing games with me. I suspected half of Berlin, just not her. I was only hot on her trail once she was threatening to blow my head off with a shotgun."

"It happens. Sometimes things don't go so well. Stein wouldn't have solved the case without you. Then Betty would've ended up abroad and gotten away with it."

"Maybe that would've been better," Jan muttered.

Bergman sighed into the phone. "When are you going to face the fact that your girlfriend was a cruel and sadistic killer who got off on making her victims suffer? Devious enough to fool you with love, and only so she could offer you up as the fall guy."

Bergman's words hit Jan hard. "I think maybe you're overstating it—"

"No more excuses! Betty was a murderer! Should I spell it out for you?" Bergman actually spat out the letters: "M-u-r-d-e-r-e-r. You're not at fault. You didn't make her do it. Start accepting the fact that you were doing everything right and that Betty's death was necessary—or go on deluding yourself, keep treasuring her memory and ignoring that you were just a toy of hers." Bergman exhaled. "Time to decide. I'll see you in thirty minutes at the cemetery or you can hand over your badge."

Then he hung up.

．　　．　　．

Bergman had a sick feeling as he headed over to the cemetery. Hopefully he hadn't crossed the line.

He had shown Jan a good deal of respect and tried to give him time to get over the trauma, but the grave murderer was not going to wait until Jan got his act together. This case was assuming startling proportions. Three victims to worry about already, and the Berlin Police were not looking good, to say the least. The press was indulging in critical mockery, and the politicians were demanding results he could not deliver.

He needed an experienced investigator. Before he shot his girlfriend, Jan had been his best man for the job, but Bergman was taking a huge risk giving him the lead now. If it got out that the chief of detectives had put a mentally unstable detective in charge of finding the grave murderer, he was ruined. An early retirement was the best they would be able to offer him.

When he saw Jan standing at the grave, he felt some of his stress fade. Jan's head was a little slumped and his eyes showed sleepless nights, but judging from his expression, Jan was actually trying to restrain himself from smacking his boss right in the face. A good sign. Bergman's harsh words were having their effect.

But Jan still did not know who the new victim was. And he was not going to like it.

• • •

The grave lay in a remote area of the wooded cemetery. The grave sites next to it were overgrown with weeds, the gravestones filthy and neglected. The glaring spotlights hardly penetrated the pelting rain.

The grave was covered with a white tent so that the rain wouldn't wash away any evidence. Two men wearing protective suits pulled the cross out of the ground. On the wood it read: *Here Lies Yuri Petrov. Born March 14, 1971. Died July 2, 2013.*

The day of his death was the day after tomorrow.

Bergman stood at the grave holding an umbrella.

Jan turned to Bergman. "Do we know who this Yuri Petrov is?"

"Yuri Petrov is a staffer at the Ukrainian Embassy. Has diplomatic status. He's currently in his home country and doesn't know about his fate yet, but he'll be landing in Berlin in a few hours."

Jan groaned. A foreign diplomat, of all things. It would only complicate matters further. Now other authorities would start interfering, ones they'd so far been able to keep at bay. He didn't even want to think about the political repercussions of failure. "As soon as he sets foot on German soil, we can't let him out of our sight. A four-vehicle convoy. Let's add a tank to it if need be."

"You have free rein," Bergman said. "Meanwhile, I get to brief him on the delightful news that he's presumably the fourth intended victim of the grave murderer. This should be going through official channels, not through me."

"He should be secure once he's inside his own embassy," Jan said. "But after the last two incidents, I'm not relying fully on strangers. The embassy itself is Ukrainian territory, so we won't be able to do anything on the premises, but I can have the place kept under surveillance. Not even the paperboy gets near without being searched and checked out." Jan pointed at the grave. "The fact that he went and found Zehlendorf Forest Cemetery doesn't make our mission any easier. The grounds are ninety-two acres. The cemetery in Charlottenburg was the neighborhood park compared to this."

"Stay alert," Bergman warned. "A fourth victim, and a diplomat at that? We can't let it happen. The police chief will grill our behinds if Petrov gets so much as a scratch."

"I'll tell investigators to operate undercover so the press doesn't notice, put two men at the grave and four more with the management. Plus I'll have every car checked out that gets too close to the cemetery. Tomorrow evening I'll send an additional thirty men who will not return home until either we have our murderer or the day of death has passed."

"I'll try to find out more on Yuri Petrov. A lot is kept under wraps when it's a diplomat, and their police record is always spotless, but what else are my political contacts good for, anyway?" Bergman sighed as if the very thought of this task revolted him. "At eight tomorrow morning, you and I are going to the embassy and I'll introduce you to this Yuri Petrov. Get some sleep. It's going to be a couple of wild days, and nothing can go wrong this time."

．　　．　　．

Jan had spent the last several hours thinking about how a Ukrainian embassy staffer could fit the pattern. Around two in the morning he finally gave up and fell asleep. Shortly after five, his unconscious decided that it was time for him to get up. He pulled the covers over his head and tossed and turned in bed but had to accept that he wasn't going to get any more rest. So he showered, shaved, pulled a white shirt from the closet, and put on a suit. He left the tie hanging in the closet. He didn't want to look too formal.

Knowing Bergman's obsession with punctuality, Jan gave himself plenty of time to get to the embassy. He pulled up a minute before his boss. The three-story embassy building had a high roof, built out for more space, and countless windows. The Ukrainian flag complemented the yellowish tone of the exterior. Compared to the many pretentious embassies in Berlin, this one looked downright modest. It could have been a private school or an administration building.

The door opened before they even reached for the bell, and a powerfully built man let them inside. He wore a dark suit, an elegant tie, and black leather shoes. His manners were refined, but his physique left no doubt that he'd worn a military uniform before his current stint at the embassy.

Jan had left his weapon at home for their meeting with Yuri Petrov. After he and Bergman had confirmed their identities, they were led into a comfortable conference room. On the table stood a carafe of coffee, several bottles of mineral water, and a small porcelain bowl of cookies.

A painting hung on the wall. It looked as though several housepainters had dumped leftover buckets of paint on the huge canvas. Even if the piece was the work of a three-year-old, it had to be worth more than a small car. Jan was wondering how much he could earn as an artist in his spare time when the door opened. He recognized Yuri Petrov from an official embassy photo. The photo had obviously been retouched, since his beaming white smile was not so white in reality; he had a few more lines and wrinkles, and his blond hair was graying.

"Dr. Bergman," he said and shook Jan's boss's hand. He bowed slightly.

"This is my lead investigator, Detective Tommen," Bergman said. Another bow. Not quite as low.

"Please, sit down." Petrov's accent wasn't too pronounced. He'd either lived in Germany a long time or had a really good teacher. The Ukrainian placed his elbows on the table and folded his hands together. His gestures looked calm and deliberate. The consummate diplomat.

"The ambassador informed you about the incidents?" Bergman asked.

"I'm to be the next target of some madman, whom the media have christened the grave murderer. The day of my death is supposed to come tomorrow."

Jan jumped into the conversation. "Have you recently received any death threats?"

"Not apart from this macabre threat."

"You have any enemies who might want you dead?"

"I am an embassy counselor. An interesting profession, but a post that has little power. To be honest, I'm almost always traveling to somewhat tedious official receptions and really have no idea how I could have made such an enemy."

"It wouldn't have to be in Germany. It does happen that murderers follow their victims to other countries."

"I come from a family of career diplomats. I've been abroad most of my life, even during glasnost and perestroika."

"Does the day of death he's given mean anything special to you?"

"July second?" Petrov thought about it a moment, tapping his lower lip with a finger. "Not that I know of. There's no birthday in my family or a holiday that I can think of."

"Did you know any of the grave murderer's victims?" Jan placed three photos on the table. Petrov eyed them thoroughly and then shook his head.

"I can't say that I did. Who are these men?"

"The older gentleman is Dr. Bernhard Valburg. Next to him, one Moritz Quast, and then Robin Cordes."

"The names don't mean anything to me either. Is there some connection between them?"

"We're still investigating in that regard," Bergman said, keeping it vague.

Which translates to "We got nothing," Jan thought.

"How can I help you, gentlemen?"

"By letting us protect you."

"Not a problem. I've canceled all appointments outside of the embassy. I will not be going out the door the next two days."

"We're posting police officers in front of the building," Jan said.

"The ambassador is also allowing us to check every visitor before they go through your door," Bergman added. "We have all the necessary information, including a list of all embassy staff and the plate numbers of your vehicles."

"Is there something else I can do for you?"

"Apart from being careful and reporting anything unusual, no." Bergman stood and shook Petrov's hand. "If you think of anything else, please get in touch with me or Detective Tommen."

Jan pulled a card from his pocket and handed it to Yuri.

The Ukrainian looked at the card. "Thank you very much for your efforts. If you have any other questions, you can call me anytime. I'll do whatever I can."

"Will do," Jan said. "And please remember to let us know if there's someone else you can think of who could have a motive, who might bear a grudge against you. We're dealing with a serial killer here—and he is extremely dangerous."

Petrov nodded gravely, and they made their way out. The Ukrainian walked them to the door and nodded at them again.

"What are you thinking?" Bergman asked Jan once the door had closed behind them.

"Something's fishy."

"He's lying?"

"He's not telling us everything. Our three victims all had a skeleton in the closet. Moritz and Robin more so, Valburg less. And they're all linked. The murderer didn't just go surf the Internet, end up at the Ukrainian embassy, and pick out his next victim. There is a reason why he selected Yuri Petrov."

"You don't believe in coincidence?" Bergman asked Jan.

"Never. We're inching closer to the murderer. We know his face, have his voice, and are getting at a motive. He's not knocking people off for fun."

"Some psychopaths want to be caught."

"That doesn't fit the grave murderer. He is cunning, well prepared. He's on a revenge mission. No idea for who or what, but when he's done doing it, he will either vanish or put a bullet in his head. He won't let himself be caught."

"What's next?" Bergman asked.

"I can't think of any lead involving the first three victims that might point to Ukraine or its embassy. Still, I'll go through it all again. When it gets dark, I'll get started on the stakeout. I want to be on hand when Petrov's day of death begins."

"At least we know where he is. If Robin would've let us watch over him? He'd still be alive."

"Maybe," Jan said, unsure. "The murderer knows that Petrov lives in a well-secured embassy and that we would find the grave. He'll have taken all that into account."

"The security personnel are all former Spetznaz, one of the best special forces on earth. You don't just brush them aside."

"Under normal circumstances, this would be pretty straightforward. But the murderer hasn't left us any clue as to what he's got up his sleeve. No idea what trick he'll pull, but we should be on our guard like hell. He's been better than us three times now."

·   ·   ·

Three more hours till Petrov's day of death. Jan sat in his car, keeping an eye on the front entrance of the Ukrainian embassy. He rapped nervously on the steering wheel. He had done all he could to secure the area and safeguard Petrov's survival. He'd gone through all scenarios imaginable and asked specialists for their opinions—but his gut feeling was telling him that it was not going to be enough.

A police vehicle was parked right before the embassy entrance, clearly visible; same for the rear entrance. Considering the plainclothes teams on the side streets, the cameras they'd installed, and all the embassy's security measures, the grave murderer would have to be a master thief with superhero powers to get into this building unnoticed.

Jan couldn't count all the nights he'd sat waiting in a car outside a house, just hoping that an offender would go in or come out. The time spent was all about boredom and weariness and would always lead to him doubting whether he had picked the right career. Few stakeouts were a success in the end, which made a long night with lukewarm coffee, fast food, and chewing gum even more frustrating.

He had wanted to meet up with Zoe, Max, and Chandu again this evening, but he had to stay near the embassy, so they'd canceled their nightly get-together. Max had suggested setting up a conference call, though. Jan had just taken a sip of coffee from his thermos when his phone rang.

"Good evening," Max said once Jan picked up. "Here on the line are, next to yours truly, Zoe and Chandu."

"Hi," Jan said, setting his cup in the holder. "How's Yuri Petrov's background looking?"

"Not much to see," Max said. "Petrov wasn't born in Germany, has a Ukrainian passport, and is embassy staff, so I've only been able to get information from diplomatic channels. As you can guess, it's all been smoothed out. Most of what I got is only thanks to Bergman's contacts. Yuri was born in Portugal—the child of a diplomat, went to international schools, and was transferred to Germany four years ago. Because of his immunity, I haven't stumbled on so much as a parking ticket. Long story short: a waste of time."

"What about the rest of the embassy team?"

"Same. All model students."

"Could any of their résumés have been falsified?" Jan asked.

"Probably. I can tell you one thing: all embassy personnel have been working there for at least a year."

"Why does that matter?" Chandu asked.

"My worry was that the murderer had maybe snuck his way into working at the embassy," Max replied. "Some cook who'd only been working there for three weeks? I would've looked at that pretty closely. The people in there are all Ukrainians or at least have Ukrainian heritage."

"Which leads me to believe the killer isn't on staff," Jan said.

"He could be delivering pizzas or repairing a broken fridge," Chandu said.

"The embassy has imposed a two-day lockdown," Jan said. "No one from the outside comes in."

"Plus the embassy has their own people for that," Max added. "Cooks, maintenance, janitors. All in there."

"I hit up a few old acquaintances from the Eastern Bloc," Chandu said. "None of them had heard of a Yuri Petrov when it came to girl trafficking, prostitution, drug smuggling, or gambling. The guy is either real discreet or he's got nothing to do with the Berlin underworld."

"I went back through all the files for the first three murders," Jan said. "I found no trace of a Yuri Petrov or the Ukrainian embassy. Nothing in the victims' personal notes or in their records, e-mails, address books."

"So this Yuri has nothing in common with the other victims," Zoe said.

"That I don't believe," Jan replied. "All my experience as a detective tells me that Petrov's got a finger in it somehow. Just because we're not finding anything on the fly doesn't mean there's nothing there."

"But we don't have the slightest clue," Chandu said, "except for the fact that he's the grave murderer's target."

"Is that confirmed?" Max asked. "Is this new grave from the same perp? Could it be a copycat?"

"Yup. Nope," Zoe said. "Wood and paint on the cross match the other three completely. It has to be the same guy. And before you ask: no, there were no fingerprints or DNA on the cross."

"Would've been too easy," Chandu muttered.

"Let's spin this around," Jan said. "How does a Ukrainian embassy staffer fit into this case?"

"That's easy," Chandu said. "First of all, the embassy premises are Ukrainian territory. Police, detectives, border patrol—no one is allowed in. There's no more secure place for stolen goods or illegal meds from abroad. They could even be producing in there."

"On top of that, he's got this crazy freedom to do whatever he wants," Zoe added. "He can't be prosecuted for any offenses, and a car with diplomatic plates can't be stopped, let alone searched. Yuri would make the perfect delivery man."

"That also applies to air travel between Ukraine and Germany, by the way," Max said. "A diplomatic bag is sacred. Makes it easy to smuggle anything from point A to point B."

"A man like Yuri is worth his weight in gold to any criminal," Chandu said. "He could easily be the brains behind this smuggling racket, or at least a big player."

"Everything you're saying makes sense," Jan said. "But I have no idea how we could prove any of it."

"With his diplomatic status? You can forget it," Zoe said.

"She's right about that, unfortunately," Max said. "Diplomats can be prosecuted, but the punishment always takes place in their own country. Even if Yuri blew someone away, German authorities would only be allowed to apprehend and extradite him. A Ukrainian court would rule on it after that."

"To sum this up," Chandu said, "we have no idea how Yuri's involved or why the grave murderer wants to see him dead."

Jan shook his head. "I just don't get it. We've been working this case with everything we have, but we're hardly any closer to nabbing the murderer. After three dead, we've got a police sketch and the murderer's voice. No names, no suspects, not even a motive."

"Better make sure nothing happens to Yuri," Chandu said. "He might cough up something with further questioning. In the words of Boba Fett: 'He's no good to me dead.'"

Chandu was right. Yuri had to survive his day of death first. All else would have to wait. "Thanks to all of you for everything you've done so far," Jan said to wrap up. "I'll check in again tomorrow morning."

He set his phone on the dash and mulled things over. It would be tough to get Yuri to work with them if he was involved in something illegal. The diplomat wouldn't admit to years of drug smuggling just to help the police in an investigation. The portable radio crackled, cutting short his speculation.

"Vehicle heading to the embassy," a police officer reported.

"What kind of vehicle?" Jan asked.

"Car. One of the embassy staff coming from the airport."

"Who's in the car?"

"According to the embassy, driver by the name of Petr Kusmin and a staffer named Galina Yefimova."

Jan pulled out his files and looked for the woman's name. On page two he found her entry, complete with photo. Galina was assistant to the ambassador. She looked young for her thirty-one years. Her smile seemed fake, and she would have looked better with longer hair, but she was quite attractive if you were into the tomboy type.

The car came around the corner. A gray Mercedes with tinted windows that allowed no view inside.

"Definitely check it out. The trunk too." Jan had to stop himself from jumping out of his car. He had good people on the case. As team leader, he had to remain in the background.

"Planning on it." It was clear that the officer was annoyed with Jan's coaching.

"Sorry," Jan muttered. When he'd been on patrol, he'd never much liked it when some smart-ass from detectives gave him advice either. He set down the portable and watched his fellow cops do their work. The men proceeded by the book. They opened the car doors and checked both driver and passenger without rushing any of it.

As they opened the trunk, Jan's hands clenched, as if expecting the murderer to pop out with pistol drawn. But nothing was in there, apart from a few small suitcases. The officers shut the trunk lid and gestured to the driver. The big metal gate opened, and he drove in to the embassy grounds.

"All okay here," Jan heard over the radio. "Driver checks out, and the passenger is Galina Yefimova."

A thousand questions raced through Jan's head. Why was the assistant flying alone? Had the woman been tense or nervous? Was any of the baggage unusually heavy? But Bergman had warned him against causing a stir. The embassy personnel weren't required to cooperate and weren't allowed to be questioned without the ambassador's consent.

Jan hated policy, politics. They weren't allowed to intervene, yet if anything went wrong they were held responsible.

He turned to his coffee, feeling testy. This was going to be a long night.

.   .   .

The portable radio crackled, jolting Jan from sleep. It took him a moment to realize that he'd fallen asleep in his car. The dash display read 5:31 a.m. The last time he'd looked, it was just before five.

"Small van leaving the premises." The police officer's voice didn't sound the least bit tired. Either this fellow cop had been rotated or he'd been throwing back a few of Max's energy drinks.

"Is the trip confirmed?" Jan asked.

"It's a kitchen employee. Drives to the big wholesale market every week. Departure confirmed yesterday."

The embassy gate opened up, and a small van rolled out. The driver wore blue overalls and a gray cap. He lowered the window to wave at the patrol car outside the embassy. The cops returned the gesture by blinking their headlights.

It was too dark for Jan to recognize the driver.

"Vehicle and plate match motor-pool records," the cop said on the radio. "All okay here."

Jan tapped his feet, suddenly restless. The trip had been confirmed yesterday. Neither time nor vehicle was suspect, but something was making Jan nervous. Maybe he was imagining things. But he didn't want to make a mistake. Yuri's survival was crucial. They needed the Ukrainian in order to get at the murderer's motive. And Jan wouldn't be able to forgive himself if there was a fourth victim.

Jan's phone lay on the dash, tempting him. A brief call to Yuri and he'd know that he was safe. Yet yanking the man out of bed at such an hour could make Jan look panicky. Bergman would have to apologize on his behalf. He had promised to disrupt the embassy's regular operations as little as possible.

Jan pounded on the steering wheel in anger. If he followed the van, he might miss something at the embassy. But something was urging him to follow the vehicle and check whether it really was on its way to the wholesale market.

Finally his gut won out. "Detective Tommen to patrol car," he said into the radio.

"Claus Plath here."

"I'm pursuing a lead and pulling myself off embassy watch. Might be just a false alarm and I'll be back within the hour. If something goes down, call me immediately."

"Will do," Officer Plath said.

Jan started the car and began following the small van.

The lack of traffic at that hour made it easy for Jan to keep track of it. He could give the van plenty of space without losing sight of it.

Jan lowered the window and drank the rest of his coffee as he drove. A new day was dawning, and with every kilometer his weariness decreased. They drove for about twenty minutes. The canal ran to his right. The first flights were coming in toward Tegel. The van was taking a direct route. Its driver wasn't going especially fast or slow, made no unusual signaling or stops. All normal.

A large sign indicated the exit to Berlin's sprawling wholesale market. Jan crept up, shortening his distance to the van. He wouldn't turn back until the vehicle was inside the market grounds.

Right before the exit, the van switched to the left lane and drove past the market, heading toward Reinickendorf.

Jan formed a fist. His gut hadn't let him down. "No clue where you think you're going, my man," he muttered. "But I'm behind you."

. . .

The detour through Reinickendorf lasted ten minutes. Jan had no idea where he was. The air smelled like chemicals and household cleaners, and the S-Bahn train clattered by. He drove over some tracks and past the old market halls to a warehouse that looked just like thousands of others in Berlin.

The van stopped at a loading dock. Jan cursed. It was still too dark for him to see anything. The area around the warehouse looked abandoned; there were no cars or trucks or pedestrians in sight. Driving right up to the building would give away his cover, so he'd have to wait until the driver had disappeared inside the warehouse.

Whatever this embassy employee was doing here, it wasn't buying fruits and vegetables.

When the warehouse's steel door slammed shut, Jan turned off his lights and drove toward the building—he wanted to keep his car close in case he had to pursue the van again. The gravel road crunched under his tires, so he approached as slowly as he could. He kept his eyes on the warehouse entrance and prayed that no one heard him coming. After what felt like an eternity, he pulled up behind a rusty Dumpster that kept him from view. He turned off his car, stuffed his phone in his pocket, and crept up to the front door.

●　　●　　●

The door didn't look rusty. With any luck it wouldn't squeak. He didn't see any cameras or other security devices, so he opened the door a crack. It swung open without a sound—the burglar gods were looking out for him. He slipped in and found himself inside a warehouse full of pallets, many of which were moldy, the wood worn gray and no good for deliveries anymore. They'd likely been sitting here for years. It smelled musty, as if the big loading doors hadn't been opened in a long time. Beams of sunlight streamed down from the skylights. A fluorescent light lit up a single spot, in the middle of the warehouse.

A loud screech pierced the silence. Jan recoiled and fought the urge to reach for his weapon. But nothing happened. Maybe the embassy cook was stashing smuggled goods or there was some other logical explanation. But the murder threat to Yuri Petrov—and the fact that the grave murderer was still on the loose—had put Jan on edge.

The pallets created a big maze. They stood nearly seven feet high, and Jan couldn't see over or through them. If they hadn't been so rotted, he would have climbed up to take a look around. But he had no choice but to sneak around, step by step.

He tiptoed forward, keeping an eye on the floor so he didn't trip or step on something. Then he found himself in an area that was lit up.

Fluorescent lights illuminated an open area about ten yards in diameter. The van driver sat in a chair in the center of it, his back to Jan. Jan followed the direction of the man's gaze but couldn't figure out why he was staring at a pile of pallets.

Maybe he was waiting for someone. Maybe he'd shot up and was waiting for the drugs to kick in. That would explain his relaxed posture and the fact that his arms dangled down at his sides.

Jan looked at the man's feet. His shoes didn't match his work outfit. They were leather loafers. Dapper ones, too, and not the least bit suitable for walking the big market hall.

Then he spied the thin plastic straps around the man's ankles. He was bound to the chair.

Jan saw something move out of the corner of his eye. He tried to turn around, but his attacker was quicker. His neck exploded with pain. Then all went dark.

·   ·   ·

Jan woke to the sound of a man screaming. It took a few seconds for the fog of darkness to clear. He had a hellish headache, and his neck hurt. He wanted to feel for a wound but could not raise his arms.

As his vision cleared, he discovered that he was sitting in a chair, his hands and legs bound. The screams were coming from the man from the embassy, who was seated beside him. He was no longer wearing his cap, and Jan recognized Yuri Petrov at once. He was screaming in Ukrainian at an unknown person wearing a ski mask. Whatever Yuri was saying, it was no compliment. His hatred for his attacker was etched in his enraged face.

The man standing before Petrov didn't appear impressed by the Ukrainian's meltdown. He was average size, not especially strong-looking. He wore dark jeans, a blue rain jacket, and the black ski mask. The hammer in his right hand told Jan that the grave murderer was standing before him. The tool was clean—so he'd washed the blood off after his last kill. The shape of the hammerhead was just as Zoe had described it.

Jan fought his restraints with all he had, but the thin plastic only dug deeper into his flesh. The murderer had done his job well. Jan's wrists and lower arms were bound to the metal chair, as were his calves and his thighs right above the knee.

He eventually gave up and turned to Yuri, who accentuated his latest torrent of words by spitting.

"What the hell are you doing here?" Jan said.

"You wouldn't understand," Petrov said.

"I understand that you're a complete idiot for leaving the embassy, and I understand that the man before you is the grave murderer who's already killed three people with that hammer he's holding."

The killer didn't react. He kept his eyes fixed on Yuri. Only a finger shifted on the hammer's handle now and then. Otherwise he was a statue.

Petrov's rage found a new target in Jan. "Fucking cop! You don't think I know I fell into a trap?"

Jan turned to the murderer. "What do you want? Why kill those people?"

No reaction.

"I asked him that already," Petrov said. "He hasn't said a word since he put you in that chair."

Petrov, trying to master his rage, spoke firmly to the murderer: "If you think I'm going to beg for my life, then you're wrong. Untie me and we'll settle this matter like men."

The Ukrainian flexed his muscles against his restraints with all he had. Blood ran from Petrov's wrist, which only seemed to make him angrier. The straining plastic made a creaking sound.

The stranger took a step forward, as though sensing that the situation was getting too dangerous. He struck Petrov in the face with his free hand. The Ukrainian's resistance broke for a moment. He convulsed, glared at his assailant, and screamed something in Ukrainian as blood dripped from his wrists to the floor.

The stranger gripped the hammer tighter. "For my daughter," his voice droned over Petrov's cursing. He held the hammer up over his head and swung it down toward Petrov's head.

Seeing the hit coming, Petrov jerked his head to the side and pressed his feet to the floor. The chair shifted sideways, only a bit, but just enough that the blow found his shoulder instead of his head.

A loud crack sounded as the hammer broke the collarbone. Petrov screamed in pain and tried to keep moving away. The chair fell over, but the restraints held him fast to it.

The stranger was clearly thrown off by his miss. He recoiled a step, as though unsure how to deal with this screaming man. The Ukrainian must have been suffering unbearable pain, yet was trying to crawl away, despite his constraints. With every pain-filled thrust, he came closer to the pallets.

Jan fought the restraints that gouged into his own flesh. But distress made him impervious to the pain. He had to free himself. He balled his fists, squeezed his eyes shut, and summoned all his strength, but the straps held.

The murderer had recovered from his initial shock. He stepped up to his victim, swung the hammer, and struck again. Lying on the floor, it was harder for Petrov to avoid the blow, which landed on his cheekbone. His screaming amplified. Blood squirted from the wound, ran down his face. He kept sliding along, but the murderer set after him.

The third blow landed on Petrov's forehead. The screaming stopped. His head rolled to the side, and his empty eyes found Jan. Yuri Petrov opened his mouth. A slight gasp escaped from his throat. Like a last request.

The fourth blow ended his suffering.

•　　•　　•

The murderer turned away from Petrov. He dropped the hammer, reached in his pocket, and pulled out a cloth. He wiped off his hands, but blood still stained his fingers. He took the fabric in his right hand and rubbed fanatically at his left. When that didn't work, he spat on his fingers and rubbed even harder.

He finally gave up and dropped the cloth on the floor. His eyes showed his revulsion for Yuri Petrov's blood.

He bent forward, breathing heavily as though he had to throw up.

"Why?" Jan asked.

"Because he deserved it."

"What about Valburg, Quast, and Cordes? They deserve it too?"

"Yes." His voice was cold, matter-of-fact, as if discussing spreadsheets.

"Why kill these men and then mutilate them?"

The stranger didn't answer. He disappeared from Jan's view. Jan heard a rustling sound, a pallet being moved. A minute later the murderer returned. He was dressed in a big plastic suit, like the ones Forensics wore, and was pushing a pallet jack with a large blue plastic barrel tied to it. The jack's supports were reinforced with metal tubing.

Chandu had been right. The murderer transported his victims inside a barrel.

Jan tried to get him talking again. "We'll get you. The fact that you've caught me will only gain you a few more hours of freedom."

The man didn't respond. That could only mean two things. Either he didn't care about getting caught, in which case Petrov was his last victim—he would drive to the cemetery and be led away in handcuffs. Or he didn't care that Jan had seen him finish off Petrov, because he planned to kill Jan next.

Jan checked how his straps were holding. His wrists hurt. The plastic straps were cutting into his skin. Blood soaked his sleeves. Maybe the blood would help him slip out of his restraints. Fighting them certainly wasn't doing him any good.

The murderer was in no hurry, and his every move looked deliberate. He released the barrel from the pallet jack, crossed Petrov's arms across his chest, and hauled him into the container with an expert grip.

Jan felt a surge of despair. True, Zehlendorf Forest Cemetery was hermetically sealed. The hearse ruse wasn't going to work a second time; when the killer showed up there, they'd catch him. But nothing here suggested that this man was bothered by Jan's arrival on the scene. He wasn't acting as though his plans had been thrown off course—it was almost as if he had some ace up his sleeve.

He had managed to summon Petrov to his own execution, and the man had come. Judging from how angry he had been, the Ukrainian had been lured here under some kind of pretense—but what could have induced him to sneak past the guards when he was supposed to be the grave murderer's next victim? It was complete madness. Whatever the reason, it must have been significant for Yuri to risk his life for it.

Ten minutes later the dead man was stowed away, the barrel tied to the jack, and the plastic suit stuffed into a bag. Petrov's blood had made a large pool on the floor, but the murderer didn't even bother with it.

The hammer was the only thing he picked up. He turned to Jan and eyed him indecisively. He walked around Jan and stood behind him.

Jan yanked at the straps with all he had, trying to slip free. One hand would be enough for him to defend himself.

"Sorry," the man said.

The plastic straps wouldn't budge.

Then came the pain.

Chapter Eleven

Jan woke to the rising sun shining down on him. The red had turned to a soft yellow and streamed down from the warehouse skylights, blinding him. He bit his lip to confirm to himself that he was still alive. The pain in his head had become a frantic staccato. The grave murderer had not killed him but Tasered him again instead.

Jan had no idea how much time had elapsed, but he had to warn his colleagues. He was still tied to the chair. He knew he wouldn't get his arms free, so he braced his chin on his chest and pushed off with his feet to propel himself backward.

Hitting the floor wasn't as painful as he'd feared it would be. He moved his legs back and forth until the plastic restraints slid off the chair's metal legs.

Sighing, he stretched out his legs. With his back still tied to the chair, he hauled himself up and hobbled over to the nearest metal girder. He stood next to its sharp edge and rubbed one wrist's plastic restraint against it. Each touch stung, but Jan maintained a constant pace.

Just when he was beginning to think it would never work, the plastic strap popped apart. He stepped over, picked up a jagged pipe, and used it to work off his other restraints. A minute later he hurled the chair across the floor. His jacket was empty. Wallet, badge, and phone gone. The murderer must have pocketed all of it. But his gun was still there, still in its holster.

Jan ran out to his car, figuring he could warn his men over the two-way radio. When he got outside, he saw the BMW's hood open. The cables had been severed from the battery—Jan wasn't going anywhere, nor would he be able to use the car radio. He gave the bumper a swift kick.

He ran out into the street and turned left. The street was empty.

Valuable time was slipping away. Every minute worked to the killer's advantage.

At the first intersection, he peered around but saw no activity. He ran on, cursing. The sweat stung his wounds. His breathing turned to gasping, but he didn't even consider slowing down. His lungs would have to collapse first.

At the next intersection, he spotted a parked delivery van. A man was hauling beverages into a little food stand. Seeing Jan, he set aside his box.

"You all right there, buddy?"

"Police officer," Jan gasped. "I have to make a call, it's urgent."

The man stared at him with a look of surprise on his face but pulled out his cell phone and handed it to Jan.

Jan dialed the Detectives Division main number. He cursed whoever invented the automated phone system. He used to know all the numbers by heart. On the third ring, someone picked up.

"Berlin CID. Hello."

"Detective Tommen here!" Jan was practically screaming into the receiver. "Connect me to the officer in charge at Zehlendorf Cemetery!"

"One moment, please."

Jan stopped himself from adding that he didn't have a moment. Classical music played as he waited. Ten seconds had never felt so long. The lead officer finally answered.

"Detective Tommen? Again? What the hell is going on now?" The static sounded harsh.

"The grave murderer got Yuri Petrov. He's on the way to the cemetery. Why 'again'?"

"You called another officer here at the cemetery a half hour ago and said the open grave at the northeast corner along Wasgensteig Road was just a diversion. The actual grave is off to the west, north of Königsweg Road. So we moved all our people over there and sealed off the area."

"That's not it!" Jan screamed into the phone.

"Is so," the man barked back. "It was your cell phone and you even gave your badge number."

"That was the grave murderer, you idiots. He stole my phone and my ID. You didn't hear the difference in his voice?"

"We got nothing to do with detectives. We only know about you from your last case. Plus the call was tough to understand with that train going by in the background."

"So turn right around and get back to the other side of the cemetery. The murderer could still be there!"

"On our way." The call was disconnected.

The grave murderer had bested them yet again.

. . .

Jan stood at Yuri Petrov's grave. Like the previous victims, Petrov lay with his face in the earth. His hair was sticky with blood. Hordes of investigators were securing clues, taking photos, discussing results. The cemetery seemed more like a beehive than a final resting place.

Jan watched the crime-scene techs as they sealed the grave's cross inside a large plastic bag. Its wood bore the day of death for Yuri Petrov. Once again, the grave murderer had kept his word. Once again, Jan had failed.

Bergman stood next to him at the grave's edge.

"You should have that looked at," Bergman said, sounding unusually calm. "Your neck doesn't look good, and there's that blood on your shirt."

That was it. No screaming. No blaming. No cursing the media.

"It's not that bad."

"This might sound like some crappy movie line—but it was not your fault."

"I'm the lead detective. Who else's fault is it?"

"We can only help people who want to be helped. Robin Cordes tried to go it alone, and Yuri Petrov willingly fell into the murderer's trap."

"But why?" Jan clenched his hands. "How can a person be so stupid? He knew about the grave murderer. He was safe in the embassy. Instead of staying there, he slips out before morning to drive to some warehouse. I've been wracking my brains for hours trying to figure out why Petrov would do that."

"There is one explanation," said Patrick, who'd just appeared beside Jan. He turned his phone around and showed him a picture of a rectangular white box.

"What's that?"

"That is a thermally cooled chest. They're used to transport organs."

"Where did you find it?" Bergman said.

"In Yuri Petrov's van."

"Petrov was an organ dealer?"

"We don't know much yet, but all signs point to it. We found two corneas in the case."

"So I burst in on an organ deal?" Jan said.

Patrick nodded.

"That explains it." Jan pointed at the corpse. "Petrov had an appointment with the grave murderer without knowing it was him. That explains all the secrecy. He didn't want us finding out about his illegal side business."

"My guess is it was a deal for a lung, but it went bad," Zoe said, climbing out of the grave.

"What makes you think that?"

She held up a pouch with a dark organ.

"Where did you get that?"

"Murderer cut it out of Yuri Petrov before lowering him into the grave here. Didn't exactly do a professional job of it, if I do say so myself. He made a long incision just below the sternum, using a sharp knife, and rooted around in there till he found the lungs. You can rule out a doctor."

"That's a lung?"

Zoe nodded.

"Why is it so dark?"

"Belomorkanal."

"Never heard of that disease."

Zoe raised her eyebrows in contempt. Jan had clearly guessed wrong. "It's a cigarette brand, Super Whiz. Yuri Petrov was a chain-smoker."

"He had a skeleton in his closet, in any case," Bergman said. "I'll put pressure on the embassy. If staffers are abusing their special status to bring organs into Germany illegally, the time for diplomacy is over. I'll have each and every one of them down at the station by tonight."

Bergman pulled out his phone and left the cemetery. His forceful stride made it clear that the Ukrainian embassy was not going to have a good day.

"I'll carry on with my new friend here." Zoe pointed at the corpse. "Should have something by this afternoon."

"Thanks," Jan said.

"Oh, and put a new shirt on. Bloodred doesn't suit you."

•   •   •

Max sat at a police computer. His right hand flew across the keys while he guzzled a glass of Ovaltine and cola with his left. The machine was slow, but this server gave him unrestricted access to the criminal database, and he was going to need it today. His phone rang, playing the title song from the Legend of Zelda video game. He set his glass aside, took the call.

"Hi, Jan. Where are you?"

"Still at the cemetery, but I feel like a fifth wheel here among all these crime-scene techs."

"What can I do?"

"Where did the last call from my phone come from?"

"The one from the grave murderer? Not far from that warehouse. The location I have isn't super exact. But if officers heard a train in the background, it has to have been a little over two hundred yards west of it. There are tracks there used by freight trains. That was the last signal. Your phone's been dead since then. I do have it on the radar, though. As soon as it's turned on, I'll know where it is."

"Anything else?"

"Forensics gave me Yuri Petrov's phone. Easy to crack the PIN. I ran across a cryptic e-mail address in the browser. It'll take about an hour till I have the password. Should I be looking for anything specific?"

"Anything having to do with organ dealing."

"Organ dealing?" Max let out a whistle. "That's high-end stuff."

"Yuri Petrov wasn't only an embassy staffer."

"Clearly. I'll get in touch as soon as I've got any news."

Max hung up, started up his password cracker, and pushed his drink away. Getting at Petrov's secrets was going to take a while; he was going to need something stronger. Time for a few energy drinks.

•   •   •

When questioning a subject, Jan always adjusted his stance to match the interviewee. If it was some tough guy, he came on tough. For a person who'd never met a detective before, he was more subtle. Statements from persons shaking in fear weren't worth much. If the subject had political influence or even diplomatic status, then he had to be doubly careful. People like that could simply get up and leave.

Galina Yefimova required a subtle approach. But Jan was in no mood for that today. He had no idea how Bergman had delivered the woman to him—from out of the embassy, without legal means—but he did know that his boss had balls of rebarred concrete. If Bergman thought he was being played for a fool, he'd show even the chancellor herself his middle finger.

Jan gave a kick to the conference-room door, which hit the wall with a little bang. As he'd hoped, Galina Yefimova flinched.

Jan abandoned everything he'd learned about interrogations done right. He didn't introduce himself and offer the person anything to drink, and he did all he could to appear hostile. He yanked the surveillance-camera cable out of the wall, slammed his files on the table, and landed hard on a chair.

Galina looked like she hadn't slept. Her eyes were red from crying. Her suit was wrinkled, and it looked as if she hadn't had much time to get dressed. That slightly arrogant expression Jan had noticed on her embassy homepage photo was long gone.

Jan glared at her. "Do you know why you're here?"

"Because Yuri was murdered." Her voice sounded fearful.

"Nice try. You want to try again?"

"Isn't this about Yuri dying?"

"This here? It's about organ dealing."

Galina looked down at the floor.

"We hacked Yuri Petrov's cell phone this morning."

"That's illegal," Galina protested. "There is confidential information on that device—"

"I don't care!" Jan pounded on the table. Again Galina obliged him by flinching. "We came across an e-mail Yuri used to set up the transports to Germany. And imagine who we found helping him do it." He aimed his finger at Galina. "You!"

Jan leaned forward. "Let's sum this up. You and Yuri didn't only use your diplomatic immunity to smuggle organs to Germany, you even used the embassy's private jet to do it. Are you aware of the repercussions for relations between our two countries?"

Galina kept her head lowered. This was the decisive moment. Either she was going to cave and start talking, or she'd retreat back into her shell and say nothing.

Jan leaned back without taking his eyes off his subject. He was under hellish pressure, time-wise, but the ball was in her court now.

"What do you want from me?"

Jan stifled a triumphant smile. "If I'm in need of an organ, how do I reach Yuri Petrov?"

"We have various contacts in Berlin and the vicinity. These can be anything from caregivers to hospital staff to well-regarded doctors. Whenever they've got a customer who's sufficiently desperate and able to pay, they turn to me or to Yuri. They get a finder's fee."

"How much money are we talking about?"

"Up to seven thousand euros, depending on the organ."

"Not bad for a tip. Then?"

"Yuri has the patient's records sent to him so he can find a donor organ the patient's system can tolerate. He sends the info on to his contacts in Ukraine. As soon as an organ becomes available, the wheels are set in motion."

"Who are his people in Ukraine?"

"No idea."

"Wrong answer."

"I was just the courier. When Yuri didn't have time. He was the brains behind the operation. I smuggled the packages through customs and collected a commission."

"And you have nothing on the people behind it all? Faces? Names? Addresses?"

Galina raised her head, her eyes welling up. "Even if I did know the people, I wouldn't talk. If I did, I'd be dead before I even made it back to the embassy. A human life means nothing to these people."

"Which is why you went out of your way to help them?"

Galina looked at the floor again. "Sometimes, a person has no choice."

"My heart's just melting with sympathy." Jan paged through his notes. "What happens once the package is inside Germany?"

"I hand the organ over to Yuri. He takes it directly to the person who requested it. With most organs, the window is really short. Often under twenty-four hours."

"Were German officials involved in the smuggling?"

"That wasn't necessary. We had no reason to need them."

"So how was the organ transported? You'd need more than a secluded back room and a nurse for that. It's not like a municipal hospital is using illegal organs."

"Yuri had connections to doctors in Berlin. Not many. Maybe four or five. But each of them is capable of doing an organ transplant.

A few falsified documents and the staff doesn't notice that the organ didn't come via the donor registry."

"What kinds of organs are we talking about?"

"Livers, lungs, kidneys, and corneas."

"A wide offering. Who are the doctors?"

Galina shook her head at the floor. A tear might have dropped there. "Again, I was only just the courier, Herr Tommen. Yuri kept all the rest from me. I received three thousand euros per smuggle. You don't ask questions."

"How many deals were you involved in?"

"Just forty."

"And Yuri?"

"Twice that."

Jan shook his head. At least eighty cases. He could guess the organs weren't obtained legally. The previous owners were probably lying buried somewhere in Ukraine.

"How long has this been going on?"

"Three years."

"Are others in the embassy involved?"

"I don't think so, but this is not exactly a topic for the coffee break. I wouldn't rule it out."

"In those three years, has anything gone wrong with any of the deals?"

"How do you mean?"

"An unhappy customer who got the wrong organ? An unexpected death? A delivery arriving too late?"

"Yuri told me so little. I think the operations always went well. Sometimes an organ is rejected despite all pre-exams and medications. Few survive such a thing, except when it's eyes."

"Was there ever a deal that failed completely?"

"No." She wiped away tears.

"Did Yuri ever get death threats?"

"No one knew who he was or where he lived. It was all done by phone. Most handoffs were managed by the doctors, not the customers. As far as I know, they kept their mouths shut."

"But why did Yuri deliver those corneas personally when the operating doctors usually get them?"

"Some customers have their own doctors. They just want the organ, and they take care of all the rest."

"So how could the grave murderer have learned about Yuri?"

"No idea." Galina's lips quivered, her eyes wet again. After a moment she said, "Two days ago I got the assignment to travel to Ukraine under some pretext and pick up the corneas. There were no difficulties. I handed over the package to Yuri last night. Eyes aren't generally a rush, so he waited until morning, took the cook's car, drove to meet his contact. I don't know anything more than that."

"Did Yuri keep any records of his business?"

"He was too clever for that. If he got caught, he could only be linked to one or two cases. Yuri wrote down the most important info, kept it in a safe, then burned it once the organ was handed over."

Jan sighed. He'd been hoping for a list he could use to match with the other victims.

"What about his contacts?"

"He wrote them down somewhere. In his address book, on his phone—that or they're lying in his safe. This list alone would not look suspect."

"You know any of them?"

"No. But I'm sure you'd find some doctors in there."

Jan observed the woman. The events clearly were hitting her hard. He couldn't tell whether Galina was so despondent because of the lost business or the death of Yuri Petrov. He figured she'd be back to her old self in a few hours. In which case the ambassador would either send her back home or take her under his protective wing.

Jan grabbed his files and stood. He'd gotten everything he could out of Galina. It was time to find out what the others had found out.

• • •

"Welcome, everyone!" Max gushed. He sat in the police conference room before a telephone and speaker. Jan was pinning the latest photos of the dead Yuri Petrov on a bulletin board. The shots showed head wounds in all their graphic detail.

"Zoe is on the line from Forensics and Chandu from home. So we're looking good."

Zoe's voice droned from the speaker: "Looking good? With a fourth victim and no sign of the killer? Have you been downing energy drinks again?"

Max straightened. "No. What makes you think that?"

"That's just swell," she growled.

"Listen up," Jan started in. "Even if the murderer slipped out of my grasp, I'm beginning to see a pattern." He pinned one last photo to the board. "Yuri Petrov didn't seem to fit the other victims at first because he looked like an embassy staffer rather than an organ dealer. Now the picture does fit, and we're getting closer to a motive."

"Which would be?" Chandu asked.

"Revenge."

"Now there's a new one," Zoe remarked.

"When the murderer killed Yuri Petrov, he spoke about getting revenge for his daughter. That's the one piece of the puzzle that was missing."

Jan went over to the board and pointed at Bernhard Valburg's photo. "Dr. Valburg was a pulmonologist who specialized in lung diseases. This will become important later. His eyes were gouged out. There's some room for interpretation, but I'm going with the obvious. Dr. Valburg didn't see something that he was supposed to see."

"A misdiagnosis," Zoe offered.

"Exactly. The murderer went to see the doctor to get treatment for his daughter."

"Sometimes there's nothing to be done, and people die even though the disease was treated correctly," Zoe said.

"Whether Dr. Valburg was guilty or not is irrelevant. Maybe he did all he could, maybe he failed. We still don't know." Jan pointed to the car salesman's photo. "Let's turn to Moritz Quast, when he was working for the health insurer. His tongue was cut out. We can assume from this that he said something he wasn't supposed to say. But what? Look at it from another angle—when he was doing his job as an administrator."

"He rejected a treatment or a medication," Chandu said.

"For pulmonology, it could be a lot of things," Zoe explained. "Ranging from naturopathic remedies and breathing exercises to antibiotics, oxygen therapy, thoracic drainage, and on up to partial lung resection."

"We don't have any details on this," Jan said, "but we don't need them for our investigation. The murderer believes that Moritz Quast, in his function as a health-insurance administrator, was somehow responsible for his daughter's death."

"Not too hard to figure out Robin Cordes," Zoe said. "Robin was supposed to get the medication the insurance rejected, but on the black market."

"But either the medicine didn't work," Jan continued, "or he wasn't able to get it."

"Thus the fingers cut off," Chandu said.

"Which brings us to Yuri Petrov, the organ dealer."

"He was supposed to get the murderer's daughter a new lung," Zoe said.

"That failed," Chandu added. "So Yuri was murdered, and his lung was cut out as a symbol."

Jan sat back down. "Now we not only have the murderer's motive, we also know why he mutilated his victims."

"But why go to all that trouble with the grave?" Max said.

"His daughter died," Jan said. "Her burial unleashed not only his urge to kill but also his desire to put them six feet under."

"How does that get us any closer to the murderer?" Zoe asked.

"We can take a better look at the names we have," Max said. "For Dr. Valburg, we'd be looking for young female patients who were with the insurer that Moritz Quast worked for. The daughter leads us to the name of the father, and then we have our murderer."

"The daughter is also deceased, which should help us narrow down the list," Chandu said. "You know his stature, and we have his voice. Identifying the murderer from there is easy."

Jan turned to Max. "How long do you need to work this out?"

"Two hours," he said. "Tops."

Jan folded his arms behind his head and set his feet up on the table. "Ladies and gentlemen, in two hours we'll know who the grave murderer is. Start chilling the champagne."

．　　．　　．

The operations room had filled up. Chairs had been removed to make space for more people. It was crowded, stuffy. Jan and his fellow cops fixed their gaze on the loudspeakers playing the SWAT team's radio communications. The raid was about to start.

The sound of the team leader's voice suggested he was used to giving commands. "We're at the location. Schwanenallee one-one-four. Begin securing possible exits."

The drumming of heavy boots sounded.

They had finally identified their man. After a week of investigating, the sleepless nights would soon be over. Jan looked forward to having a weekend again and a normal work schedule. No more stress from the media. Once he questioned the killer and finished up his report, he would be ready to party.

"Doorbell reads Elias Dietrich. Fifth floor confirmed."

It had taken Max less than an hour to track down the name. Elias Dietrich. An unassuming name. A spotless record. Nothing that could connect him to serial homicide. No irregularities.

Until June 23, 2013. That date would soon describe the murder of Bernhard Valburg. And in the days that followed, those of Moritz Quast, Robin Cordes, and Yuri Petrov. Four murders. The reasons, vile. Planned in cold blood. Elias Dietrich would die in prison.

The drone of a drill sounded. Something metallic hit the floor.

"Reached the stairwell."

More drumming of boots. SWAT must be storming up the stairs. No panting could be heard over the speakers. Apparently sprinting up four flights wasn't too strenuous for these men. Even in protective gear.

"Reached target residence."

A bang sounded. The front door being knocked open with a battering ram.

"Accessed."

Jan dug his fingernails into his palm. The room was deadly still. Everyone was staring at the speaker. Patrick pursed his lips.

"Clear," one of the men shouted.

"Clear," another.

Room by room, they searched the place. No shots sounded.

Then it was quiet. The connection hissed slightly. Jan took a deep breath. *What is going on?* he wanted to bark. But he kept silent.

Bergman's voice on the line was like salvation: "Your status?"

"The residence is empty."

"The target?"

"Not on premises."

"Fled?"

"Negative," said the SWAT team leader. "The residence is cleared out. No furniture. No clothes. Floor and windowsills dusty. Target is long gone."

●　　●　　●

Jan studied the photo of Elias Dietrich. Full beard, thinning hair, a hint of a smile. The jacket faded, the tie knot too small. No contemptuous smirk, no treacherous gleam in his eyes. A completely normal man. *But isn't it always that way?* Jan thought.

His résumé revealed just as little. Completed middle school. Employed by Berlin city government. Twenty-year job anniversary. That explained the photo with the suit and tie.

"The manhunt continues," Patrick said. "We're also questioning his relatives. Everyone from uncles to nephews. Maybe someone put him up without knowing they were housing the grave murderer."

"It's not going to be enough," Jan said.

"We're not dealing with a habitual criminal," Patrick said. "Up until his first murder, he was a dull city official."

"His crimes were planned too well. He gave us the shaft with Robin Cordes and lured Yuri Petrov out of the embassy despite the death threat."

"He's the most wanted criminal in Berlin. At some point he'll run into a patrol."

Jan scratched at his head. "I need more intel. What else is there for background?"

"The police database doesn't tell us much. He didn't even have a car. Two officers are questioning his former boss."

Jan turned to Max, who was tapping away at his keyboard as if his life depended on it. "Got any leads off the Internet?"

"Elias Dietrich does not exist online. No credit cards, no e-mail address for him, not even a cell phone. I'm on his bank records," he added.

Jan's phone ringing interrupted his thoughts. Jan longed for the age of cable phone lines, before answering machines were invented. He didn't recognize the number.

"Detective Tommen here."

"Hello, Matthias Lerger here." Jan had never heard the name. "I'm with Section Sixty-Four in Lichtenberg, and I had checked the main cemetery in Friedrichsfelde as part of the search for the grave murderer."

"What is it?"

"We were about to be taken off the case, but an hour ago a cemetery employee called me to say they had a new grave."

"A new grave? That has to be some kind of a joke."

"That's what I thought too, so I drove over to the cemetery and took a look for myself. Near one wall of the cemetery grounds, someone has dug a new grave. It matches the grave murderer's specifications. Announced to no one. Between a foot and a half and two feet deep. Simple wooden cross with name, birthday, and day of death, just like with the previous victims."

The hairs on the back of Jan's neck were standing up. "What's the name on the cross?"

"Chandu Bitangaro."

Chapter Twelve

Jan's hands were trembling so much that he almost dropped his phone as he tapped his friend's number into it. He had no clue how Chandu could be involved in this, but that was beside the point. If Elias Dietrich was responsible for the new grave, Chandu was in danger.

He picked up after the third ring.

"Thank God." Jan sighed.

"What's wrong?" Chandu asked.

Jan felt his heart thumping. "We have a new grave."

"How? I thought you sent SWAT to get Dietrich."

"He wasn't there. Doesn't matter. Is your door locked?"

"Of course. You know that. Why are you so worked up?"

"Your name is on the grave. The day of death, July fourth."

"What?"

"I don't know anything more yet. I'm having the grave checked out, but I'm getting you to safety first."

"I'm safe here. This place isn't even registered to me, and no one knows I live here apart from you, Zoe, and Max."

"Not risking it, old friend. Pack your underwear. You're spending the next two days here."

"At the police department?" Chandu said. Jan could hear how upset his friend was. "You know how many pieces I got under the bed? Probably more than your entire armory put together."

"No excuses. Grab your piece, stay near the door, and wait for reinforcements."

"Look, please, no cops in here. I'd have to find a new hideout. Have your officers wait nearby and come up on your own."

"Okay. But do not leave the building."

"Wasn't planning on it. I'm watching reruns of American football. When will you be here?"

"Twenty minutes." Jan was already heading out to the parking lot. "You have any idea what this guy would want with you?"

"This Elias Dietrich? I just heard the name for the first time this morning."

"Your computer on?"

"Sure."

"Go on Berlin.de."

Jan heard Chandu walking through his apartment. Then computer keys began clicking.

"What now?"

"Go to Politics and Administration. Then Police Ticker and click on Wanted."

"I'm there."

"The top entry is Wanted for Murder. It's got a photo of Elias Dietrich."

"Hmm," Chandu said after a pause.

"Don't tell me you know him."

"Could be."

Jan had reached the parking lot. "You at all involved in this meds-and-organs business?"

"Of course not. I've never had anything to do with organ dealing. I was a debt collector, a bouncer. I'm not moving any lungs."

"Doesn't matter for now." Jan was inside his car. "I'm on my way. Once you're here, we'll figure out Elias Dietrich's background. Maybe we'll find something you two have in common."

A loud crack sounded.

"What the hell?" Chandu began. Then came an explosion.

"Chandu!" Jan yelled into this phone.

They got cut off.

Jan dialed the number again but his phone couldn't reconnect. "Shit!" he screamed in frustration.

He tossed his phone onto the passenger's seat, started up the engine, and gunned it.

•   •   •

Patrick was paging through precinct reports. Elias had few relatives in Berlin. One cousin, a brother of his wife's. His parents had died long ago. Looking into family members wouldn't take long. He'd check into Elias's relatives' real estate at the same time. Maybe one of them had a little lakeside bungalow or a summer cottage.

Patrick was pulling up a photo of Elias's cousin when his phone rang.

"Hi. What's new?" he said to Jan.

"Send all units to Oranienburger Strasse, corner of Tucholsky!" Jan barked.

"What is—"

"No time," he cut in. "I'll explain later. I need every man. Quick!" He hung up.

Patrick froze. Jan often resorted to frantic hustle and barked instructions into the phone, but a new sound—fear—permeated his voice this time. Something serious must have happened.

Patrick got up and stood on the table. All heads in the room turned to him. "Drop everything!" he shouted. "Send all available units to Mitte. Seal off Oranienburger Strasse and be on the watch for Jan's car. Wherever he is, send him a patrol car to follow as backup."

He leapt from the table, grabbed his jacket, and ran to his car.

•   •   •

Jan ignored the pedestrians' angry shouts, cut off a bicyclist going the wrong way, and steered his BMW into the lot next to Chandu's building. He jumped out of his car and drew his weapon from his holster.

The trip had lasted twelve minutes. Twelve minutes during which he'd gotten no connection to Chandu's number. Twelve minutes that felt like a goddamn eternity.

This time he wasn't going to jump right into the fight without backup. On the way, he'd requested more reinforcements. The approaching sirens told him that his fellow cops were driving just as fast as he had been. The Oranienburger Strasse would be sealed off within a minute. Two minutes later the block would be surrounded. Then not even a fly would be able to escape.

The front entrance door was slightly ajar. Jan ran upstairs. No time for weighing tactics or sizing up the premises. His friend might be fighting for his life. Every second counted. He'd already lost twelve minutes. Too many seconds.

The stairwell was empty. In a building like this, residents didn't go calling the cops when something blew up at the neighbor's. They bolted the door and hoped it would be over soon. No one wanted to get trapped in a mob feud or stuck between two gangs battling it out.

On his way up, Jan kept his eyes peeled. He intended to take care of Elias Dietrich, and fast. Didn't matter if he was armed or not—the man was going to take a beating. Fuck the regs. The bastard had earned it. For a second he regretted that his weapon wasn't loaded. Then he remembered the moment when he'd last shot it, and all regret vanished.

The door to Chandu's apartment was busted open. It was broken off at the frame, as if it had been smashed in with a sledgehammer. Even the big crossbars securing the door had been ripped away. Jan ran in and ducked, ready to attack anyone harming his friend. "Chandu!" he shouted.

No answer.

Jan pivoted.

Chandu's apartment was practically untouched, in stark contrast to the demolished door. Only the chair at his computer was tipped over. But instead of that gentle scent of incense, a stink of blasting powder filled the room. That explained the explosion Jan had heard over the phone.

"Chandu . . ." Jan stormed into the bedroom. The bed was made. Jan ran to the bathroom, gave the door a kick, and dropped to his knees.

Empty.

Shouts were coming up from the staircase. Boots sounded on the steps. A moment later, two uniformed cops were storming the apartment.

Jan met them. "We're too late," he said. He was in no state to elaborate.

• • •

Patrick showed Jan a bag of plastic shards. "A stun grenade."

"Where did Elias Dietrich get a stun grenade?"

"Black market. Not too hard to get."

"That's what caused the explosion."

"It'll knock down even a tough bull like Chandu," Patrick explained. "The thing is one hundred and eight decibels. A human's pain threshold is about one thirty. Add in the flash of blinding light, and Chandu was disoriented for at least thirty seconds, probably even unconscious."

"Tell me how it went down," Jan said.

"Once again, the grave murderer was precise, and really clever." Patrick pointed at Chandu's doorway. "Even with a sledgehammer it would have taken him some time to get through here, so he used a heavyweight rock hammer."

"What's that?"

"It's a sledgehammer with a point on one end. Most of them are over ten pounds, used for splitting stone. He would've had no problem bashing a hole in the wood door and throwing in the flash grenade. The door shielded Dietrich from the flash blast, and he probably wore soundproof headphones."

"Chandu was at the computer when we were on the phone. So not far from the door. The apartment has no hallway. You walk right into this big living room. So there was no way to escape it."

"I'm guessing that the perp was listening at the door and waiting for just the right moment. After the explosion, he had enough time to smash the door off its frame without Chandu being able to defend himself. Then he probably injected Chandu with something. That wouldn't have taken more than two minutes."

"How did he get him out of the house?" Jan asked. "The kind of barrel he used to get Yuri Petrov to the cemetery is too small."

"In a wheelchair."

"Wait, a wheelchair? What makes you think that?"

"We have a witness. A construction worker was patching the street nearby. After the explosion, he came over to the building and noticed a man pushing a large black man in a wheelchair into a vehicle. The description matches Elias Dietrich as well as Chandu."

"Wheelchairs are too small for Chandu."

"No, those days are over. People are getting fatter and fatter, so the wheelchairs have to fit."

"What kind of vehicle can you get a wheelchair into?"

"A minivan. Converting one isn't a problem. You can get a ramp for a couple hundred euros."

"Do we have a plate number?"

"Unfortunately not. The man was focusing on the explosion, not on what he thought was ambulance service."

"The vehicle?"

"A dark-colored VW Sharan. The APB is out. Streets are blocked."

"It might already be too late for blocking streets."

"Maybe we'll get lucky, and he's holed up somewhere," Patrick said.

"Let's go over it." Jan went to the door. "From the moment of the explosion till the door was knocked off its hinges, we'll give Elias two minutes."

"At the most."

"Giving Chandu an injection and tying him up, another two minutes." Jan counted it out on his fingers. "A minute for hauling him into the wheelchair."

"Hard to imagine with such a big, powerful man."

"I saw how fast our murderer did it with Yuri Petrov. Let's say two minutes."

"Which puts us at six."

"I needed twelve to get here from the station. So he had six more minutes to get Chandu downstairs and into the vehicle . . ."

"Two more minutes. Three tops."

"Then up the ramp and out. One minute."

"Which brings us to ten minutes."

"Those last two minutes were just enough for him to make a break for it." Jan pounded on the busted door frame.

"We have all available units on it," Patrick said, trying to calm him. "We'll get him before he can do anything to Chandu."

Jan nodded. "Thanks." He exhaled deeply. He needed a clear head. Rage would only get in the way. Time was too short.

• • •

Smoke from Zoe's cigarette floated toward the ceiling. Smoking was forbidden inside Detectives Division, even in their team's little room, but it wasn't bothering Jan. The smell of Zoe's Gauloises provided the comfort of familiarity.

"What's the date of death on the cross?" Zoe asked. She looked uncommonly tense. She held a cigarette between her fingers for a minute without taking a drag. Her free hand was clenched.

"July fourth."

"Day after tomorrow?" Max asked.

Jan nodded.

"Why Chandu?" Zoe's voice was almost a whisper. "How does he fit this scenario?"

"He must have had something to do with Elias Dietrich's daughter dying," Max said.

"I find that hard to believe," Jan said. "Chandu isn't the type. He's threatened and extorted people and done nasty things to them, sure. But that all went down in the criminal world. None of those people was a respectable citizen."

"The day after tomorrow," Zoe muttered. "What's he waiting for?"

"No clue, but the next twenty-four hours are going to be crucial. We should be thankful."

"I know why." Max flipped open his laptop. "I've been merging all the data on Elias Dietrich. The fourth of July is the day Charlotte Dietrich died. Elias's daughter."

"That explains it."

"The Dietrichs were a normal family. Eight years ago, his wife Dolores died of cancer." Max turned on the projector, and a photo of a woman with short blonde hair appeared on the wall. She had a prominent chin but a warm smile. That of a loving mother.

"After she died, Elias had to care for his daughter himself. He got his work hours reduced and moved into a smaller apartment."

The wall showed a picture of an apartment building. "This was his last known address."

"Which we raided. It was cleaned out."

"It was tough for him to get over the death of his wife, but things really started going downhill four years ago, when Charlotte started complaining she was having trouble breathing."

Max pulled up a picture of a young girl. She was the spitting image of her mother. The same warm smile and oversized chin. She beamed into the camera with all the joy of youth.

"Look at her expression," Zoe said. "So much life there." She lowered her eyes. "No one should outlive their child."

"Let me guess. Elias saw Dr. Valburg about his daughter's breathing troubles."

Max nodded. "According to the doctor's records, Charlotte was treated for asthma."

"But the diagnosis was false," Jan added.

"Charlotte had sarcoidosis."

"My God," Zoe said.

"What kind of disease is that?" Jan asked.

"An immune-system disorder. Inflammation crops up all over the body, leading to shortness of breath. You feel pressure on your chest, accompanied by coughing."

"Why didn't Dr. Valburg see it?"

"Sarcoidosis is rare in children. It usually hits adults between about twenty and forty." Zoe turned to Max. "Any other details from Dr. Valburg's notes about this?"

"Does 'Stage Four' mean anything to you?"

"The poor child." Zoe shook her head. "Stage Four brings a fibrotic change in the lung tissue. The connective tissues of the lungs start reproducing. Collagen fibers harden the tissue, eventually leading to loss of function." She pressed out her cigarette. "An awful way to die."

"How do you treat such a thing?"

"In the early stages, with immunosuppressants like chloroquine. That can have nasty side effects, though, like increased risk of infection and the production of malignant cells that create cancers. There's no guarantee of a cure either."

"Which brings us to Moritz Quast," Jan said. "Once Elias realized what the disease was, he probably needed a medication that insurance denied."

"Lungs aren't my specialty," Zoe told them, "but this disease is multifaceted—so approaches to treating it are too. Corticosteroids are sometimes used, or TNF blockers like infliximab." She shrugged. "All pricey stuff, and the effects are disputed. Infliximab hasn't yet been approved as a generic in Europe. That's where Robin Cordes could have come into play."

She lit up another cigarette. "Even if he did obtain the meds, there's no guarantee they would have cured the girl. In which case Robin could be innocent of that little girl's death. Dr. Valburg did earn what he got, though, when he misdiagnosed sarcoidosis as asthma."

"That left one last resort. A lung transplant," Jan said. "How long are wait times for an organ like that?"

"Can't say exactly," Zoe answered. "A good year. At Stage Four, twelve months is too long."

"So Charlotte died before Yuri Petrov obtained the organ," Jan said. "Either that or something went wrong during the transplant."

"Dr. Valburg's records don't confirm that and neither do Petrov's notes," Max said. "What we do know is, Charlotte Dietrich died at Charité Hospital on July fourth, 2009."

"Four years ago?" Zoe asked. "Why did he wait so long to exact his revenge?"

"Elias suffered a nervous breakdown at the hospital. He ended up confined to the mental hospital in Pankow for a few years."

"How long was he there, exactly?"

"Just under four years. He was released on March first, 2013."

"Do we have records on his stay there?" Jan asked Max.

"It's tough getting at confidential records like that because Elias is still alive, but I trust Bergman to get them. Otherwise I'll hack their system."

"But we still don't have any connection to Chandu," Zoe said. "How does he fit in with Elias and the victims?"

"I mentioned Elias Dietrich when I was on the phone with him. He'd never heard the name, but he seemed to recognize his face when I asked him to pull up a photo."

"Seemed to?"

"He wasn't sure. We got disconnected before he could explain."

"Did Chandu keep notes about jobs he did?" Max asked.

"Never." Jan shook his head. "He only got assignments in person. Chandu is far too smart to keep notes that could be used against him."

"I've searched for Chandu's name in all the records involving the case," Max said. "Notebooks, contact lists, e-mails. Nothing."

"He didn't know any of the victims," Jan told them. "He told me that."

The door to the conference room opened. Bergman came in, closed the door behind him, and leaned against it. "The manhunt for Elias Dietrich is on. We've called in every reinforcement available. I even called officers back from vacation."

"Thank you. I really want to—"

"No reason to thank anyone," Bergman cut Jan off. "That's not why I'm here. Sitting in the interrogation room is Dr. Wieland Maria Beringer. Psychiatrist by profession. Happens to be the doctor who treated Elias Dietrich. Maybe you'll want to have a few words with him."

•   •   •

Wieland Maria Beringer had shoulder-length gray hair, a full beard, and narrow metal-rimmed glasses that reminded Jan of John Lennon. He wore a white shirt that had yellowed at the edges and a dark-brown sweater-vest that didn't match his blue pants.

As Jan sat down at the interrogation-room table, the psychiatrist removed his glasses and observed Jan with narrowed eyes, as if Jan were one of his patients.

"Dr. Beringer, thanks for your time," Jan began, keeping it formal. "My name is Detective Tommen. Jan Tommen. I'm working the serial homicides committed by the so-called grave murderer. As you've heard from Bergman, our prime suspect is Elias Dietrich. I understand you treated him for several years. What can you tell me about him?"

Dr. Beringer cleared his throat. He put his glasses back on. "Elias Dietrich was hospitalized and confined to the psychiatric ward after suffering an acute stress disorder." The psychiatrist's nasal voice sounded artificial, as if he were reading from a note card. He blinked continuously. "According to ICD-10 F43.0, if that means anything to you." He folded his hands and stared at the ceiling as if contemplating the genius in his words.

"I'm less interested in technical jargon than in the reason why a normal family man suddenly mutates into a serial killer."

"I find that difficult to believe," Dr. Beringer said. "Elias Dietrich exhibited no signs of violent behavior. Are you certain that your assumptions are correct?"

Jan clawed at the desktop. His friend was in the clutches of a madman, and here he was wasting his time with psychobabble. "Sorry to disappoint you, but all the evidence points to Elias Dietrich."

"I've treated a lot of violent criminals in my life. Elias showed no signs that I saw."

Jan leaned across the table until his head was nearly touching Dr. Beringer's forehead. "Your peace-loving Elias has killed four people and is holding another man against his will—who he plans on killing the day after tomorrow. I don't give a shit if you do or don't believe Elias Dietrich capable of murder, and I don't give an even bigger shit how many violent criminals you've treated. I want to know all about Elias Dietrich. What was his daily routine, who did he talk to, why did you release him." Jan showed Beringer his fists. "And if you even think of using the words *doctor-patient confidentiality* or anything like them, I'll go out to my BMW, remove the battery, and give you a dose of electroshock treatment until I know what I want to know."

Wieland Maria Beringer stopped blinking and pulled off his glasses.

"Detective Tommen," he said, clearly unimpressed. "I work with violent criminals, rapists, sexual sadists. If threats like that had an effect on me, then I've chosen the wrong profession." He permitted himself a smile. "So perhaps you should consider taking a different approach with me."

Jan sat back down in his chair. "Listen, Dr. Beringer. We are convinced that Elias Dietrich is a serial killer. Evidence from four homicides supports our belief. It's only a question of how many more people he's going to kill before we catch him." His voice was calmer now. "We have twenty-four hours to find him before he murders his next victim. No one knows Elias Dietrich better than you. Anything you can tell us is going to help us apprehend him."

The psychiatrist gently wiggled his thumbs without taking his eyes off Jan. Jan held his gaze but said nothing. The next move had to come from Dr. Beringer. Jan wanted nothing more than to head out in search of Chandu, but this psychiatrist just might give him a crucial lead.

"What do you want to know?"

Jan exhaled. He'd been holding his breath without even realizing it. "What condition was Elias Dietrich in when he was admitted to your care?"

"A strong acute stress disorder or nervous breakdown, whatever you want to call it. His daughter died at the age of eleven. He was initially quite aggressive. He busted up some hospital furniture. Some male nurses had to give him an injection to sedate him so that he wasn't a danger to himself or to others."

"If he ripped apart furniture, why would it surprise you that he's a serial killer?"

"This type of aggression is a normal reaction to severe grief. Many people feel anger at such moments. He had alternating outbreaks of violence and lethargy for about three days. His stress reactions—such as sweating and nausea—were in the acceptable range."

"If he calmed down after three days, why did you wait years to release him?"

"Acute reactions are one thing. Processing it all is far more difficult." He removed his glasses again. "Certain intrusions occur that we can't predict."

"Intrusions?"

"Intrusions, or flashbacks, are a way of reliving the past. A person recalls an incident with frightening accuracy. It propels the subject right back into that very moment of suffering."

"How did this play out with Elias Dietrich?"

"It was quite severe in the first few months. Much of the time, he was rolling around on the floor as if in physical pain. Then there came a phase of emotional apathy, and eventually a return to normality."

"What does normality mean in Elias's case?"

"He behaved like any other person suffering a loss. He was sad, but had life under control. He read books, conversed with other patients and psychiatry staff, helped out in the kitchen, and enjoyed taking strolls for fresh air."

"What books did he read?"

"Harmless stuff," the psychiatrist answered. "Classics like *Anna Karenina* and *Moby-Dick*. We don't have horror or crime novels. Nothing that could get the patients worked up."

"Which other patients did Elias Dietrich talk to? What kinds of illnesses were they suffering from?"

"There's a wide spectrum in our psychiatric ward. They range from severe depression, schizophrenia, and borderline personality to obsessive-compulsive disorders."

"Were there violent criminals among them?"

"Of course we have patients who have their issues with violence, but we keep murderers and other dangerous felons isolated. Elias had no contact with them."

"Let's get back to his daily life. Did Elias ever do unusual things, things that don't fit the image of a normal person?"

"I'll spare you a lecture on what's normal," Dr. Beringer said, clearing his throat again. "You probably mean things like pulling the wings off flies, writing down violent fantasies, or drawing disturbing pictures, things of that nature."

"Yes, something like that."

"No. The only unusual thing about Elias was perhaps his long meditative phases after intrusions occurred."

"Meditative phases?"

"A phase of emotional apathy often follows after a flashback and all its side effects. These vary in length, but as I mentioned, the subject eventually does return to normalcy. In Elias's case there was an added intermediate phase in which he entered into a sort of meditative state. He sat in the middle of the room with his eyes closed, as though thinking hard about something."

"Did you ever talk to him about it?"

"Of course."

"What did he say?"

"Elias said that meditating would help him overcome his pain. He imagined some lovely place and put himself there in his mind."

"What place was that?"

"Forest, meadow, the sea, a lake. Depending on his mood."

"And you believed him?"

"Of course. Have you heard of *samatha*?"

"Afraid not."

Dr. Beringer rumpled his brow. "Samatha is a Buddhist meditation technique. The person meditating concentrates on an image, such as a meadow or the sea. This extreme focus leads to a deep calming of the spirit."

"Could Elias have been thinking about something else?"

"Such as how to carry out a murder?"

"For example."

"I might be a psychiatrist but I can't read minds, Detective Tommen. I suppose Elias could have been thinking of murder, but meditative behavior of this nature is uncommon for a violent criminal. I know of no such cases."

"Did Elias Dietrich ever talk about what happened to his daughter?"

"Of course. That is a crucial component of the healing process."

"Did he ever make any accusations? Mention anyone he held responsible for her death?"

"At first, Elias complained about his fate in general terms. The death of his wife, and his daughter Charlotte's illness."

"Did he name names?"

"He considered the doctor who treated Charlotte to be guilty for her death."

"Dr. Valburg."

"That's his name."

"Didn't that make you suspicious?"

"No. It's an understandable reaction."

"Wanting to kill a doctor?"

"Elias never said anything about killing anyone. Perhaps about revenge, but not murder." Dr. Beringer leaned forward. "I'm no pulmonologist, but diagnosing sarcoidosis as asthma is a grave mistake. How would you have reacted if a doctor more or less caused your daughter's death?"

"Elias Dietrich clearly got his revenge."

"You're not going to make me feel guilty that easily. Elias Dietrich only talked about revenge during his first few months with us. Then he never mentioned Dr. Valburg again. It seemed highly unlikely he would carry out such an act."

"Did Elias mention the names of his other victims?"

"Which were?"

"Moritz Quast, Robin Cordes, and Yuri Petrov." Jan deliberately left out his friend's name. He refused to count Chandu as one of the victims.

"Those names don't mean anything to me."

"Are there any records of your conversations?"

"I've got my notes. I don't do audio or video recordings."

"Could you give them to me?"

"If you don't tell anyone else and promise to leave me in peace. They won't help you much—most of it's jargon."

"Doesn't matter."

Dr. Beringer shrugged. "I'll send them to you when I get back to the clinic."

"Did Elias write anything down? Did he keep a journal, recollections, anything like that?"

"Not a word. Elias was well read and smart, so it did surprise me that he never wrote anything down. When I asked him about it, he told me, 'My thoughts are clear.' I left it at that."

"Did Dietrich have Internet access?"

"No. We're as careful about that as we are about books."

Jan shut his eyes, fighting the frustration that was welling up inside him. Elias Dietrich had done everything he could to make sure no one would be able to follow his trail.

"Why was he released?"

"He had recovered—that is, to the extent we considered possible."

"Possible?"

"He hardly ever had flashbacks, and the magnitude of his intrusions had lessened. He had a better handle on his loss. We release a patient when we're sure that he's neither a danger to himself nor a danger to society. Returning to the real world does have its risks. A man might function well inside the controlled environment of the psychiatric ward, but that doesn't always mean he will succeed on the outside."

"Did you get the feeling that Elias was coping?"

"We met daily the first week, then only occasionally after that. I didn't perceive any deterioration in his condition. Later, I could only assume that he was getting through March twenty-ninth, June twenty-third, and July fourth."

"Why are those dates important?"

"The first is the day his wife died, the next is his daughter's birthday, and the last was the day she died. His intrusions were particularly bad on those days. Especially on the last two."

"June twenty-third was the day his first victim died—Dr. Valburg."

Dr. Beringer folded his hands on the table and stared at his fingers, deep in thought. He looked ashamed. "I handled Elias on those days. Of course he was angry and might have thrown a chair over, but he didn't do anything to suggest he could be a serial killer. If he had given any clear signs indicating that he was capable of such behavior, I never would have released him. I'm not looking to reach some quota of rehabilitated patients."

"What do you think happened, then?"

Dr. Beringer appeared to choose his words carefully. It took him a long time to answer. "The first possibility is that Elias tricked me. He was fantasizing about murder the whole time and simply pretended to behave when he was with me so that he could be released from the ward." He took a deep breath. "Unlikely, but not impossible."

"Second?"

"He was released too early. In the psychiatric ward there were few aggravations to remind him of his losses—he only had photos of his wife and daughter. But in the outside world, the triggers for flashbacks increase exponentially. A child's laugh that sounds like Charlotte's, places they visited together, his wife's and daughter's graves. It might have been too much for him."

"When did you release him?"

"On March first, 2013."

"So, four weeks before the anniversary of his wife's death?"

"That was a conscious decision. It would give him some time to find his way. Of the three dates, March twenty-ninth would have likely triggered the mildest reaction. I wanted to test his reaction to the day of his wife's death."

"So how was it?"

Dr. Beringer paused a moment. "I had a longer appointment scheduled for him that day, but he didn't show up for it."

"That didn't seem strange to you?"

"It did. So I drove over to his house. But he wasn't home. I asked a neighbor, but she hadn't seen him. Then I drove to the cemetery and visited his wife's grave. There was a fresh bouquet of flowers there, but no trace of Elias. I sent staff to his apartment and the cemetery regularly over the next few weeks, but Elias had disappeared for good." Dr. Beringer shook his head. "I'm sorry if I was wrong about Elias. But after March first? I lost all contact with him."

·   ·   ·

Jan had just seen Dr. Beringer out when Max came running up to him. "I got something," he said, out of breath.

Max raised his laptop up high like a trophy, grabbed Jan by the sleeve, and pulled him into the conference room.

"The crime techs analyzed the flash grenade and stumbled on a fascinating detail." He pressed a few keys and turned the laptop screen to Jan. It showed a document, a form of some kind that Jan could hardly read, owing to its small text.

"A couple years ago, SWAT reported a case of flash grenades gone missing."

"Someone stole from SWAT?"

"It's not phrased exactly like that. It turns out one of the cases in a shipment contained fakes instead of the real grenades. Since the case had already been in storage for a year, they never found out if the swap happened during delivery or in SWAT's building."

Max pressed a key, and an image of grenade splinters appeared. "The grenade that took out Chandu belonged to the missing shipment."

"Were there any suspects?"

Max pulled up a photo of a man about Jan's age. He was staring into the camera with a spiteful grin as if to say, *You got nothing on me.*

"The suspect was Linus Keller, who did time for owning illegal weapons and selling firearms. There was no hard evidence, but your fellow cops would've bet their lives that Linus was involved."

"We know where he lives?"

"Better than that," Max said. "I've tapped his cell phone. We can follow his every step."

Jan slapped Max on the shoulder. "Time for the cavalry."

•　　•　　•

"This is police brutality!" Linus shouted as SWAT officers led him into the interrogation room. Linus's head was bent forward, his arm twisted back in a painful hold that gave him no chance to make a move.

"I'm going to sue all of you."

The SWAT officers pushed Linus down into a chair and cuffed him. Jan sat down across from him.

Linus tugged at the handcuffs. "What is this shit?"

Jan didn't address the question. "I'll be brief," he said. "I need some info on a missing shipment of flash grenades. Come clean and you can stroll out of here, and we'll drop the illegal-weapon charge."

"What weapon is that?"

"The Heckler & Koch P8 we found on you, that you seem to have scratched the serial number off of."

"That? I just happened upon it."

"Don't tell me: free prize, came with your carton of cigarettes?"

"In my parking lot."

"Such a coincidence."

"I wanted to bring the gun down to the station. Just didn't have time."

"And the hundred rounds of ammo that were lying right next to it?"

"You said it."

"I'm going to try one more time nicely. We found a flash grenade that was used in a kidnapping. I need a name. Then we'll forget all about this."

"And otherwise?" Linus grinned wide, exposing his yellowed, gap-filled teeth.

"Then you end up in custody awaiting trial. I'll stick a nasty-ass thug in your cell and pay him ten euros for every blow that lands on your face." Jan pulled his wallet from his pocket. "I have a hundred on me. It's gonna be a real good time."

Linus shook his head. "Jesus Christ. Who got kidnapped? The pope?"

Jan leaned across the table. "My friend Chandu. And he's more important to me than the pope."

"Wait, Chandu? You don't mean Chandu Bitangaro?"

"The very same."

Linus laughed out loud. "So there is justice."

Jan pounded on the table. "You think this is funny?"

"I do." Linus displayed that repulsive grin again. "Your friend Chandu tossed me out of a club a few years ago for being too drunk—the sluts in that joint supposedly said I was harassing them. I was of a different opinion and wanted back inside."

Linus pointed to a scar on his forehead. "This is the result of our little difference of opinion. Had to be sewn up with a bunch of stitches. Reminds me every morning how much I hate that friend of yours."

Linus spit on the floor. "I'll tell you something, pig. You're not getting a thing from me. I'll go to jail even with a hundred thugs waiting for me in there. I'll just lie there on my cot grinning while Chandu gets what he deserves."

Jan pushed over the table and rammed it into Linus's stomach; Linus fell back onto the floor, chair and all. Jan came around and grabbed him by the hair.

"Listen to me, you rat puke. If anything happens to my friend, you're leaving jail in a plastic bag."

He let go of Linus's hair and went to leave the interrogation room. When he reached the door, Linus shouted, "Hey, pig."

Jan turned to the man. He still lay on the floor, but he'd raised his bound hands and showed Jan both middle fingers. Then he laughed.

•   •   •

Jan kicked at the door to their team's room. "Motherfucker."

Max looked up from his computer. "No luck?"

"Depends," Jan said. "Linus Keller had something to do with it, but the minute I mentioned Chandu's name, it was over."

"They knew each other?"

"Apparently Chandu roughed him up good outside a club a while back. Now Linus would rather go to jail than help him."

"He have anything we can hold over him?"

"Not really. Unregistered weapon. I can't put much pressure on him with that."

The door opened, and Zoe came in. She looked tired out, tense.

"Hi, Zoe. I thought you were over in Forensics?"

She shook her head. "Corpses are more my game. I've been watching over the crime-scene techs' shoulders while they work, but there's nothing new, apart from that grenade. I can't just go home on a workday, so I thought I'd see if you'd made any headway."

"Not really, but we still have enough time for me to go question Chandu's employers."

"Employers?"

"I know a few clubs where he used to be a bouncer. Maybe he came into contact with Elias Dietrich."

"As a bouncer?"

"I don't have any better ideas," Jan growled. "Chandu's neighbors are being questioned, the manhunt for Elias Dietrich and his vehicle is going full bore, and the few clues we have are being analyzed. Chandu had to have come into contact with Dietrich while on a job. Maybe one of his bosses can tell me something."

"I'll go through video footage from the traffic and surveillance cameras," Max said. "Maybe I'll find the van. Then we can narrow the search area."

"Can I help somehow?" Zoe asked.

"I got the records from Dietrich's psychiatrist, Beringer, and I don't understand a single word. But all that jargon might not be a problem for you." Jan pointed to a stack of paper. "I printed them all out. Maybe you can find something in there."

"And if it starts to get late, I got this here." Max set down an energy drink for Zoe.

She picked up the weird-looking can and studied it like it was some alien technology. On the tin was a cartoon character with a wide mustache and a blue hat. Jan expected her to make some snide remark, but Zoe looked like she was out of words. She blinked, sat down at the table, grabbed Dr. Beringer's notes, and started to read.

"I'm heading out," Jan told them. "If anybody out there from Chandu's world knows Elias Dietrich, I'm going to track them down."

•　　•　　•

Chandu opened his eyes. He could hardly remember a thing. The phone call with Jan. The noise at the door. That ear-splitting explosion. A trip in a minivan. But these were just flashes of memory that he couldn't piece together too well.

The dim room was spinning. Chandu shook his head, but his dizziness ebbed only gradually. Not even the nastiest bout of drinking had ever given him such a headache.

He tried to stand but found he was bound to the chair. Several wide belts were strapped around his arms, legs, and torso. He tried to flex his muscles, but he lacked the strength.

As his vision cleared, he saw a table before him with a small lamp that illuminated a photo of a child. Next to that lay a hammer.

Then Chandu noticed a digital alarm clock resting against a table leg. It was counting backward. And in twenty-four hours, it would reach zero.

Chapter Thirteen

Jan was on his way to his old hood. Before becoming a detective, he had been a patrol cop in Kreuzberg. Back then, he'd gotten called out to this disco every weekend to deal with angry drunks and customers who'd started fights with the bouncers.

The place hadn't changed. The walls were plastered with posters and graffiti; cigarette butts, beer cans, and empty bottles littered the sidewalk outside. Not exactly a place you'd like to loiter during the day, and yet few clubs in Berlin were more popular at night.

This was where he'd first met Chandu, back when he worked there as a bouncer. A coked-up nut job had pulled a pistol and shot Chandu in the shoulder. The shooter hadn't seen enough blood, so he pointed the gun at Chandu's head. But Jan had been quicker and shot the crazy man dead. Chandu never forgot Jan's good deed, and they eventually became friends. A cop and a prominent underworld type. It wasn't exactly something that would help his career as a detective, but Jan had never regretted their friendship. Not too long ago, the big guy had returned the favor by saving Jan's ass. Now it was Jan's turn again.

Jan hadn't been back to the club for years and didn't know the new bouncer. So he flashed his badge and the bouncer showed him inside. The music was louder than a blasting operation, and Jan could feel the bass in his stomach. He fought an urge to plug his ears as he was led down a narrow hallway to the owner's office. Once the door shut behind him, the worst of the noise was blocked out.

The bouncer left Jan with a man who was watching the dance-floor action through a small window. Jan put the man in his late forties. His hair was clipped short, and he wore a black jacket over a white shirt. He had on faded dark jeans and leather biker boots that creaked as he approached Jan.

"Herr Tommen. Nice to see you again." The man shook Jan's hand.

"Sorry," Jan said, "but do we know each other?"

The man laughed. "I was still assistant manager when we had that shooting outside the club. I had long hair back then and a beard."

"Jo Mafeld," Jan blurted in surprise. "I didn't recognize you. Back then you were . . . more in-your-face."

"That would be one way of putting it." He gestured to the couch. "My days of rhinestone jackets are over, though. The wife broke me of that."

He poured them each a glass of water. "I hear you've made detective." He raised a glass. "Congratulations."

"Thanks."

"What can I do for you?"

"Unfortunately, this visit is of a professional nature." Jan took a sip of water. "I'm sure you've heard of the serial killings in Berlin?"

"That grave murderer?"

"Exactly."

"Have you caught him?"

"Not yet. He's kidnapped another victim."

"Who?"

"Chandu."

"You mean, our Chandu? Who watched the door here for years and whose ass you saved?"

"The very one."

"Goddamn," Jo said. "How did Chandu get mixed up in this?"

"That's what I'm trying to find out." Jan pulled the photo of Elias from his pocket and laid it on the table. "Know this man?"

Jo set his glass aside and studied the photo. "No. I'm afraid I don't. Who is it?"

"Elias Dietrich."

"The grave murderer?"

"Probably."

"What's the connection to Chandu?"

"I was hoping you could tell me."

"I don't know the face, but I'll go show the photo around to the staff. Maybe one of the bouncers or a bartender knows him."

"The name's not ringing a bell?"

"Elias Dietrich." Jo shook his head. "He's not a regular. I'll go through our contacts list right after this. See if I can find something." He shifted his gaze from the photo to Jan. "Why come to me?"

"It's more about the club than you. Chandu crossed paths with the man at some point, and the encounter did not go well. My guess is, Elias wants to get his revenge."

"It happened here?"

"Could have."

"Like I said, I don't know the man, but we're still the hip club these days. We end up having to throw out troublemakers every night. We see a brawl now and then, but an incident that would justify murder? No way. The only time a fight really escalated was with that shooting a few years back, and you shot the attacker dead."

Jan shut his eyes and sighed. He'd been hoping to get more out of this conversation.

"How bad is it?" Jo asked.

"Real bad. Twenty-four hours left. Then Chandu's a dead man."

"And this guy in the photo abducted him? How did he do it? With a bazooka?"

"With a flash grenade and a stun gun. Maybe an injection too. This Elias busted a hole in Chandu's door with a hammer and threw in a flash grenade. That was enough to take him down."

"How did the murderer get Chandu's address?"

"What do you mean?"

"He was always peculiar about that. I only ever had his phone number. Even his girlfriend didn't know where he lived."

"That had more to do with his debt-collector gig. He was worried someone might come around who wasn't too happy with his methods. But it's a good question—how could the murderer have gotten his hands on Chandu's address?"

"Definitely not out of the phone book."

"I know of three people who know Chandu's address. I'd trust each of them with my life. I've never seen anyone else at his place, ever."

"It must have been someone from the red-light scene."

"Those are the ones he was hiding his whereabouts from."

"I've had my share of dealings with characters like that," Jo said. "They'd know just how to play it, find out exactly where they could seize him should it become necessary."

"So one of them gave Elias a tip."

Jo nodded. "Find this traitor, and he'll lead you to the grave murderer."

•   •   •

Jan called Zoe from his cell phone.

"Got anything?" she asked without preamble.

"Not yet. But remember that guy you paid a visit to with Chandu?"

"The Rat."

"That's the one. You know his real name?"

"Tim Ratinger."

"Thanks."

"What have you got in mind?"

"I'm going to pay our Rat a visit. Someone leaked Chandu's secret address to Elias, and I want to know who. You know where we can find this Tim?"

"No idea. We met in a public place."

"No worries. I'll go rattle the bushes, see what my informants can tell me. If I find anything, I'll be in touch."

Jan hung up and ran to his car. It was time for a little detour to *Kotti*—Kottbusser Tor in Kreuzberg, which was less than three minutes away by car.

Jan couldn't help checking his watch. Midnight. Twenty-four more hours and Dietrich would bash in Chandu's skull. Jan clamped his fists around the steering wheel. He couldn't let thoughts like that distract him. He would track down the grave murderer. Chandu might even escape on his own. His friend was stronger than anyone he knew. A measly pair of plastic cuffs would never hold him back, and once he was free, he would rip this Elias Dietrich to shreds.

Jan slowed down as he approached the entrance to the Kottbusser Tor subway station, then cruised around the surrounding square, which looked busy for a Tuesday night.

A group stood outside a closed-up food stand. Kids were racing around the pedestrian zone on their mopeds, and a man in a fur coat was walking his bull terrier. Jan wasn't interested in any of these people, however. What did get his attention was a figure leaning inconspicuously against a streetlight, playing a game on his phone and keeping an eye on the road. Jan was hoping that no one recognized his car—otherwise the drug dealers would vanish within seconds.

Jan reached another subway entrance not far from a pharmacy. A young man with Rasta dreads was leaning against a "No Parking" sign, puffing away on a self-rolled cigarette. He wore a multicolored knit cap and jeans three sizes too big for him.

Jan rolled down the passenger's-side window and stopped the car. The young man glanced around to check his surroundings, then approached the window.

"What'll it be, boss?" The dealer's gaze indicated he was high as a kite.

Jan pulled his pistol and held the barrel to his face. "Get in or I'll give you a third nostril."

The young man's head cleared in an instant. He raised his left hand and carefully opened the door with his right.

"Dude, hey. What is up with you?"

"It's Detective Tommen to you, Adrian."

"This any way to treat an informant?"

"Ever since you fucked me over, I consider you my ex-informant."

"Still no reason to go spraying lead all over."

"I've got no time for this; I need intel. Give it to me and you'll never have to see me again. Lie to me, and today is the last day you'll be in business."

"What is this, some new cop technique?"

"Go submit your complaint at the station tomorrow. Where is Tim Ratinger?"

"Who?"

Jan cocked and pointed the gun at Adrian's forehead. "I'm going to repeat the name one more time. Tim Ratinger. Also known as 'the Rat.'"

"Okay, okay," Adrian said. "Go try Café Meier on Kurfürstenstrasse, not far from the subway station. Tim chills there a lot."

Jan lowered the pistol and waved him out of the car. "To your continued success."

Adrian hadn't even shut the passenger's-side door completely when Jan took off. It was almost four miles to Kurfürstenstrasse. A ten-minute drive if he obeyed the traffic rules. He figured he'd only need five.

•   •   •

Zoe came racing up in her Z4 as if trying to win the German Grand Prix. Two kids holding beer cans saved themselves only by leaping aside when she drove up onto the sidewalk.

She climbed out, slammed the door, and rushed over to Jan. "Glad you texted me. Is the Rat still inside?"

"I think so. It's supposedly his favorite bar," Jan said. "Since I've never seen him, I need you to ID him."

It was a seedy joint. The plaster was flaking off the walls of the building, the windows were grimy, and the customers loafing around on the sidewalk out front looked as though they'd gotten to know each other in the slammer.

"Classy," Zoe remarked. "You got a plan?"

"The mad pig."

"How's that go?"

"Storm in, grab him, drag him out. Someone has a problem, shout them down, show the badge, and wave the gun around if need be."

"Sounds reasonable. And what if he's not in there?"

"Then we bribe the bartender."

"And if he's not bribable?"

"I doubt that'll be a problem. If it is, grab him and drag him out. You know the rest."

"You ever heard of the word *subtle*?"

"No. Should I have?"

"I'll explain it some other time." Zoe gave him a sly grin. "So let's head on in." She pushed a young guy out of the way, opened the door, and stepped inside.

Jan had to admire Zoe. At least a hundred years' worth of jail time was sitting in this bar. Most had likely been in for assault or manslaughter, but here she was waltzing into the place looking calmer than any cop he knew. She positioned herself at the door, folded her arms, scanned the room.

"So? Do you see him?"

She shook her head.

"Let's try the bar."

The bartender was several inches taller than Jan, his bald head covered in tattoos. The big ring in his nose didn't make him look any more simpatico. He was serenely polishing a beer mug.

Jan placed a twenty-euro bill on the bar. "I'm looking for Tim Ratinger; he goes by 'the Rat.'"

The bartender looked at the bill and raised his eyebrows in disapproval.

Zoe reached into her pocket and laid a hundred-euro bill next to it. "Now talk!"

The bartender set the mug down on the bar and took the money. He gestured toward the restroom with a slight nod.

"We need a minute," Zoe said. The bartender nodded and went back to polishing the mug.

When they reached the restroom, the door swung open. Tim came out and stopped in front of Jan and Zoe. All three stared at each other for a second, unsure what to do next. Zoe was the first to react.

Her punch sent him and his glasses flying back into the restroom.

Jan turned to Zoe. "Not your usual hello."

"We're old friends."

Jan stood by the door and waited for the man to pull himself back up.

"What in the hell was that for?" Tim said. He held his nose, picked up his glasses. "I don't have anything new on Robin Cordes."

"Robin's history. I'm more interested in Chandu," Jan said.

"Ask crazy boxer chick here. She's the one who hangs out with him."

Jan ignored the remark. "If I was looking to find out where Chandu lives, who would I ask?"

"I've got no idea."

Jan turned to Zoe. "Want another go?"

Zoe cracked her knuckles. "All righty . . ."

Tim raised his hands and took a step back. "I'm telling you all I know."

Zoe sighed, disappointed. Tim glanced back and forth at them as if he wasn't sure who was crazier. "What happened?" he added.

"Let's just say that Chandu got a visit from someone who wasn't too nice to him."

"How's he doing?"

"Not good."

"Chandu worked for some tough guys. He was mixed up with dudes who can hold grudges. Some of them might have wanted to get their revenge. It's a long list."

"How did they know where to go?"

"Well . . . seeing how it's such a long list, a person could make some money off knowing Chandu's hideout."

"So you sold Chandu's address to them?" Zoe said.

"No, no one ever even asked me for it. A few years back I trailed him until I found out where he lived. But I never told anyone. It was a waste of time."

"Anyone else know?"

"Sure. The guys he collected dough for. Those are some real control freaks. They eventually put their own people on it."

"How much is that worth?"

"Hundred euros. Maybe two hundred."

"Can you tell us a couple names?"

"Not exactly." Tim shrugged. "Top of my head, I can think of twenty-odd people who'd sell info like that."

"What about his former employers?"

"You couldn't get within ten yards of them before they'd bump you off."

Zoe reached in her pocket again. She pressed three hundred-euro bills into Tim's hand. "You're working for me now." She showed him a photo of Elias Dietrich. "I want to know who sold this guy here Chandu's address and where I can find him. And I want to know as fast as possible."

"How fast?"

"In twenty-four hours. Otherwise, Chandu's a dead man."

Tim rubbed at his aching nose. "Listen, I'm not going to lie to you two. I'll go without my beauty sleep tonight and really get on the case, but one day isn't much time. I'd have to land a lucky strike, and fast." He looked Zoe in the eye. "I'll give it my best shot, but you two really should have a plan B."

•　　•　　•

"What do we do now?" Zoe asked Jan as they left the bar. "I have no desire to put Chandu's life in the Rat's hands."

"I don't intend to," Jan said. "They're releasing Linus from custody first thing tomorrow morning. I'm going to pay the bastard a visit tonight and question him a little more persuasively this time."

"*We* are, you mean."

"Just me," Jan insisted. "After I question him I'll be suspended, maybe even arrested. My career is over, and I'll go down in history as a prime example of the violent cop. Court trial. Media circus. All the beautiful things in life." He pulled his car keys out. "But it'll be worth it."

"I'm coming along anyway."

"There's no reason for you to sacrifice yourself."

"And there's no point talking about it. We're losing time. I'm going with you, and there isn't a thing you can do to stop me."

Jan turned to Zoe and looked her in the eye. Her usual spite had been replaced with a firm resolve. She had no idea what kind of avalanches they might trigger tonight. But it did feel good to have a partner.

"Well, then, you're driving. Let's hit it."

. . .

As Zoe raced through Berlin traffic, oblivious to whatever damage she might cause, Jan pulled his badge from his pocket. He'd dreamed so long of reaching detective—sat through countless night shifts, spent hours studying for the tests in his free time, and improved his shooting skills. Getting called up to Homicide had been one of the proudest moments of his life.

The Detectives Division had demanded a lot of him. Sleepless nights, nightmares, long weekends, and canceled vacations, but he had accepted all of it. He loved what he did.

He was going to pay a high price tonight, but his friend's life was at stake. The friend who had saved him as he lay dying on the sidewalk. The friend who had risked it all for him.

I had a great run, Jan thought wistfully, running his fingers over his badge. Tomorrow morning it would be over for good, and he'd never get it back.

•   •   •

"I had no idea they had cells here," Zoe whispered as they made their way down the stairs to the basement of police headquarters.

"These aren't meant for a long stay; sometimes we just have to keep a suspect locked up here before transferring to Moabit prison."

"So where's Linus Keller being held?"

"In the third cell."

"Keys?"

"The officer watching the cells has them. I'll tell him Bergman needs to speak to him and that I'll keep watch meanwhile. Two minutes or so ought to be enough."

Jan put on a smile and strode down the corridor toward the cells. He had no idea who was on duty down here, but he needed to lure him away from his post one way or another.

The officer sat at a table watching the video monitor of the cells. He turned when he heard Jan's and Zoe's footsteps.

It was Fabian Gisker.

"What are you doing down here?" Jan said in surprise. "I thought you were still on leave."

"I got myself transferred down here for the night. No pay."

"How come?"

"To save your ass, young 'un."

Jan's hands curled into fists. "You're not going to stop me."

"Am so."

Jan pounded on the table. "Linus Keller is a weapons smuggler. Arrested four times for assault. This bastard sold a flash grenade to a sick serial killer. Give me one good reason why he hasn't earned a good roughing up."

"Because we're on the other side," Bergman said from behind him.

Jan spun around at the sound of his boss's voice. He hadn't heard him coming. "Not tonight."

"We'll find him," Fabian said, trying to reassure him. "There's still time."

"We've been on the case all day, and we've got nothing," Zoe said. "We have no idea what he's done with Chandu—who knows whether he's murdered him already? And the only thing standing between us and saving him is one goddamn gunrunner who just laughed in all your faces when you questioned him."

"Beating a confession out of him won't get us anywhere," Fabian said.

"Will so," Zoe said. "It gets us closer to our friend."

"You have any idea what the consequences would be?"

"Sure. Saving a life."

"No. It throws us back to the stone age."

"What's so bad about forcing a convicted offender, who abetted a serial killer, to tell us what he knows?" Zoe asked.

"It's not about Chandu, Elias Dietrich, or even Linus," Bergman said. "It's about crossing a line. When is it ever legit to beat up a prisoner? When it's Linus, maybe. What's next, though? A drug dealer? And then someone who was caught speeding?"

"Someone who was speeding isn't holding back intel that could save a life."

"What if we got it wrong? Say we wrongly accuse an innocent medical examiner and beat a confession out of her?" Bergman stepped closer to Zoe. "How would you like it if a cop came into your cell and broke your fingers for a crime you didn't commit?"

Zoe coolly returned Bergman's glare. "The fucker is guilty. No doubt about it."

"It's not going to happen."

"But we've got nothing else," Jan said, desperate now. "We've been at it day and night and don't have a clue where Elias Dietrich is holed up. We don't even have any idea why he kidnapped Chandu— and in a few hours he'll be dead. We need a lead."

"Not at this price."

"What price, then?" Zoe shouted. "What's worth more than a friend's life?"

"You have no idea how things work in Detectives. You dissect your corpses, analyze your clues, and write up a report that might help solve a crime. Or not. I have to play God. I have to weigh what's moral, what's a legitimate course of action. I have to make decisions that no one should ever have to make."

He looked Zoe in the eye. "I've let child molesters walk, been spat on by murderers and cursed as a dirty racist. I've watched friends die and had to let colleagues go who were doing nothing more than their duty. And while you get to go home and dream of sharpening your scalpels, my memories of these cases stalk me, always. Say Chandu dies. His face will be with me for the rest of my life, always reminding me that I failed. You think I'm a heartless bastard. I have to live with that. My soul might've gone to Hell a long time ago, but I will not sacrifice the system."

"If the welfare of a motherfucker like Linus Keller is more important than Chandu's life, then the system has been broken for a long time," Zoe hissed.

"Perhaps. But I still believe in it."

Zoe turned away from Bergman and spat on the floor. "Take that as my notice," she said and ran off for the stairs.

Jan pulled out his badge and slammed it on the table. "I've been playing this game for twenty-four hours now. And I've been playing by your rules," he added. "If anything happens to my friend, I won't ever step into this fucking joint again, and I'll tell every tabloid reporter who'll listen just why Chandu had to die."

He followed Zoe out.

"They're right, you know," Fabian said to Bergman once Jan was gone.

Bergman stuffed Jan's badge in his pocket. "I know."

.   .   .

It was three o'clock in the morning, but the restaurant was still open. The "Trattoria" sign illuminated two open parking spots in a dim yellow light. The green curtains had been pulled shut. Two boxwoods in ochre tubs framed the entrance.

Zoe hesitated. If she entered this restaurant, her life as she knew it would be over. She had built a good life for herself in Berlin, with an interesting job and even a little of what people called a social life. All that would be over as soon as the door closed behind her. She looked at the sign as though expecting to read something other than "Trattoria." Maybe "Abandon Hope, All Who Enter Here."

She wasn't religious, but she did believe in Hell. For her it was no fiery dungeon beneath the earth, populated by tormenting demons. Hell was a life that you despised and could not escape. A life that you hated waking up to in the morning, one plagued by joyless days, one in which sleep was the only respite. That would soon be her future. She could still flee, just get in her car and drive back to her apartment. But the price for doing that was Chandu's life.

She reflected on those long evenings with Jan and Max in Chandu's apartment, his cooking skills and booming laugh that could make the walls quake.

She made her decision and stepped inside.

She was greeted by lilting Italian music. The tables were covered with red-and-white-checkered tablecloths adorned with candles and napkins folded into stars. Two couples and a man who looked to be deeply absorbed in his newspaper occupied the main dining room. Zoe went past the bar and down the hall. A man of Chandu's stature stood in front of an elaborately carved wooden door. He wasn't quite so muscular as Chandu, but his chest did strain against his dark jacket. Chandu could win anyone over with his broad grin, but this man's mug was that of a thug who took pleasure in carrying out his job. When he saw Zoe, he pulled off his sunglasses.

"Wasn't expecting you here," he said in his raspy voice.

"Morning, Maurice. Is he here?"

"Where else would he be?"

"No clue. Bordello, jail, in Hell."

Maurice laughed. "Just like her mom."

Zoe slapped him hard across the cheek. It made a loud clap. "Never mention my mother again, you filthy bastard."

Maurice's eyes smoldered with rage for a moment, reminding Zoe just what sort of violence he was capable of. But his anger subsided, and a smile returned to his face.

"He'll be glad to see you." Maurice opened the door and let Zoe in.

The adjoining room looked just like the main dining room— same decor, same tablecloth and candle—but there was only one table in this room. A man sat there digging into a plate of spaghetti. He coiled the noodles with the fork in his right hand while reading a notepad he held in his left. A layer of styling gel ran through his black hair—just enough so that it didn't look greasy. His tailored suit fit perfectly, and his browned skin gave him that Mediterranean look. With his wealth and his ostensibly fine manners, he could have passed for a successful businessman anywhere. But Zoe knew better.

She sat down across from him, grabbed the wine bottle that was on the table, and poured herself a glass. The man set his work aside and raised his head.

"What a surprise," he said, smiling.

"Hi, Tony." Zoe took a sip of wine. It smelled of currants, and she could taste the oak barrel the wine had aged in. She nodded in appreciation.

"I'd prefer it if you called me Dad."

Zoe set down her glass. "You might have made your sperm available, but you weren't much of a father otherwise. Tony's good."

"It wasn't my idea to write 'unknown' for father on your birth certificate."

"What choice did Mom have? There were all those people looking for ways to put pressure on up-and-coming Tony. If the cops had found out, we'd have been under constant surveillance."

"Your mother knew who I was."

"That was her biggest mistake. Believing you would give anything up for her."

"There's only one way of dropping out of this life—as a corpse." He bristled. "You might have despised what I do, but you two sure have enjoyed the quality of life my money has brought you."

"I didn't want a *quality of life*. I wanted a father. Someone who took me to school and put presents under the Christmas tree for me."

"You think I didn't want to?"

"No. Your career was more important."

"In my field there is only up. Down below there's a black plastic bag waiting."

"Which is about what you're worth."

Tony contorted his mouth in anger and balled up his napkin. Then he laughed gently. "I've missed you."

"Can't say I feel the same way."

He let go of the napkin and crossed his arms over his chest. "You definitely didn't come here to voice your complaints about your screwed-up childhood. So what do you want? You need money?"

"If I needed money I wouldn't be asking you. What I need is information."

"Information?"

"You know a gunrunner named Linus Keller?"

Tony hesitated. "Possibly."

"The shitbag sold weapons to some nutcase who then went and abducted a friend of mine. Linus is refusing to talk, so I need to ask you to have a chat with him."

Tony picked up his glass of red and took a gulp without taking his eyes off Zoe. "I'm surprised. I thought you hated my business."

"I do."

"But you want me to rough someone up for you?"

"The motherfucker earned it. No room for scruples."

"You seem attached to this friend of yours."

"Doesn't concern you."

"Let's say I do it," Tony said. "Our noble Linus is a small fish, but he has influential customers. If I go interrogate him, it could cause me trouble."

"You'll survive."

"I will, but my business would suffer. All that for your friend I don't even know?" He shrugged.

Zoe leaned forward. "I'll make you the following proposal, Pops." She spat out the last word with contempt. "If you get the information I need out of Linus, to save my friend, I'll come with you. That's what you've always wanted, right? To spend more time with your daughter? For years you've been crying your eyes out about it. Now you have your chance."

"You know what I do. I'm hardly ever in Berlin. You'd have to leave everything behind—your work, your place, even your friend, whoever he is. Your life as you know it would be over."

"Just save his ass, and we have a deal."

Zoe's father stared into his wine. It shone bloodred in the candlelight. He drained it in one slug.

"So. Where do I find this Linus?"

Chapter Fourteen

Jan sat alone in his office. The dull red light of daybreak suited the photos of murder victims, suspects, the bizarre-looking autopsy close-ups. The grave murderer had sent him to the brink, but Chandu's abduction had driven him beyond that.

He had read files all night, speculated on possible hideouts with Patrick, and weighed the accounts from witnesses who'd called in, but Jan nonetheless sensed that Elias Dietrich was going to outsmart them yet again. He would fall into their net eventually, but time was working against them. If they didn't get that decisive lead soon, his friend was going to die tonight.

Jan fought the urge to push over the table. Every second he wasted on rage or sorrow was one less they had to help Chandu. He felt like a total failure, because he was the one who had let the grave murderer get away. He'd been so close to him. But Dietrich had instead made a mockery of him by diverting officers from Yuri Petrov's grave with his own cell phone. He sighed audibly. There was no time to wallow in sentimentality or self-pity. His friend was counting on him.

He drew his weapon from his holster. He eyed the cold steel that he had despised for so long. And he made his decision.

•   •   •

Max had four monitors set up before him and the surveillance-camera tapes all running at the same time. He rubbed his aching eyes, but he didn't avert his gaze, not for one second. It was eight in the morning. The sun was shining through the windows of police headquarters. Sixteen hours to go.

He'd been watching these goddamn films all night but had seen no trace of the minivan. They still had no clue where Elias Dietrich had taken Chandu. The APB on the vehicle was still going full bore, but if the grave murderer had parked the minivan inside a garage or warehouse? They would never find him.

Max edged closer to the monitors. Time was running out, so he sped up the recordings to double speed. People walked faster, autos whizzed through the frames like in some old black-and-white movie when cameras still had hand cranks. Max's head hurt and his neck was stiff. All of a sudden he saw a dark VW Sharan. He slapped at the keyboard and the images stopped. He played back the recording in slow motion. It was a camera along the Tiergarten, not high res but good enough to make out plate numbers. The camera angle wasn't great, and a car passing the VW hid any view of the driver, but for a single moment he could make out the license plate.

Max almost knocked over the chair with joy. His fingers flew over the keyboard as he loaded all the video footage around the Tiergarten onto his hard drive.

They had their first clue.

•   •   •

Klaus Bergman sat in his office with the door closed. He was drinking his eighth cup of black tea, which was doing little to stave off his exhaustion. The TV was turned on. It was eight a.m. and the local news was starting. He turned up the volume.

"The Berlin Police are asking citizens for assistance in the grave murderer case," the female news anchor said. An image of Dietrich appeared.

"The prime suspect is Elias Dietrich. He is five foot eight, of slight build, with dark hair. He's driving a dark-colored VW Sharan minivan. He is armed and dangerous. If you know anything about his current whereabouts, please report to the nearest police station. A reward of ten thousand euros has been set aside for any information leading to the suspect's arrest . . ."

Bergman turned off the TV. He had done everything he could. He'd pulled all officers back from their vacations, extended patrol officers' shifts, and drummed it into each of his cops that they were to squeeze everything they could out of every informant who had ever worked for the police. He'd played his last trump card with the public manhunt. There was nothing more he could do, but he still felt horrible.

In a few hours he'd have to release Linus Keller, probably the only person who knew anything about Chandu's whereabouts. Keller would strut off with a big grin on his face, knowing they had no leverage on him. He could charge Keller for the HK in his possession but not hold him.

Bergman set down his cup. Though time was running short for Chandu, he'd built up a hard-hitting troop these last few years. This was, without a doubt, their toughest test. He'd have to trust that they'd prevail.

He didn't want to imagine the alternatives.

•   •   •

The operations room was buzzing with activity. The investigators sat at their computers, talked loudly into their phones, or huddled in small groups comparing their findings. The air reeked of stale sweat, old coffee, and half-eaten street kebabs.

Patrick came running up to Jan with a stack of files under his arm. He looked like he hadn't slept in a while. His hair was a mess by his standards, and he'd taken off his jacket and tie and rolled up his sleeves.

"We know how he obtained the vehicle." Patrick handed Jan a copy of a rental agreement. "He rented it."

"In his own name?"

Patrick nodded. "He paid for three weeks, in advance, cash."

"What about the plate number?"

"It's gone out to all officers. But we're stopping every VW Sharan just in case he swapped plates."

"Does the vehicle have GPS?"

"Struck out on that, unfortunately. The rental doesn't come with any bells and whistles. So we won't get him that way."

"Any progress on the manhunt?"

"Not yet. It's like the earth swallowed the car whole."

"What else can we be doing?"

"Not much. All officers are on the case. I put a few people on Chandu's background. If we find any connection between him and the grave murderer, we might get to him that way." Patrick placed a hand on Jan's shoulder. "I know how much your friend means to you," he said kindly. "We're searching for him like he's one of us. There's still time. Don't give up hope."

Jan returned the gesture. "Thanks. You and your troops have been a huge help. We're going to find him." He tried to sound optimistic.

The door flung open. Max came bounding up to them, holding a few color printouts he almost dropped in his hurry. "I can narrow it down!"

His voice was nearly breaking. He stood in front of the map of Berlin. All eyes turned to him.

"I located the Sharan twice. Once here . . ." He circled the Tiergarten with a pen. "And a second time here in Friedrichshain." Another circle. "The first hit was on the Strasse des 17. Juni. The second was on Karl-Marx-Allee. If we connect these two points, as seen from Oranienburger Strasse, then we significantly narrow down our search area."

"Well done." Jan patted his friend on the shoulder. "That eliminates two-thirds of Berlin."

"It's still a huge area, I'm afraid." Max shrugged in apology.

"If we assume from this that Dietrich remained in Berlin," Patrick said, "then his likely destinations are either Lichtenberg or Marzahn-Hellersdorf."

"He could, of course, have driven to the left, into Petersburger Strasse, or right into Warschauer Strasse," Jan added. "In which case we'll have to figure in Prenzlauer Berg and Treptow."

"I'm ordering all units off the west-side neighborhoods and over there." Patrick ran to a phone and frantically tapped in a number.

"I haven't gone through it all yet," Max said. "I'll keep searching. If I see the Sharan again, I'll be in touch." The young intern gave a little salute and left the ops room.

Jan grabbed his car keys. "Reach me on my cell," he shouted as he left the room and ran out to the parking lot. He wasn't going to just sit on his butt while his friend was waiting to die.

He looked at his watch. Fifteen hours left.

•   •   •

Bergman watched from his office as Linus Keller was released from custody. They couldn't hold him any longer. This thug was their key to the grave murderer, and yet here he was leaving the station with a big fat smile on his face. Linus seemed to savor every step. He pivoted around and clapped his hands in a poor imitation of a show dancer.

"Had a lovely time with you all," he shouted into the lobby. All heads turned to him. "But I have to go prepare for a little party I'm throwing." Another pivot on the balls of his feet. "My good old friend Chandu will be killed by the grave murderer soon, so I need to make sure I have enough champagne in the house."

Linus raised a hand and waved at the officers present. "Have fun, you guys," he said. Then he left the station.

Bergman slammed the door to his office. On days like this, he hated his job.

· · ·

Jan peered at the cars parked along the side of the street. His car smelled of French fries and a slowly fermenting milkshake that had spilled all over the floor when he'd had to slam on the brakes earlier. He hadn't allowed himself anything more than a brief detour to a drive-in window—and even that made him feel guilty, as though he were somehow betraying his friend by eating.

His phone rang, startling him.

"What have you got?" he barked, hoping it was Max calling, that he'd been able to further narrow down the search radius.

"It's Tim Ratinger."

"Did you find the informer?" Jan asked, suddenly hopeful.

"I did, but he's gone underground."

"Who is it?"

"Name of Jordan, last name unknown. A small-time fence working out of the Wedding district who must have been doing some big business these last few weeks. He's closed up shop and disappeared without a trace."

"How did you figure out it was him?"

"Jordan was giving a lot of work to people. Nothing huge—procuring information, spying, just little stuff—but the guy he was supposedly working for matches the description of Elias Dietrich."

"So he wanted Chandu's address?"

"Yes."

"There any chance of getting to Jordan?"

"His buddies are saying that he's cleared out and gone abroad. With a little time I could get a lead, but not by midnight."

Jan cursed and pounded on his steering wheel.

"I'm sorry, Detective Tommen. I'll keep my ear to the ground, but that's all I've got for now."

"Thanks for your help."

"Good luck," Tim said. Then he hung up.

Jan took a deep breath. Yet another dead end—but it wasn't too late yet. He steered into the traffic circle around the Victory Column. His next destination was Rummelsburg. He would drive down every street in that neighborhood. Every single one. Until he found that VW Sharan.

•   •   •

All the waiting was driving Zoe insane. Sitting at home, she stared at her designer watch. It had cost as much as a small car, but it was still just a watch, its minute hands ticking forward with no mercy, on and on toward midnight. Linus Keller had been released that morning. More than ten hours had passed since then.

10:03 p.m.

Chandu had just under two hours left to live. She thought about her friend. Elias Dietrich was a joke on two legs compared to Chandu. How could he ever have overpowered him?

A buzz interrupted Zoe's thoughts. She had a text. She picked up her phone and read. Two words.

Trattoria. Now.

She grabbed her car keys and stormed out the door. Time to break the speed limit a few times.

•   •   •

She entered the trattoria's back room to find Maurice wiping blood off his hands. The result of his work sat bound to a chair, the very one Tony had sat in to consume his evening meal a few hours before.

She barely recognized Linus. His eyes were swollen shut. Blood dripped from his broken nose, and his lips would need plenty of stitches. His jaw was broken and his head hung limply to the side.

Zoe was sickened by the sight. She had seen much worse, of course—accident victims whose bones had been crushed, tough guys who'd been beaten to mush with baseball bats—but Linus was different. She was responsible for his condition. She had sicced Maurice on him. Maurice's hands had created these wounds, but every drop of blood that had been shed was on account of her. Linus was scum, but she was nonetheless ashamed.

Maurice set the bloody towel on the table and pulled his jacket back on.

"Have something for me?" she asked, trying not to show her revulsion.

"Linus was one tough puppy," Maurice said, adjusting his tie, acting like a businessman who'd just successfully wrapped up some big deal. "But I managed to persuade him to cooperate."

He handed Zoe a note. Blood had seeped into the white paper, leaving a brownish stain. But there was an address.

Elias Dietrich's hideout.

.   .   .

The clock was ticking. The moon disappeared behind dark clouds. Jan shone his headlights down yet another ordinary side street in Lichtenberg. No minivan. His phone rang. He pulled over and saw Zoe's number on the screen.

"I knew you wouldn't leave us hanging."

"You always did believe in the good in people."

"In your case I still do."

She fell silent for a moment. "Thank you."

"For what?"

"For accepting me just the way I am. You, Chandu, Max. It meant a lot to me—even if I do have a funny way of showing it."

Jan didn't know what to make of this call. He'd never heard Zoe like this. Like she wanted to get something off her chest.

"Don't worry about giving notice. We'll get Bergman to come around—"

"That's not why I'm calling," Zoe cut in. She suddenly sounded as though she was in a hurry. "I know where Dietrich's hiding."

"Where did you—"

"There's no time to explain. You know that industrial area in Lichtenberg?"

"I'm right near there."

"Then step on it. I'll text you the address and description. You'll find Elias Dietrich there."

Jan pulled into traffic and sped up, flying around the other cars with no regard for anyone's safety. A chorus of car horns blared, but he was already heading into the industrial zone.

"Once I've sent the text, I'll call for all available units to be sent your way."

"How did you get it?"

"Don't ask. Just put a bullet in the motherfucker."

"Will do."

"And give Chandu a kiss on his nice big nose for me," Zoe added.

Then she hung up.

. . .

Jan parked his car out on the street and headed down a dark foot-path that ran alongside a large industrial building. As he headed into the darkness, he knew he never would have found Elias Dietrich's hideout without Zoe's directions. At the end of the path, he came upon a rusty and dilapidated corrugated metal outbuilding that must have once been used for storage or as a garage. The Sharan was parked right beside it.

As soon as he caught sight of the minivan, he wanted to run right at the building, kick in the door, and shoot at anything that wasn't Chandu. He forced himself to be patient. Dietrich was clever—he might have set up a cam or a motion detector. But Jan couldn't waste too much time either. Thanks to Zoe's call, an army of cops would be descending on this spot in no more than five minutes.

Jan worried about how Elias Dietrich would react once he realized he had no way out. He might kill Chandu, might blow them all sky-high. Jan didn't want to give him those options.

He'd left his flashlight in the car, knowing that even the dimmest beam of light could give him away. The weak moonlight would have to do. The ground around the shed looked parched. Dry branches and leaves littered the area, forcing Jan to consider his every step.

He was ten yards away when he spied light coming from inside the shed. Someone was home. Jan crouched down and pressed on. He closed in, step by step, his pistol trained on the door in case Dietrich opened it.

Two yards from the shed, an LED started blinking next to the door. Seconds later a chiming sound kicked in.

Jan cursed the darkness. Dietrich had a motion detector hidden somewhere.

He sprinted forward.

So much for stealth.

•   •   •

The howls of hyenas accompanied them as they made their descent. The howls were not as deep as lions' roars, nor did they sound like the hiss of jaguars—they were more like the spiteful laughter of children.

They came with torches and started setting the first huts aflame. His friend Amaru lived in one of them. With his mother and brothers and sisters. There had been no rain for days, and so it wasn't long before the fire had consumed their home. He heard their screams, the firing of machine guns.

Chandu's mother came running over to him. She had his little sister in one arm and she pulled him from his bed. He wore only shorts and an old T-shirt. She grabbed his hand and ran out with him.

"Run," she cried. People were scattering in all directions, wild with panic. They were his friends, his neighbors, his relatives. Their screams were deafening.

His aunt ran up to him. Her dress was coming off. She grasped at the hem as she tried to tell his mother something. Then her head exploded, spattering blood everywhere. A jeep's headlights closed in on him, and he stared at them as though mesmerized. He wanted to keep running but his legs wouldn't budge. The lights held him captive.

His mother grabbed him by the arm, yanked him away. The jeep raced on, accompanied by the sharp hammering of a machine gun. They ran between huts, past the school and the goat corral, into the jungle. Stones bored into his feet. Branches struck his face. He began to cry, but his mother kept pulling him onward. Tears ran down his sister's cheeks. Only two of them would survive the night.

And the hyenas laughed.

A loud bang woke him.

The tiny room spun. His head pounded, and he thought he might throw up. He felt the restraints on his arms, his legs.

It was all a blur. He was still sitting in that strange room, the hammer and photo on the table, the digital alarm. Then the door opened, and Elias Dietrich came rushing in with a pistol in his hand.

•   •   •

Jan expected a hard impact as he threw himself shoulder first at the corrugated metal siding, but the section of wall gave way surprisingly easy. He rolled inside and drew his pistol.

Around him stood countless blue barrels. Tall enough for him to hide behind but low enough to allow him some visibility.

Jan pivoted around. One corner of the room had been cleared, and a cot and bare lightbulb were evidence that someone was living here. Next to the cot were an old fridge and a gas cooker. The floor was glossy with grease. It reeked of used motor oil and some kind of stinging chemical that reminded him of bleach. To the right was a room partitioned off by more corrugated metal and a small wooden door. There was no sign of Chandu.

Dietrich could be hiding anywhere. Behind a barrel, beyond the door, or back in some corner—even inside a barrel. Jan kept his pistol aimed in front of him and began marching through the sea of blue plastic containers. Chandu had to be on the other side of that door. Jan didn't even want to think about what might happen if Zoe's informant had gotten it wrong. Time was almost up.

Jan made some noise as he cleared a few barrels out of his way. He didn't need to be quiet anymore, and yet he had to consider every step he took for fear of a trap.

When he finally reached the door, he pulled it open and peered inside. A table lamp illuminated a small room. Chandu sat on a chair, bound with straps. His gaze was dull, as though he'd been drugged. Dietrich knelt behind him, hiding behind his captive, a gun to Chandu's temple.

"Detective Tommen. I should have guessed."

Jan kept his pistol aimed at Dietrich. "It's over. Gun down."

Dietrich laughed—a dry, contemptuous laugh devoid of humor. "You didn't wonder why I stole your phone back in that warehouse with Yuri and then disabled your car—but left you your gun?"

Jan didn't reply.

"I noticed that it wasn't loaded. I have to admit, I was a little surprised. But then I did some research on your last case."

Using his free hand, Dietrich pointed at Jan's weapon. "Is that the one? The pistol you used to kill your girlfriend? Tell me, do you get nightmares? Keep reliving that moment again and again and again?"

Jan tightened his grip on his weapon.

"Explain one thing to me, Detective—how do you think you'll stop me with an unloaded weapon?" Dietrich laughed smugly, clearly enjoying himself. "I'll make you a proposal. I'll give you ten seconds to clear out of here. In which case I'll finish the job quick.

Otherwise, I'll let Chandu suffer. He'll die either way. You just get to decide if it's going to be quick or agonizing."

Dietrich lowered the pistol to Chandu's right side. A shot into the abdomen would be fatal, but only after a long and painful struggle.

"You do a thing to Chandu, it's your death that'll be agonizing."

"Is that a threat?" Dietrich sneered. "My whole life is an everlasting Hell. Dying like that would be all too fitting. Besides, my mission is fulfilled." He pulled back the hammer on his pistol. "Eight seconds."

"Do you think that your daughter would want you avenging her death like this?"

"That psych crap doesn't work on me. Six seconds."

Jan studied Chandu's eyes, which were blurry and vacant. His friend was barely conscious and had no idea what was happening. Jan couldn't expect any help from him.

He changed the subject. "You know the problem with all those crime shows?"

"Don't care. Four seconds."

"We detective types are always portrayed as too sensitive."

"Two seconds."

"In reality, we get over the worst experiences all on our own. It's just a matter of time."

Jan pulled the trigger.

●　　●　　●

Jan finally felt the stress begin to ebb as Chandu was being lifted into the ambulance. His knees buckled and he had to sit down on the ground.

He had done it. His friend was alive and the grave murderer had been captured. The doctor had assured him that the drugs in

Chandu's system would wear off soon and he'd be back on his feet in no time. One of his eardrums had ruptured, but he was otherwise unhurt.

The entire Berlin police department seemed to have descended on the corrugated metal shed that evening. His fellow officers from Detectives, other investigators and techs, the patrol cops. The scene was more packed than a Christmas festival with free beer.

Even Max had abandoned his spot at the computer. His sister had apparently left, since his jeans had ketchup stains on them and his *Star Wars* T-shirt was thoroughly wrinkled. Only his clean-cut short hair hinted at his recent transformation. It was a start, in any case. The young hacker came over to Jan and sat down next to him. He handed him an energy drink and then opened a can for himself.

"Nice shot." He toasted Jan. "I hope for Dietrich's sake that he's left-handed, because his right one isn't going to be good for much."

"At least he won't be able to hold a pistol anymore."

"He won't be able to hold a thing with that hand."

Jan opened the can and took a slug. He'd never tasted anything so disgusting. It tasted like a mixture of lemon candies, Play-Doh, and toilet cleaner. "How can you even drink this stuff?"

"You get used to it. Gets better after a couple sips." Max drained the can in one chug.

Jan looked at the weird character on the side of the can. Jan was probably too old for junk like this, but the drink did live up to its name. He felt his weariness evaporating.

Max raised his empty can. "A toast to the Berlin Police. May our friend recover quickly and may the grave murderer rot in prison."

"I'll drink to that." Jan took another sip and shuddered. "I thought it was supposed to get better."

Max shrugged. "Okay, I might have lied."

Bergman was pushing his way through the throngs of cops. He stopped before Jan with arms folded over his chest. Sawdust coated

Jan's shoes, his pants were splattered with old motor oil, and he hadn't changed his shirt in two days. He hadn't seen a shower in a while either. He must have looked pitiful.

Bergman reached into his overcoat pocket and tossed Jan his badge. Then he gave a slight nod and disappeared.

"What was that about?" Max asked.

"A compliment."

"All he did was nod."

"From Bergman, that means, *Great job and I'll see you tomorrow.*"

"Ah," Max said. "He's an emotional one, isn't he?"

Jan looked at his detective badge and ran his thumb over the dull metal. He allowed himself a smile and closed his eyes. A few hours' sleep would be a fine thing.

After that, he would interrogate the grave murderer.

Chapter Fifteen

Elias Dietrich sat motionless in the interrogation room. He stared at the wooden table before him as if engrossed in a book. Only his blinking eyes gave any indication he was alive.

His hands lay in his lap. His right was heavily bandaged. The bullet had passed clean through it, breaking bones and shredding tendons, but Dietrich had refused to take any painkillers.

"So there he is." Patrick stood next to Jan, observing the grave murderer through the one-way glass. "Neighbors will describe him as friendly and reliable. He always paid his taxes on time and never even got a traffic ticket." Patrick shook his head. "What made him do it?"

"That's what I'm going to find out," Jan said, and he entered the interrogation room.

As Jan shut the door behind him, Dietrich's gaze remained fixed on the table. Jan sat down across from him. Over the years, each offender Jan had interrogated had been different, but they always fell into one of two groups. The first group was unrepentant and filled with hatred—they were the born criminals. That type had to be locked away and never let out again. The second group was remorseful or at least cooperative, acting as if they'd only just now grasped the gravity of their deed. For them, there was still hope.

Elias Dietrich didn't fit either of these two groups. He was apathetic and indifferent, seeming not to fear punishment nor showing any contempt for the man who had snatched his last victim from him and shot his hand to pieces.

"Silence isn't going to help you," Jan began. "We're going to sit here for as long as it takes me to understand exactly why you committed those four murders. A day, a week, a year. This room will be your home for however long it takes."

"You don't have children," Dietrich said. His voice was calm, void of emotion. He didn't even bother to look up.

"What does that have to do with it?"

"You'd understand if you did."

"I doubt I would. You're not the only person who's lost a child. But not every grieving parent mutates into a serial killer."

"I didn't neglect my daughter. I didn't lose her in an accident. She died because of inept and greedy people with no respect for life."

Elias Dietrich raised his head and looked Jan in the eye. Jan couldn't detect any anger or hatred in the grave murderer's gaze; in fact, he displayed only a startling lack of concern.

"When I first held Charlotte in my arms, I thought my heart was going to burst. It was such an overpowering moment that no words can describe it. Whatever you had thought happiness was up until then suddenly paled by comparison. When she reached for my finger with her tiny hand, I swore to her that I'd protect her and do everything in my power to provide her with a good life, even if it cost me my own." Dietrich shut his eyes. "Charlotte had so much energy. She had such a zest for life, sometimes so much that you couldn't hold her back." He looked lost in memories now. "One day, I took her to a performance of *The Nutcracker*. When she saw the tin soldiers marching around, well, that was it for her. That very evening I had to sign her up for ballet so that she could dance like Svetlana Zakharova."

He opened his eyes. "Four years ago I buried Charlotte. And with her, her dreams."

"So that's why you killed those men?"

"I believe in atonement, Detective Tommen. Whoever takes a life should pay with their own."

"But you've taken four lives."

"Every one of them could have saved Charlotte. None of them did so."

"So you blamed all of them for her death?"

"They were all to blame. I can accept that you might not like my idea of punishment. But every one of them was a nail in Charlotte's coffin."

"Let's begin with Dr. Bernhard Valburg, your first victim."

"What is there to discuss? He made the wrong diagnosis. That was the start of Charlotte's suffering. If he had detected sarcoidosis right away, Dr. Valburg would still be alive and I would not be sitting here."

"As tragic as that misdiagnosis was—don't you think it's a bit extreme to kill the doctor for it?"

Elias laughed. A fleeting, derisive laugh. "Did you look into the victims' histories during your investigation?"

"Thoroughly."

"Then you must have noticed something about Dr. Valburg, something that did not make him a respectable doctor."

"You mean his drug use?"

"I'm no junkie, but I'm pretty sure cocaine impairs coherent thought."

"According to his assistant, he only did cocaine occasionally."

"And of course you believed that."

"I'm with Homicide, not the drug squad. It was my job to track down Dr. Valburg's murderer, not investigate his cocaine habit."

"We saw Dr. Valburg daily for a while. I have no experience with drugs, so I didn't see his strange behavior for what it was. I'd never seen him any other way."

"So when did you start to notice?"

"Far too late. A patient made a random comment to me that got me thinking. She didn't care herself; she just wanted her usual prescription. He was able to do that much for her."

"Did you confront him about it?"

"No. I left his office and took Charlotte straight to the hospital. Getting the proper diagnosis took several days, but they finally confirmed that she had sarcoidosis."

"So that's why Dr. Valburg had to die?"

"Of course!" Dietrich sounded outraged. It was the first time he had displayed any emotion. "If he hadn't been snorting coke, he would've diagnosed her correctly."

"Dr. Valburg had personal problems."

"We're not talking about some coke-addicted salesman who pressured me into buying an ill-fitting suit. In that case, I'm just losing money. With a lung specialist, it's another matter altogether."

"His wife had died."

"You're really going to offer that up as a legitimate excuse? I buried my wife too. Unlike Dr. Valburg, I didn't have the salary of a pulmonologist. Plus I had a daughter. I never resorted to drugs, nor did anyone get hurt!" He continued in a calmer voice. "I did the world a favor by killing him. Who knows how many more people he might have misdiagnosed?"

"So what led you to Moritz Quast?"

"Moritz was my contact at the insurance company. He helped me out when we first went to the hospital. But when the treatment wasn't working, I had to consider alternative options. A clinic in Switzerland was having some success with a new form of therapy. Nothing that would have cured her entirely, but it would have slowed down the progression of the illness and reduced the symptoms."

"And Moritz Quast rejected it?"

"Insurers have degenerated into business operations. They don't care what happens to their customers. It's all about profit, not the health of their customers. If he had only had the courage to tell me that. But he kept hiding behind regulations and assessments. He couldn't approve treatment abroad that wouldn't result in a comprehensive cure. But it was never about a cure for him. It eventually became clear to me that Charlotte wouldn't survive without a transplant, but she wasn't even on their list of organ recipients. Not to mention the waiting period for a lung." Dietrich shook his head. "The insurer made millions upon millions in profit that year—and dividends increased."

"You were denied the chance to do it the legal way, so you went looking for other channels."

"Robin Cordes, you mean."

"Exactly."

"Once I realized I couldn't count on Moritz, I found him waiting for me at my front door one day. Told me how bad he felt and gave me the number of a friend who was importing meds that weren't approved in Germany. Two days later, I'm meeting with Robin Cordes, a supposed pharmaceutical rep. After ranting for a while about all the rules and regulations in Germany, he promised me a remedy that would significantly slow down the progress of the sarcoidosis."

"And you believed him?"

"In a hopeless situation like that, Detective Tommen? You believe anything. The doctors had written Charlotte off. They hadn't said it in so many words, but I could see it in their eyes. They were helping her cope with the pain, but no one believed there was any chance of a cure. And then Robin Cordes comes along, pretending to understand my situation and leaving these glossy brochures on my table for a substance that had very promising results in early tests."

"I'm guessing the results were falsified?"

"Of course. There was such a substance, and it was used for sarcoidosis, but the chances of success were minimal. Robin said he could get a modified version, one that was more effective, but that hadn't yet been approved in Germany."

"So you agreed to it?"

"For the desperate, God is the person who gives you hope."

"Why didn't you ask the doctors about it?"

"Robin warned me explicitly not to do that. They could not give it to Charlotte because it wasn't approved. I had to secretly put it into her food."

"How much did you pay Robin for it?"

"Two thousand as a deposit. Then four thousand more on delivery."

"When did you realize it was worthless?"

"When Charlotte's condition hadn't improved and she only had a few weeks left to live."

"Did you get back in touch with Robin at that point?"

"I couldn't reach him on his cell phone, and Moritz had made himself scarce. I didn't have any more money. The doctors said I should start getting ready for my daughter to die."

"So what led you to Yuri Petrov?"

"Nothing. He came to me."

"Just like that?"

"It was late one night. Charlotte was asleep, and I was just heading into the bathroom when Petrov called me. He'd heard about my daughter. He offered to procure a lung for her, complete with a doctor who would perform the operation."

"And you believed him?"

"I had a moment of clarity and asked Petrov for proof. We met two days later on Friedrichstrasse. He had me get in his car and then explained to me that he was a diplomat who smuggled illegal organs into Germany and could have them transplanted into patients by doctors he was friends with. As proof, he showed me his diplomatic passport and a cooler containing a liver he was about to transport. Then he let me out on the next corner and handed me a card with his cell-phone number."

"That liver could've been from a pig."

"True. But just like with Robin, I didn't have anything to lose. My daughter was dying. I couldn't imagine life without her. Yuri Petrov was my last chance. So I called him."

"I thought you were broke. Where would the money come from?"

"Petrov had offered me the Full Wellness Package. That evening he took me to a money lender who would let me borrow fifty thousand euros."

"Which would go directly to him?"

"That was the deal."

"And you weren't worried about any of them pulling a fast one on you?"

"Detective Tommen, haven't you been listening? I wasn't taking out a car loan. My daughter was about to die. Even a one-in-a-billion chance was better than anything the hospital could offer me."

"How were you going to pay back the money?"

"At the time, I didn't care. If my daughter was saved, my friends and I would've worked the rest of our lives to pay back the debt. If not, owing fifty thousand euros would hardly matter to me."

"But Petrov didn't deliver. And the first payment was due."

"Two months later, a debt collector paid me a visit."

"Chandu Bitangaro." It was tough for Jan to hear that his friend could be one of the bad guys. He still hadn't gotten the image of Chandu on a stretcher out of his head.

"Chandu was waiting at my apartment. I was on my way to the hospital and wanted to bring Charlotte some freshly washed pajamas. He grabbed me by the collar, lifted me up, and demanded the first installment on my loan."

"But you couldn't pay."

"Of course not."

"What happened then?"

"I told him that my contact still hadn't delivered the organ and that I wasn't going to start paying back the loan before that. Of course I didn't tell him I didn't have the money. I was just hoping to buy myself a bit more time. I wanted to get back to the hospital as fast as possible. Each day could have been Charlotte's last."

"But Chandu didn't let you go."

"He was good at his job."

"So, since you still didn't intend to pay—did he rough you up?"

"I guess I shouldn't have called him a son of a bitch." Dietrich shrugged. "By the time our little talk was over, I had a broken wrist, three cracked ribs, and a torn shoulder tendon that still gives me trouble today. I don't even want to talk about what he did to my face."

"So that's why Chandu had to die?"

"I explained to him what I was using the money for—that my daughter needed me—but he showed no mercy." He paused for a moment. "During my daughter's final days, I sat next to her bed like a cripple. When she saw my face beaten all black and blue, she started crying."

He closed his eyes and fell silent for a long while.

"They had her pumped full of painkillers, so she spent the final hours of her life in a delirium. By the end I was praying that she'd go quickly."

He swallowed hard. "God didn't listen."

"When did you start thinking about murder?"

"From the start. After my breakdown, I contemplated suicide for a long time. My family had been everything to me. I had no interest in a career as a city manager. I didn't care about material things. After my wife and then my daughter died, I had nothing left to live for."

"Why didn't you commit suicide?"

"Dr. Beringer. He saw my despair for what it was and tried to help me make sense of my life again. One day, we were talking about my desire to kill Dr. Valburg, and I realized that that thought aroused me like nothing else did. Not in a sexual way. But here was a way to punish him." Dietrich laughed. "When I was released, Dr. Beringer was so pleased to have shown me a way back into the world. He had no idea it was all founded on my fantasies of killing people."

"Why didn't you ever alert the police?"

"To which part? Dr. Valburg's misdiagnosis, or Moritz Quast rejecting treatment? Maybe Robin Cordes's crooked business, or Yuri Petrov's organ-smuggling operation?" He snorted in contempt. "Even if the police had arrested Robin, he would've gotten nothing more than a suspended sentence. Yuri Petrov was a diplomat—untouchable. Not exactly suitable punishment for my daughter's death."

"So you planned the murders."

"I had nothing but time on my hands. Four years in an institution is enough for a hundred murders. I secretly obtained access to the Internet and did research when I could. I mostly did it at night when Dr. Beringer wasn't on the premises."

"Once you were released from the ward, when did you disappear?"

"I was grateful Dr. Beringer put so much effort into me, but my sessions with him gradually got on my nerves. I wasn't sure how fast you would figure out it was me, so I couldn't go back to my apartment."

"You were released on March first. Why did you wait so long before killing Dr. Valburg?"

"Dr. Valburg was not the issue. It was tougher figuring out Robin Cordes and Yuri Petrov. Those took some planning."

"Let's start with Bernhard Valburg. How did you get into his house?"

"That was easy. I only had to wait till he was too high to remember to lock the door or shut a window. I went inside and got a house key. The doctor didn't even notice it was missing. The night I killed him, he was just standing in his living room staring absently out at that absurd garden of his. He didn't even notice me coming through the door."

"Why gouge his eyes out? Was that some kind of religious nonsense? Eye for an eye, tooth for a tooth?"

"A man who buries his wife far too soon and witnesses the agonizing death of his own daughter—that man does not believe in God anymore. At least not in a God like the one portrayed in church."

"So nothing religious?"

"You read too many crime novels."

"What was it, then? Boredom?"

"While I was keeping watch at my daughter's bedside, I read a book about the Native Americans. There was a tribe that believed in the physical integrity of the human body. Whatever happens to a person's body during life, that person will carry beyond death onto the eternal hunting grounds. A tribal member who was guilty of a serious crime was not just punished while he was alive—his dead body was also disfigured. The mutilation would follow him in the afterlife and torment him forever. I found it comforting to think that Dr. Valburg would be blind forever."

"His death wasn't enough for you?"

"The life of some drug-addled old man for the life an innocent child with big dreams? I ask you."

"Then you packed him into a barrel, loaded him into the VW, and drove him to the cemetery."

"It was just as easy as it sounds. You know where I got the barrels. I cleaned one of them out and then used bleach to remove all traces of dirt. Then I printed the words 'Green Waste' on the barrel in case I ran into anyone inside the cemetery."

"So how did you feel afterward?"

"Good. Excellent, actually. An emotional state I no longer knew."

"Then you turned your attention to Moritz Quast?"

"I was so excited, I dug the grave for him that very night."

"How did you know where to find his parents' grave?"

"For that I have Bernd Pietsch to thank."

"Who the hell is Bernd Pietsch?"

"I'd have to back up a little."

"I have all day."

"Bernd Pietsch was one of my fellow inmates in the psych ward. He had some scary sexual tendencies, but I was in no position to be choosy. Bernd had a half brother named Jordan who ran a little pawnshop here in Berlin. Jordan also traded in stolen goods."

"And this person knew Moritz Quast?"

"Patience, Detective Tommen. When I first broke in to Dr. Valburg's house, it wasn't just for the key. The doctor also provided me with the money for my plans. As you can imagine, I was flat broke. I'd sold all my furniture, and that kept me above water for a few weeks, but I needed more."

"You plundered Dr. Valburg's house?"

"Not the whole house, just things the doctor wouldn't immediately notice were gone. He completely failed to notice that some watches and jewelry had gone missing."

"How much money are we talking about?"

"Quite a bit. I swiped two original Glashütte watches and his wife's whole jewelry box, which was a gold mine. I took it to Jordan's pawnshop. And, because I was a friend of his brother, he gave me forty thousand euros for it all."

"A hefty sum."

"There's a certain irony to the fact that Dr. Valburg's bounty is what made my plans possible."

"Why did you need so much money? You were living in a shack in Lichtenberg."

"Let's go back to Moritz Quast and his parents' grave a moment. Jordan didn't just take the stolen goods, he also served as go-between for services of a different nature."

"What kind of services?"

"Information, mostly. For a thousand euros I received the name of Moritz Quast's new employer and his home address, as well as directions to his parents' grave."

"How did your contact get his information?"

"No idea. They must have bribed some office drudge somewhere. I didn't even know their name. Everything went through Jordan."

"Maybe I should pay the man a visit."

"Waste of time. Jordan got enough money to split for good. He's probably at some resort in Thailand enjoying his retirement."

"You've told me how you located the grave. But why didn't you kill him at home like Dr. Valburg?"

"I have never in my life humiliated myself the way I did with Moritz Quast. I fell to my knees in tears in his office and pleaded with him for that treatment in Switzerland. He assured me that he would do everything in his power, but by the end he wouldn't even return my phone calls, and he made sure I wasn't allowed to enter insurance-company premises anymore. I wanted him to see what he'd done. I chose that cemetery so I could take him past Charlotte's grave."

"But first you had to eliminate the cops on watch outside."

"Moritz was a spineless coward. All I had to do was threaten him with a pistol and he became as obedient as a lapdog. The two cops on watch made it easy for me by splitting up. The first was out cold before he knew what hit him. The second was more cautious, but he wasn't counting on Moritz coming at him. Once the two cops were tied up in the living room, it was a piece of cake."

"How did you get into his house?"

"Moritz was a mess. I drove by his place every day to have a look at the house. Wearing city work clothes, carrying tools and instruments, you're completely invisible. I went in through a back window, made an impression of his cheapo key, then slipped right back out. I checked the nearest power box to make my disguise seem credible, and was on my way." Dietrich smiled. "When you questioned the neighbors, I'm guessing none of them recalled a city worker checking the meters a few weeks before."

Jan said nothing. He was always surprised how easy it was to break into a house. Even an amateur like Dietrich had no problem doing it.

"The cops were watching the front," Dietrich continued. "I entered the property through the neighbors' backyards and came in through the back door. Moritz was such a pathetic sight, shivering with fear, clutching his pillow like it was a stuffed animal. Now it was his turn to beg and cry. I really only came to kill him, but it was pretty satisfying to see him drop to his knees and plead for his life."

"So you prolonged his agony by driving him to the cemetery to make him face what he did. Then you killed him at his grave?"

"Is this another of your sorry attempts to appeal to my conscience?" Dietrich asked. "You checked Moritz Quast's background, right? So you know as well as I do that he was a greedy, unscrupulous worm who betrayed his own partner."

"Robin Cordes."

"Not that I was sorry to see Robin go to prison."

"How did you get to him? He went into hiding after the first two murders."

"That was tough. I was pretty sure Robin would disappear when he got wind of what had happened to Dr. Valburg and Moritz Quast, so I put a tail on him right away. His prison stay nearly wrecked my plans, but as soon as he was released I knew what he was up to around the clock."

"That's what led you to the poker games."

Dietrich nodded. "Robin worked hard. Two weeks after his release, he'd gotten himself in a game and then he's organizing a group of players himself. At a charity poker event, I met several people who were happy to invite me to games; after all, I was a lousy player with lots of money. That's what brought me to Nina and Paul Hauren, who made me aware of Robin's poker group."

"He didn't recognize you?"

"It had been years since we'd last seen each other. I'd lost weight since then, my hair's grayer, and I grew a beard."

"How did you kill him?"

"That was easy. After the game was over, Robin stayed behind to clean up. When he left the restaurant, I was waiting for him. By the time he saw what was coming, it was too late."

"How could you have been so sure we would let the hearse through?"

"You underestimate the power of money, Detective Tommen. A desperate small-time criminal? He'll do anything if you promise him a few euros for his next fix. Jordan had an inexhaustible supply of men and women who'd hang around a cemetery all day for a few hundred euros. We were careful only to use people who had a clean record so they wouldn't look suspect if they were checked. I figured you'd be staking out the grave. So I had to come up with another way in."

"So you broke into the cemetery's office?"

"Before my daughter died, I'd never had anything to do with criminals. I was just an ordinary city official. I got an experienced burglar to help me on this one. He led the way, and I just kept close behind."

"Weren't you worried that one of your helpers would blackmail you?"

"Do you really think that a wanted offender would go running to the cops and betray the man who's handing him money?"

"Who were the men?"

"Don't even bother. I'm not ratting on anyone."

"You don't really believe your helpers are going to get off so easily."

"Word's already gotten around that I've been arrested. And even if I did tell on them? I only know their first names. They'd be underground before you ID'd the first one."

Jan made a note, as he still planned to hunt down Dietrich's helpers. "Now. How did you get Yuri Petrov to leave the embassy?"

"It didn't take much imagination. I pretended to be a rich businessman in urgent need of two corneas for his son. I rented a limo and showed up at our first meeting wearing a pricey suit. The beard was sufficient as a disguise. I put twenty thousand euros on the table and promised Yuri one hundred fifty thousand more if he could deliver fast. That greedy gleam in his eye told me all I needed to know. You yourself saw what so much money will do to a person. Even with his life in danger, he still got in a car and evaded his own bodyguards."

"All except for me."

"I'll admit I wasn't counting on you. But that gravel in the driveway gave you away."

"Why didn't you kill me?"

Dietrich sighed. "I don't enjoy killing. My goal was to punish the men responsible for my daughter's death."

"How were you going to lay Yuri Petrov in his grave? You couldn't have known I was coming, that you'd be able to call off my officers using my cell phone."

"I'd signed up a couple young guys to create a little diversion, which would enable me to get the body in the coffin and have it buried by the gravediggers. Thanks to your help, that wasn't even necessary. Once I ordered all units to the far side of the cemetery with your phone, I had no trouble putting the corpse in place."

"Which left only Chandu Bitangaro."

"The most dangerous one of all. I knew I wouldn't be able to handle him with a stun gun alone, so I went with something more serious."

"The flash grenade."

"Jordan made contact with Linus, who advised me well. After I'd checked out Chandu's apartment door, the rest was easy. I waited until he was home, punched a hole in his door, and threw the grenade in. You wouldn't believe the impact it made. I was standing to the side of the door with headphones on and almost got knocked over myself."

"But that wasn't enough?"

"I had to be absolutely sure he wouldn't wake up on the way down, so I gave him an injection. The sedative would suffice till I got him to my hideout."

"If I hadn't arrived in time, would you have killed him too?"

"Chandu might not have been directly responsible for my daughter's death, but I couldn't forgive him for humiliating me. My mistake was meeting Linus at my hideout. I never thought he would cave. How did you manage that?"

"We have our methods," Jan lied. He still had no clue how Zoe had obtained the intel. "But why graves?" he asked. "Why dig an open grave for each victim and put a cross there?"

"I hoped I could save Charlotte right up until the very end, so I hadn't given any thought to her burial. But my daughter was one step ahead of me. She had come to terms with dying. In the few lucid moments her painkillers allowed her, she asked about her tombstone. When she was asleep, I left the hospital, took some photos of gravestones, and showed her where she would be buried, right next to her mother."

Dietrich rubbed at his eyes as if trying to fight back tears. "Against the doctors' advice, we drove to the cemetery because Charlotte wanted to see her grave. I pushed her emaciated body there in a wheelchair. She had a tube running from the oxygen bottle into her nose. Her breathing rattled, and she could barely lift her hand, she was so weak. Charlotte looked at her grave and said, 'A beautiful spot.' Two days later she was dead."

Dietrich looked Jan in the eye. "The men who murdered my daughter should feel what it was like to stand at their own grave. The terror of knowing they are going to die should rob them of all sleep and drive them mad. They should share all my daughter suffered, if only for one day."

•   •   •

"I wish every murderer would be so cooperative when it came time to confess," Bergman said once Jan had finished his questioning.

"He didn't have anything more to lose," Jan said. "When his daughter died, his life was over, as far as he was concerned. Only vengeance kept him going."

"What do we do next?" Patrick asked.

"Prepare for a massive media circus," Bergman told them. "The trial won't take long now that he's confessed. His story will make it hard for the state prosecutor to present him as a brutal serial killer. In this day and age, Dietrich might even get a lucrative book deal before the trial's even over."

"I had enough of that with the last case." Jan sighed. "A little less press would be nice."

"As long as the public doesn't hear anything about his motives, things will settle back down after a few days. But when the trial begins, the media storm enters a new phase. You should take some time off," Bergman said to Jan, glancing at his tired eyes.

"Will do, but first I'm going to go visit Chandu."

"How's he doing?" Patrick asked.

"Now that the drugs are out of his system, he's almost his old self again. Apart from a busted eardrum, he's good as new."

"Physically, at least," Patrick said. "Who knows how captivity affected his spirits."

"He's got me to help him through that," Jan said.

• • •

After the cell door closed behind him, Elias Dietrich sat down on his narrow cot. He eyed the lunch tray that the guard had left on the stool. It held a meager portion of bread and sausage, but that seemed fitting for a day like this.

Four years ago, he had held his little girl in his arms one last time, feeling her last breaths as her fragile body finally gave up the struggle.

That was so long ago, he thought sadly as he pulled Charlotte's photo from his pocket. At least she had left him this. A final memory of a lovely time—her tenth birthday. She looked so happy just then, so full of joy, anticipating the hours to come.

He kissed the picture and studied it as though wanting to imprint its every detail on his mind. Then he put it away and stood up.

He looked out the barred windows, noticed how green a tree was, how the leaves shone in the bright yellow sunlight. A strange smile appeared on his face. He'd had no reason to smile for so long.

He picked up the thin metal tray and bent it until it buckled and a piece broke off. Then he drew its sharp edge across his neck.

"Your daddy is almost there," he whispered as the pool of blood grew.

•   •   •

Jan found Chandu at Charlotte's grave. Chandu had his head lowered and was holding a bunch of roses. Jan stood next to him, his hands clasped respectfully. On the gravestone was a photo of the little girl.

"She had a wonderful smile," Chandu said without raising his head. "She would've made a lot of people happy if she'd lived."

"Her death was not your fault," Jan said, trying to console his friend.

"I know," Chandu said, "but I did beat up her father and humiliate and demean him, right before she died."

"You couldn't have known."

"I work as a debt collector for one sick bastard, a man without scruples, with no conscience. I always told myself that his customers weren't any better. Gamblers, junkies, pimps. No one who didn't deserve a beating. So I always went home with a clean conscience and slept well."

Chandu wrung his hands on the bunch of roses. "When I woke up in his hideout, he took off his ski mask and looked me right in the eye. His eyes were full of a merciless hatred that ran so deep. It took a moment, but then I remembered when I'd met him before.

"I'd been waiting for him at home. He smelled like sweat, his hair was ruffled, his shirt all wrinkled. He had come bounding down the stairs like he was on the run. He hadn't looked any different from any other criminal borrowing money from my employer. And, like every one of them, he'd told me some sappy story about his wife dying, and how his daughter was about to die."

"But in this case it was the truth."

"I should have realized it." Chandu shook his head. "I've always considered myself a good judge of people. But that night, I was so wrong."

Chandu set the roses on the grave. Bending down was clearly difficult for him.

"You should've stayed in the hospital."

"My legs are a little shaky, but I'll be okay. I'll see about the eardrum another day." Chandu took a step back. "Wouldn't we have done the same thing?" he said. "If either of us had a daughter like Charlotte?"

"I don't think so," Jan said after a moment's hesitation. "Revenge didn't make Elias Dietrich any happier. And he'll have to answer for quadruple homicide. He'll never get released. Wherever Charlotte is, she never would have wished this for her father. Let's just hope neither of us is ever faced with such a choice."

Chandu folded his hands as though in prayer. "I'm going to quit. No more debt collecting. I never want to make a mistake like this again."

"How will you make a living? For you and your mother? That nursing home of hers isn't cheap."

"I'll find something. Something less crooked. Where I don't have to harm anyone who's just trying to help their dying child."

"Sounds good. You need help, you give me a call."

Chandu placed a hand on Jan's shoulder and nodded in thanks. "How did you find me?"

"The nurse told me you'd taken off. You weren't at home, so—"

Chandu cut in. "No. How did you find Dietrich's hideout?"

"Zoe."

"Zoe? How did she pull that off?"

"I don't know. She just called that night and told me how to get there."

"How could she possibly have known?"

"Ask me something I do know. I've been trying to reach her all day. Cell phone and voice mail are turned off. Max checked the connection. Her last call was to me, when she told me about the hideout. She's not at the office. I even sent a patrol car to her house and had the concierge open her door. She's not home."

"She called you, told you about the hideout, then hung up? And now she's disappeared?"

"In hindsight, it was a weird conversation. First she thanked us for all being so nice to her and for making her part of the team. She was oddly melancholy, like she wanted to get something off her chest. Then she told me about the hideout and said I should give you a kiss on your nice big nose once I got you out."

"And that was it?"

Jan shrugged. "She just hung up, without another word."

"Has she gotten herself into some kind of trouble?"

"I sure hope not. Maybe the stress was too much for her, and she took off for a bit. Maybe she'll show up again when all the hysteria dies down."

Chandu made the sign of the cross. "I'm not waiting that long. Let's go find her." He turned away from the grave.

"Oh, and Jan," he added. "You can forget about that kiss."

Epilogue

Zoe stared at the latest headlines on her new phone. *Serial Killer Caught. Latest Victim Rescued.*

She let herself smile. Jan was no high-flying genius, but he was a good detective. She hadn't doubted him for a second. The murderer was caught, and Chandu had been freed. Not a bad swap for her own life, which hadn't been all that great for a while now.

She would miss Jan, just like she'd miss Chandu's cooking. Even that annoying keyboard clatter coming from Max's laptop. There hadn't been a single day when one of the three hadn't irritated her, and yet they had become something like friends. She put her phone in her pocket and raised a hand to wave good-bye. One moment of wistfulness.

Then she got on the airplane, and the door shut.

Acknowledgments

To Franz Edlmayr for his amazing collaboration, Simon Jaspersen for the constructive comments, Andreas Hartel for the feedback, and Steve Anderson for the English translation of *Bis alle Schuld beglichen* (*Until the Debt is Paid*).

Thank you all for your invaluable help.

About the Author

Alexander Hartung lives in his hometown of Mannheim, Germany, with his wife and young son. He discovered his love of thrillers and historical fiction while studying economics at the University of Heidelberg. His bestselling book *Until the Debt Is Paid* is the first in the Jan Tommen Investigation series, and *Grave Intent* is the second. Both are set in Berlin

About the Translator

© René Chambers

Steve Anderson is a translator, a novelist, and the author of the nonfiction Kindle Singles *Double-Edged Sword* and *Sitting Ducks*. Anderson was a Fulbright Fellow in Munich, Germany. He lives in Portland, Oregon.